NEWARK CONFESSIONS

Historical Fiction Noir
by R.J. Kinch

Comley Place Publishing
Bloomfield, N.J. USA

Cover Design Concept by Erica Thompson

Printed in the United States of America by Book Baby
Pennsauken, N.J. 08110

Names: Kinch, R.J.
Title: Newark Confessions

First Edition

ISBN 979-8-35095-266-7

ISBN 979-8-35095-267-4 (e-book)

For Joel. I hope he would have liked it.

PREFACE

Many of the events in this book actually took place while elements surrounding the characters' participation in these events are fictionalized. I chose to use the vernacular of the time period inclusive of ethnic and racial slurs to present an accurate picture of the attitudes of the day.

R.J. Kinch – March 2024

"History is a nightmare from which I am trying to awake."

James Joyce -*Ulysses*

CONTENTS OF THE BOOK

PART THREE

PART FOUR

THE IRISH WAKE

Joe shut the arched, heavy oak door behind him, but that barely muffled the loud voices emanating from the other side. Some of his father's old friends were getting drunk on the whiskey that Tom had generously supplied to celebrate the life of a woman whom, in reality, they'd hardly known. Joe grabbed the handrail in disgust and hurried down the front steps to join his brother.

He didn't feel like driving in late afternoon traffic, but he wanted some time alone with John, who was now the family elder. The two men sat in the car, peering ahead stoically as drops of rain landed on the windshield. Joe waited for more water to collect so that he could wipe away a good portion of the city grime that had built up on the glass.

"I'll turn the rain rubber for you when you're driving," John said as the drizzle picked up in intensity.

Usually very patient about letting the engine of his nineteen-year-old car run a bit before driving, Joe found himself wondering when the old heap was going to stop sputtering so they could leave. Eventually, he pushed in the choke, put the car in gear, and set out for St. John's Church on Mulberry Street in Newark. Every building they passed seemed even drearier than usual with the heavy cloud cover absorbing most of the sunlight.

"It don't seem right," he said to his brother. "I know it's an Irish tradition to have a party, but celebrating is the last thing I feel like doing."

"Mom claimed to have lived a full life. The last thing she would want is to have all of us moping around, lamenting her death."

"Now that they've both passed, I feel different—maybe a bit like an orphan feels," said Joe. "I'm also plenty offended that these paddies showed up today for one reason only: free booze."

His brother ignored the comment. "Mom was my guiding light before I took my vows. That's why I'm not dressed like a priest today. I wanted to take this day to honor her by just being her son."

"Your speech at the church had everyone choked up. Mom really had the power to influence people. I felt it every day."

"Even being such a wee thing?"

Joe let out a chuckle. "Don't you think Mom's accent got stronger in the last few months, during her illness? I know she regretted not going back to at least stand on the soil of the Free State of Ireland."

"No, not really, but I wasn't around her as much as you. I do know she felt better knowing they'd cleared up some things there before she died. 'Brothers fighting brothers for no good reason. Let the British keep the factories in the north if it means peace,' I remember her saying."

Joe nodded. "She was always worried sick I'd get killed fighting in the trenches of Europe." He reached into his pocket and pulled out a handkerchief, wiping his eyes before they could start to tear.

"I know you aren't religious," said John, "but my faith is providing such comfort. I'm just as sad as you are about Mom, but I can think about how many lives she touched, and how she's looking down on us from heaven right now."

Traffic virtually stopped as Joe made a right onto Market Street from Springfield Avenue. They only had a few blocks to go, but they needed to cross the busiest intersection in Newark—and deal with the powerful smell of car exhaust lingering in the air now that the rain had stopped.

Joe loosened his tie and unbuttoned his collar, pulling out the chain holding the sterling silver Celtic Cross his mother had given him on that fateful day back in November 1915. "I may not be religious, but I'm still wearing this. I believe in something. Maybe it's about having good luck. Maybe it's just about Mom."

John replied, "I know Dad wasn't too fond of going to church. He told me, 'With all these saints in the family, I don't think I'll have anything to worry about if I miss a mass or two.' He was a good husband to her. He protected her from a distance, allowing her to be herself. Grandma told me he saved her life with his love."

Joe's thoughts immediately switched to his father and the sordid circumstances around his death. "Before he died," he said, "I got sick of hearing how alike we were. But when I was a kid, I tried to be like him in every way. All he would have to do was look at me to know when I needed his help. Even though I'm the youngest. Dad saw himself in me more than you or Tom."

Traffic at Broad and Market was finally waved forward, and Joe put his foot on the gas and sped eastward down to Mulberry Street, then turned left. All the open-air stands that lined the street were closing up for the day. He beeped his horn and wove his way around several pedestrians who were paying more attention to the food they were carrying than any threat from oncoming traffic.

He pulled over in front of the soup kitchen that was supported by John's parish. Both men got out of the car and embraced on the sidewalk.

"Brother," said John, "thanks for the ride. Let's get together more often. I'd like to see everyone, and I don't mean getting you all to come to church."

Joe replied, "We'd like that. About church, I'll be paying you a visit real soon. I've got some things that I need to get off my chest, and I want you to hear my confession."

PART ONE

CHAPTER 1

THE LAND OF PROMISE

Margaret Keane was twenty years old. Most of her friends were married and had at least one child. She'd observed the routine of ritual courtship in her small town in Ireland: Handsome lad charms the pants off pretty young maiden. Maiden gets in a family way, and there is a rush to have a church wedding. Two months later, the handsome lad is spending more time at the pub drinking Guinness with his mates than supporting his pregnant wife. Margaret vowed that this would not be her fate.

She was just over five feet tall, with long chestnut-brown hair and dark brown eyes. Music was her passion, and people loved to listen to her sing. Early on at the parish school, they'd tagged her as a young star. St. Patrick's used her celebrity to attract people to fill the pews and the offering basket.

The Keene family ran and lived in a modest guest house of eight rooms in Fanore, a seaside village in northern County Clare. It was a perfect place to visit to enjoy ocean breezes and day adventures into the Burren. The guest house was usually quite busy, except for during the dark days of winter—starting after Christmas and ending a week before Saint Patrick's Day.

Margaret's beautiful singing voice had enthralled Robert Stroud, the owner of the guest house. "Margaret, my dear, you are far too talented to stay in Ireland," he'd told her. "No one here appreciates your abilities the way people in London or Manchester would. I have connections in both."

"Mr. Stroud, thank you for your kind words and your offer to help. I just might take you up on it one day," she said, trying to be polite.

Margaret tolerated the English. Her mother, Ellen, had lost over half of her family in the potato famine and frequently would go on diatribes about how the English could have done more and how they treated the Irish worse than the Americans treated their slaves. Margaret stayed current on the issues of Home Rule and was a big supporter of Charles Stewart Parnell. She'd even made the trek to Ennis to see one of his speeches. Her passion for Irish politics and world affairs projected a level of intensity that was uncommon for a woman of her age and off-putting to potential suitors, who eventually gave up trying to win her favor.

The defeat of the First Home Rule vote in both houses of Parliament in 1886 dashed Margaret's hopes for a more independent Ireland. At almost the same time, she received an offer to understudy as Josephine in a London production of Gilbert and Sullivan's *HMS Pinafore*. When she overheard the sponsor of the offer, Robert Stroud, telling a guest that he hoped Margaret wouldn't embarrass him with her "bloody Irish accent," she finalized her decision and had the difficult discussion with her parents.

"I'm sorry, Mother, but I've got to leave. I love you and Father dearly, but I'll not be happy marrying one of the local boys and singing in church every Sunday."

Ellen, fighting back the tears, had said, "Dearie, I understand, but I don't have to like it. At least you are going to America, and not London to entertain the English. You have people in New Jersey who'll help you get settled."

‡

Fighting away the tears that had welled in her eyes as she left her family, she'd stepped aboard at the dock in Galway and had soon become violently ill as the *RMS Clarence* made it to the high seas. After two days of nausea and very little sleep, she'd started eating again, and halfway through the trip, she began to feel like herself once more.

February passage meant rough waters, cold temperatures, and high winds. Her mother had told her she needed to get at least an hour of fresh air every day. She quickly learned that her wool coat and scarf would not be enough to keep her warm, so when sitting up on deck, she wrapped herself in the blanket from her small bunk.

By the end of the journey, day thirteen, it had warmed up considerably, and she could stay out longer on deck. Her excitement built as she thought about beginning this new chapter in her life. She was eager to see the new statue that the American president, Grover Cleveland, had dedicated just a few months earlier. She did not sleep well that last night, as the passengers had been told they would disembark the ship in the morning.

The *RMS Clarence* entered the narrows between Brooklyn and Staten Island and headed toward Castle Gardens in Battery Park. Margaret was one of the first passengers on deck. Lights began slowly emerging on the port side of the ship. It was difficult for her to see beyond the shorelines because of the early morning fog, but within a short time, Margaret could make out the likeness of a very large copper figure holding a torch. In seeing the famous statue, she was overcome with emotion and began crying tears of joy. She was convinced that America, despite all the uncertainty of her adventure, was the land of promise for her future.

She'd been told processing could be a bit of an ordeal, but if you were healthy, you would eventually get through. After about five hours of being shuffled through various lines, being poked and prodded, and listening in on a variety of fellow immigrants' conversations, Margaret finally got her papers stamped. She exchanged her British pounds for just over ten dollars. Her destination now was Fraunce's Tavern on Pearl Street, less than a ten-minute walk from Castle Gardens.

Making her way across the cobblestone streets with her two bags, she maneuvered around a pile of horse dung, then scooted past a trio of grubby "gentlemen" who wanted to carry her luggage for her. A policeman, who had been keeping his eyes on the ne'er-do-wells, escorted her down the remaining block to the front of the tavern.

After taking two deep breaths, Margaret opened the door to a dark staircase and carefully climbed up two flights of stairs to the landing, where a small sign that read "Guest Quarters" hung. Upon entering, she noticed a group of rather worn furniture and an upright piano in the corner of the large sitting room. A thick layer of dust hid its mahogany finish. She wondered if it was in tune.

A tall blond girl about the same age as Margaret came to the desk. After they'd exchanged pleasantries, Margaret learned that she would need to wait for someone to come and escort her to her Aunt Mary's home in Newark, across the river in New Jersey. They would have a note from her aunt.

She could rest today, but tomorrow she would need to help serve meals and clean to pay for her room and board. Margaret thought about how long she'd had to save up money for the boat voyage. The modest sum she'd exchanged earlier that day needed to last her until she started working.

"Would anyone mind if I play the piano and sing when I've some free time?" she asked Emma, the girl at the desk.

"Been here for over a year, and I haven't seen anyone play that piano. Let me check for you, but I don't think it'll be a problem . . . as long as you're good!"

Margaret winced, but responded assuredly, "I'm glad it won't be a problem."

Emma grabbed Margaret's bags and told her to follow her. The pair walked down a dimly lit hallway and up to the fourth floor, where Emma opened the door to their room, revealing a bed that the women would share. There were large patches of peeling paint on both the ceiling and walls. Margaret immediately began shivering from the wintry draft coming from the window, which was not properly seated on its sill.

"You'll be staying with me. We can eat after the guests finish dinner, so come down at seven o'clock," instructed Emma, pointing to the alarm clock sitting on a small table in the corner.

Margaret put on her nightclothes and jumped straight into bed, pulling the tattered quilt over her head. As she warmed up under the covers, exhaustion took over, and she slept through to four the next morning. She remained quiet until six, when Emma got up.

When she noticed Margaret was awake also, Emma said, "You'll be helping me today. Breakfast begins at seven and ends at nine. After that, we'll make up the rooms with fresh linens. We'll finish around one or one thirty. My boss told me that, after your chores, you can use the piano and sing until four o'clock, when we need to start preparations for dinner. If you hurry now, you can sit and have a cup of tea and some of the day-old bread and rolls."

Margaret was used to attending mass on most mornings, but realized her schedule would not allow that here in New York. After serving breakfast, she decided she would head to Saint Peter's, a church she'd passed the previous day, and say a rosary after her morning chores.

Because she was in a hurry, Margaret had a difficult time finding the church. The building façade was unlike that of a traditional Catholic church, but eventually, she noticed the cross and walked up the front steps. After pulling open the heavy wooden door, she put a penny into the poor box, blessed herself with holy water, and sat down in the back row. She fixed her eyes on the beautiful white marble altar and the painting of Jesus being crucified and began praying. "Dear Jesus, please be gentle with my parents, because they have been through so much. Please keep them in your loving care. Please help me find my way in this foreign land." She opened her small bag and pulled out the rosary beads she'd received when she made her first communion.

When she got back to the tavern, she decided she would just play the piano today, as she only had a little over a half hour. Margaret was self-conscious about her piano skills, since practice time had been very limited back home. She played a song she knew well—"Siúil a Rún." Tomorrow, she would sing, too.

‡

It was day four of her stay at the tavern, and Margaret enjoyed having access to the piano and a small audience on occasion. She sang, "I wish I was on yonder hill / 'Tis there I'd sit and cry my fill / And every tear would turn a mill."

While she was playing, an impeccably dressed man in his late twenties came into the lobby. He had on a very stylish brown sack coat and a matching derby. Just under six feet tall, he was clean-shaven, his dirty-blond hair slicked back.

He walked over to Margaret. "My dear, you've the voice of an angel," he told her. "I've never heard anyone sing so sweetly."

Margaret was used to receiving such compliments, but blushed when she looked at him. "Thank you so much." She took notice of the man's stature, dress, and rugged good looks and thought about how different he was from the men back in Fanore.

He walked over to the desk in the lobby. "My name is James O'Mara. I'm here to pick up a young lady who has recently made passage from Ireland and escort her to her aunt in New Jersey."

Margaret, who had been listening carefully, jumped up and said, "Sir, please give me about five minutes while I go pack my bags. I don't want to keep you waiting."

"Please call me James," he replied. "Your Aunt Mary's a friend of my Aunt Maeve's. It'll be my pleasure to escort you. First, please read the note I brought with me. It's a good idea not to take anything for granted these days. May I call you Margaret?"

"Of course, James." She smiled coquettishly and took the letter from Emma.

Dear Margaret,

I picked James O'Mara to bring you safely to me in Newark. I've known him for a long time, and you will be perfectly safe with him. He is not so hard to look at, and he is very charming, but he has quite a reputation as a ladies' man, so I warn you to be careful. I don't want you to get hurt. Your mother says that you handle yourself well, but you are very inexperienced in these matters.

Aunt Mary

"Emma, do I have anything you need me to do before I can leave?"

"No, you're free to go today. While you're upstairs packing, I'll keep your escort entertained."

Margaret raced upstairs and got her things together. She sensed Emma had only been trying to be funny, but she felt jealous and did not want James talking with her. She put on her best clothes and her wool coat, but she felt self-conscious about how shabby she looked in contrast to her escort.

Butterflies were fluttering in Margaret's stomach as she brought her bags downstairs. She was nervous in the way she would get before singing in front of a large audience. Reminding herself of how she calmed her nerves before a performance, she had settled down by the time she made it to the front desk.

Margaret was happy to see James had taken a seat by himself in the sitting room. She walked up to Emma and thanked her. With a sly smile and a wink, Emma replied, "Good luck with everything."

James grabbed both of Margaret's bags, and they began their walk to the ferry that would take them to New Jersey.

‡

Powerful gusts came in from the west, blowing the smell of soap from the Colgate factory onto the deck of the ferry. Because it was quite noisy on board, Margaret inched closer to James and started asking questions about living in America. Because of the wind, James took off his derby and held it while Margaret tucked her hair into her coat. James listened intently and provided her with an excellent picture of what life was like in the Newark area. His manner was down-to-earth and unpretentious.

As she stared into his penetrating light blue eyes, she realized James was attracted to her as well. More than anything, Margaret wanted to be taken seriously and respected for her intelligence as much as her talent and beauty. James's earnest responses when she spoke made her feel acknowledged. She was tired of men dismissing her and treating her like she was just some young girl from the country. What if she had met James in Ireland?

Desire, as strong as the gales on the Hudson, suppressed all her notions of modesty. As Margaret looked into his handsome face, she imagined James taking her into his arms and passionately kissing her right on the deck of the ferry.

Panic began to set in as the trip was nearing its end. The dock on the Jersey side in Hoboken was now in plain sight. She acknowledged to herself that she truly was inexperienced with men. Rather than deal with the consequences of James being unaware of her feelings for him, Margaret decided to act rather than rely solely on fate.

"James, you're so patient with me, answering all of my silly questions. I've just one more for you."

"Of course. What is it?"

"Do you have any interest in kissing me?"

"Margaret, we've just met. I'm trying hard to be a gentleman."

"You didn't answer my question. So you've no interest in kissing me?"

"I didn't say that. If I'm being honest, I'd say it is all I've been thinking about since we started talking on this boat."

"James, please kiss me. I want you to."

He gently pulled Margaret closer and bent down to press his lips against her open mouth. She put her arms around him and pulled him tighter, her bosom thrust against his chest. She felt alive, like she had never experienced before. The embrace ended when the ferry bumped into the dock and the enfolded couple almost fell over. They both laughed as they drew apart and gained their balance, then walked arm in arm off the boat to the train station.

Time passed quickly as they held hands on the thirty-minute ride to Broad Street Station. They spoke about vaudeville. James told her, "With your voice, they'll hire you on the spot. You'll melt the heart of anyone in the audience with Irish blood who listens to you sing these old ballads. I hear that the starting pay is twelve dollars a week, and it'll go up if they realize people are coming to see you. They won't want to lose you to New York."

Once they arrived at their station, they began the half-hour walk to Walnut Street and Aunt Mary's flat.

CHAPTER 2

AUNT MARY

Newark in the 1880s was a bustling city of manufacturing and commerce. Railroads and waterways made it very accessible, and industries began to grow. The smoke and smell from the factories could be quite overwhelming on most days, as production of a diversity of goods—such as leather, iron, beer, and celluloid—took root in the city. The increase in manufactured goods provided employment opportunities for a growing class of factory workers, made up mostly of Irish and German immigrants.

Walnut Street was a typical street in the Ironbound section of Newark, referred to as "Down Neck" by locals. Small multifloor houses were packed into a cramped area to provide housing so that workers could easily get to work by foot. The city infrastructure could not handle this population boom and, together with poor sanitation practices, made Newark one of the riskiest places in the US when it came to disease and death.

‡

As the pair walked toward Walnut Street, Margaret regretted having been so forward with James on the ferry. She started wondering if this was all a little too good to be true. Not only had she become attracted to the first man she met in the States, but he had connections to get her started in her singing career. She tried to think about it pragmatically and was able to get past the feeling of regret. What harm was there in finding out more?

"I've a favor to ask of you. My Aunt Mary has only known me as a little girl and from what my mother told her about me in her letters. I'm afraid she thinks of me as being very naïve and likely to get into trouble. I truly want to see you again soon, but can you give it a little time before you call on me?"

"I understand completely. I'll be by in a few days—after you get settled—and we can walk to the theater. It's close to here."

"James, this is all happening so fast. Thank you for understanding." Margaret squeezed his hand and then released it for the rest of the walk.

Mary Riordan was Margaret's mother's younger sister. She had emigrated from Ireland twelve years earlier after she married her husband, Mike, who worked long hours at the Ballantine Brewery and frequented local taverns on his walk home. They had three young children, two boys and a girl.

"Come in, both of you," she said, after opening the door for James and Margaret. "It's cold out there. Well, will all of heaven's angels look at what a beautiful woman you have grown up into!"

While embracing her aunt, Margaret noticed a rather potent smell of whiskey. "Thank you, Aunt Mary, for letting me stay with you until I can get on my feet."

"Of course, my dear, that's what family is for. James, please join us for dinner. I've got some fish and potato soup cooking on the stove and fresh bread that I've just pulled out of the oven."

"That sounds lovely, but I'm afraid I can't. I need to be getting back." Addressing Margaret, James said, "I don't live so far away, and I would like to check in on you and tell you more about H.C. Miner."

"I'd be disappointed if you didn't. I'd love to hear more."

As soon as James had left, Mary lectured her niece. "Maggie, no respectable woman works at a vaudeville house. You can find honest work during the day. I also need help around here."

"Aunt Mary, no one's called me Maggie since I was ten. I prefer to be called Margaret, and I've every intention of finding out more from James. Trust me, if it's not respectable, I won't be interested."

"Well, I can tell by the way you look at Mr. O'Mara that vaudeville is not the only thing you are interested in seeing him for. I wish I could put that cunny of yours under lock and key until you find a respectable man to marry."

"Please, Aunt Mary, I don't like when people talk that way."

"Fine, have it your way, Margaret. I won't be getting you out of any trouble, and I'll not be telling any lies on your behalf to your mother. Let's bring these bags to Nora's room, where you'll stay. Then come into the kitchen and have some supper."

"Thank you, but if you don't mind, I'm going to turn in early. I'm not used to all this city noise. It makes my head hurt. What can I help you with tomorrow?"

"We'll talk about it in the morning when we have a cup of tea," Mary said. "Good night."

Margaret put on her nightclothes and got into bed, thinking about her aunt's suspicious attitude. Was her affection for James that obvious, or had Mary just been fishing for a response? She thought about the woman's appearance and how the years had not been kind to her. Mary seemed much older than Margaret's mother, although Ellen was three years her senior. Margaret would be respectful, but she hadn't come all the way to America just to have some bitter woman boss her around. Twelve dollars a week sounded like a lot of money, and surely she could find a place to live on that.

Margaret slowly drifted into sleep, thinking about James and their kiss.

‡

Margaret woke up suddenly to the sounds of a pot being clanged with a metal spoon right next to her bed. "Maggie, no one sleeps past seven in the morning in this house. You need to get up and earn your keep."

"Forgive me, Aunt Mary. I guess I'm still tired from the journey. Please give me a few minutes and I'll come and help with the chores."

Still half asleep, Margaret hurried to change into her clothes and then combed the tangles from her hair. Looking into the small mirror on the dresser, she felt a sudden rush of guilt. Being so forward with James yesterday had been so unlike her.

In her dreams, she had picnicked with him at her favorite spot back in Fanore, where they'd watched the ocean. She thought about the way James had looked at her as she sat on the blanket, as one lover looks at another. Facing the mirror, she said out loud, "Margaret, stop torturing yourself. You just turned twenty-one years old, and being attracted to a man is hardly a sin at your age."

Once she'd finished getting ready, she hurried into the kitchen to greet her aunt, who addressed her coldly. "I made you a cup of tea. There are some beans and toast for your breakfast. When you finish, sweep out the entire flat and scrub all the floors. I'm going to walk the children to school and be out for a few hours, and I expect everything to look spotless when I return. Then you can get started on some laundry this afternoon."

"Yes, Aunt Mary."

When she arrived the day before, Margaret hadn't noticed how dirty everything was. After finishing her breakfast, she put up her hair so it wouldn't get in the way, then got down on her knees and began scrubbing the kitchen floor.

‡

Time passed quickly as Margaret attempted to complete the chores. After a few hours, she heard the key jingle in the lock for a few moments, and then the door creaked open. She still had a considerable amount of work left to do.

"Maggie, come put a kettle on. I want a cup of tea," called her aunt from the hall.

"Yes, Aunt Mary."

When she entered the kitchen, all Margaret could smell was whiskey. She looked at Mary and noticed several unfastened buttons on her dress. Her hair, which had been in a bun earlier this morning, was now flowing down her back.

"Sit with me, girl, and have some tea with your aunt."

Margaret obliged her, sitting down on the other side of the kitchen table and pretending not to notice anything peculiar about the woman's appearance.

"We need to find you a husband. A pretty thing like you shouldn't be so hard to match up." Mary cackled with laughter. Taking out a small flask from her coat pocket, she poured some whiskey into the hot tea.

"Aunt Mary, with all respect, I didn't come to America to just get married. If that's all I was interested in, I would've stayed in Ireland."

"Oh, so you're going to be one of those loose women, are you? Scurrying from one bed to the next?"

"I've no intention of doing anything like that. I'm not opposed to marriage if I meet the right man."

As Margaret finished her sentence, she noticed her aunt had closed her eyes and fallen asleep. She left the table and went back to cleaning the bedroom.

‡

Margaret tried to snap out of her bad mood. This was the beginning of her second full day of nonstop work. After her many hours of chores yesterday, she went to bed right after supper. During the night, she dreamed James never showed up to take her to the theater and she couldn't earn enough money to move out. A knock at the front door got her attention back to the present moment, and she listened carefully.

"Oh, it's you. Surprised you waited this long," bleated Mary as she answered the door.

"I brought some fish, being that you have an extra mouth to feed," Margaret heard James say.

"Don't think I can't see right through you. I don't know what I was thinking when I asked you to get her. I should've gone myself and had someone look after the children."

"Mary, I've only the best intentions. I don't know why you would think otherwise. I want to help Margaret get started around here, nothing more. You have my word on that."

Margaret hurried down the hall and into the kitchen. "James, what a pleasant surprise to see you. It is such a lovely morning, and I'd enjoy going for a walk and seeing the theater you told me about the other day." James smiled at her. "Aunt Mary, I'll not be gone too long and will help with chores when I return."

Mary scowled. "It's quarter to ten now. If you are not home by one, I'll come out looking for you."

Margaret and James left and walked one block in silence, as if Mary could still hear them. Margaret began to sniffle, and James quietly asked, "What's wrong?"

"It couldn't be any more awful staying with them. I imagine prison might be better. Last night, Mike—her husband—awakened me when he came home drunk, trying to get up the stairs. As soon as he got inside, they argued. Eventually, they went to sleep. Poor little Nora was awake and heard everything. Aunt Mary walks the children to school every day and goes to Lord knows where, returns drunk, and then sleeps it off before the children come home. And she has said some terrible things about my intentions with you. She wants to control me. I can't stay there. *I can't.*"

"Margaret, I don't want you to stay there either. I've always thought Mike was a lunkhead, and the burden of the household falls completely on Mary. I've seen her tight a few times. My, she could be the life of the party. I didn't realize she'd become a drunk."

James then talked about the boarding houses in the area. There was one on High Street for women only, managed by a German lady who ran a tight ship. "It's not the most cheerful place in the world, but you'd be safe. I'm happy to pay for you to stay there while you get settled. She charges one to two dollars a day with meals—to keep out the riffraff."

"You're very sweet. I'm afraid I'm going to have to take you up on your kind offer. However, I've every intention of paying you back when I get work. I don't want to rely on you for everything. By the way, how come you know so much about this woman's boarding house?"

James hesitated for a moment before he answered. "It's because I courted a girl who lived there."

"Are you still courting her?"

"No, it ended five months ago."

"My dear James, I'd expect a handsome man like yourself to have had relationships. I appreciate you telling me. All I care about is what happens in the future." Margaret felt helpless, but she knew she needed James. She also believed she could control the pace of the relationship. Her feelings for him were strong, but she wanted to ensure this was not infatuation potentially blinding her common sense. Taking a deep breath to build her courage, she said, "I want to be with a man who is only interested in me."

Without a moment of hesitation, James replied, "Margaret, I've never met a woman like you before. The moment I laid eyes on you and heard you sing, I fell for you. All I thought of when we were apart was when I'd be able to see you again. You have my heart."

"You've been so kind to me. However, it's only been a few days since we met. I'd like our courtship to go slowly and develop as we get to know each other better."

"You've just made me the happiest man in New Jersey."

A smile graced Margaret's face. She grabbed James's hand and said, "Let's hurry to meet this German lady. Hopefully she has a room for me."

The two hastened to the boarding house, which was just a few doors past the Newark Technical School. The three-story stone building had a distinguished look to it, built on a hill with a big flight of stairs leading up to the front entrance. The pair quickly hurried up the steps and were greeted by the manager as soon as they entered the foyer.

In a thick German accent, Mrs. Schmidt asked, "So, you have just come from Ireland? The only room available is $1.50 a day with one week in advance. If you can do some work for me, I'll give a discount. You are so small, I'm not sure about you working."

"Mrs. Schmidt, I'm a hard worker. My parents ran a guest house. I helped with all the chores from the time I was ten years old."

"I just lost my helper. She is going to have a baby. She is a colored lady, almost two times your size. If you can do the work she did, I will give you the $1.50 room for $7 a week."

Margaret thought about the great expense. It also seemed like Mrs. Schmidt would be quite the taskmaster. Hopefully, she would have enough time to sing as well as work at the boarding house.

"Mrs. Schmidt, can I see the room before I make my decision?" she asked.

"Yes, of course. I can show you on the third floor. Your man needs to wait here."

The space was more than she could have hoped for. It was a large corner room, painted a bright white, with lots of light and views of a garden in the backyard. There was a chair for her to read in and a dresser to store her clothes. On this February day, it was nice and cozy in there, a steam radiator gently hissing by the window. The five guests on the floor shared a bathroom with a tub and a flush toilet, and Mrs. Schmidt told Margaret she could take two baths a week as they walked downstairs, where James was waiting patiently.

"It's settled," Margaret said. "I'll move in today. It's an absolutely perfect room with a delightful view. Mrs. Schmidt, I shall return later with my things. I can start working for you tomorrow."

She felt relief for a moment, but then began to anticipate the big confrontation with Aunt Mary when she revealed her plans. "On the way back to the house, I'd like to look in the theater and stop by a telegraph office, if it's possible," she told James. "I want to get word to my parents before they get any communication from Aunt Mary."

There was a telegraph office that was on the way to the theater on Market Street, and from there Margaret sent out her missive.

> *Arrived safely in America. Unable to impose on Aunt Mary any longer. Friend helping me move to safe boarding house for women. Will write soon to explain.*
>
> *Margaret*

"When she reads this, my mother will know that I couldn't get along with Aunt Mary. Sending it is worth the money, for peace of mind. Do we still have time to see the theater?"

"I'm afraid it's getting late," James said. "Let's handle Mary first, and then we'll go to the theater on the way back."

On the walk to the flat, to calm her nerves, Margaret prepared a little speech that she would give her aunt regardless of her response. She and James picked up the pace and made it to Walnut Street five minutes before one.

"I was about to go out looking for you," Mary shrieked as she opened the door. It seemed she had returned to the flat just a few minutes before Margaret and James.

"Aunt Mary, I've decided to move to a women's boarding house on High Street," Margaret told her. "It's not right for me to impose on you and Uncle Mike. I'm grateful to you for letting me stay these days. I'll get my things and move this afternoon."

Mary sneered at her. "Your mother didn't tell me what a little whore you are. I know what you'll be doing with this hoodlum. Don't come back here when he gives you the boot."

James rapped his fist on the kitchen table. "Shut up, Mary. You don't know what you're talking about. When did you get so mean, or is it just the drink that's talking?"

"Wait until she finds out about you and all your dealings around town. Maggie, the minute you leave, I'm writing a letter to your mother telling her what you're up to."

"Aunt Mary, write that letter. My parents know I'm not capable of doing anything like what you're suggesting."

Margaret ran into the bedroom, grabbed her things, and threw them into her bags. She caught James's eye as she raced into the kitchen. He quickly opened the door, and the pair whooshed through, rambling down the steps to the street, doing their best not to listen to Mary's drunken rants.

"James, I'm shaking. I've never been through anything like that before "

"Forgive her," he said. "That isn't your aunt talking. The drink is making her crazy. The walk to the theater will clear our heads. I'm pretty sure we'll be able to get inside this time of day."

The H.C. Miner Vaudeville House was still a work in progress, as it had just opened a few months earlier. There were woodworkers inside putting in some flourishes, and they had left the door open. The theater had twelve hundred seats with a lower level and a mezzanine, and the band played below the stage, which was outfitted with a violet velvet curtain. Margaret had only ever been to a music hall in Galway that was about half the size.

Standing on the stage and pretending to look out at an imaginary audience, she said, "I'm impressed. This would be a grand place to sing. My only worry is being able to sing loud enough for such a big place."

"I'm glad you like it. It's easy to picture you singing to a packed house," James told her.

"Well, I still need to get hired. They might not like me."

"Not a chance."

"Well, I'm glad you're confident. Just a small request: before we walk back to the boarding house, would you be so kind as to show me where the nearest church is?"

Holding hands, the pair walked to Saint Joseph's, which was less than a ten-minutes from the boarding house. The façade of the church looked like St. Patrick's in Fanore. It felt like a good omen to Margaret. As James opened the heavy oak door, she pulled out her little cloth money purse and took out a penny, which she put it in the coin box. James put in a nickel. They both blessed themselves with holy water, moved into a pew, and kneeled.

Margaret prayed silently. *Lord, forgive me for treating Aunt Mary so poorly. Please watch over her children and keep them from harm. Please keep my parents in Your grace. Finally, please watch over James and me. I haven't had time to think things through properly. I know what my heart tells me. Help me remain virtuous and stay in Your grace. Amen.*

She noticed that, after an initial period of contemplation, James's demeanor changed to one of obvious delight. "James, why are you smiling?" she asked. "You'll have to join me at church frequently if it's going to make you this happy."

"I felt I gave the good Lord a proper thanking in His house for bringing you into my life, that's all."

Upon leaving the church, the pair made the short walk to the boarding house. Before going up the steps, James bent down and kissed Margaret, who obliged and pulled him closer. He finished by kissing her on the forehead, then looked into her eyes and told her, "You know I'd do anything for you, Margaret".

"I absolutely believe you . . . Now help me get these bags up the stairs to the house before Mrs. Schmidt changes her mind."

CHAPTER 3
FAMILY

James O'Mara had become an orphan at thirteen, in 1874. Reluctantly, his mother's sister, who lived in Newark, had taken him and his two younger sisters in. With all those extra mouths to feed, James had to go to work to support his siblings.

He started out in a fish market down neck. Soon, he began frequenting Morphy's Billiards Hall on Mulberry Street on Sundays and found he had a natural talent for the new game of fifteen-ball pool. He quickly realized he could make more money by hustling pocket billiards and doing odd jobs for Clancy, a local bookmaker, than working a respectable job.

James continued contributing to the household, but the rest of his earnings he used to enjoy his newfound spare time. By the ripe old age of eighteen, James had built an appreciation for good whiskey, steak dinners, and expensive clothes. He knew how to stay on the right side of the law by doing favors for the police, who would look the other way when James was involved in something illegal. When the H.C. Miner Vaudeville House opened in the fall of 1886 in Newark, they hired him to ensure patrons didn't get too rowdy during the performances.

James had a well-deserved reputation as a lady's man around town. Because of his good looks and deep pockets, he always had a pretty girl on his arm. These relationships did not last, however, because James quickly grew bored and moved on.

‡

James got Margaret settled in the boarding house and secured her an audition at H.C. Miner. He also quit his own dubious employment with Clancy, keeping the job at the vaudeville house. This allowed him to spend more time with Margaret and support her in building her career.

Margaret became an instant hit as the "Celtic Sweetheart from County Clare," and her renditions of Irish folk songs and ballads played well to a large percentage of the audience. James was always at her side, whether it was escorting her to church or work.

As her fame grew locally, Margaret found it increasingly difficult to sing at the levels necessary to fill the theater. One morning, six months after starting at H.C. Miner, she was in tears when James came to escort her to morning mass. "I'm going to have to leave the theater for a while. I can barely talk above a whisper, let alone sing," she told him. James took her to the hospital that day.

The doctors diagnosed Margaret with tuberculosis, and she spent nearly two months at the Hospital of the Sisters of the Poor of St. Francis. James paid for a small private room rather than allowing her to be put up in the tuberculosis ward, and the nurses opened the windows fully during the day to let the fall breeze blow through.

After a month had passed, Margaret began to feel healthier and even regained the weight she had lost. Eventually she went back to Mrs. Schmidt's boarding house and spent the following months trying to build back her full strength. During this period, James exhausted almost all his savings. He decided he needed to find full-time, steady employment, and using some of his old connections in the Republican party, he secured a job as a policeman in Orange, a city a few miles west of downtown Newark.

In the mid 1800s, they separated the city of Orange into four distinct parts: South, East, and West Orange, with Orange proper in the center. Industry grew the fastest in Orange, along with housing for workers. The town soon had over twenty factories producing hats, making it the hub of hat-making in the States. West and South Orange were decidedly more affluent, with more spacious houses and much less industrial production.

‡

James had not revealed to Margaret that he had run out of money. He started getting anxious about seeing her again and asking her to marry him. He was not afraid of being rejected, but thought it a distinct possibility she might say she wasn't ready yet, which would significantly lessen the time they could spend together.

After procrastinating for a week, he finally decided that this would be the day. "I've some good news, Margaret. They've offered me a job as a policeman in Orange," James told her.

"Well, that is good news," she agreed, "but doesn't it mean we won't be seeing each other as much?"

He bent down on one knee and took a silver ring from his pocket, slipping it onto her finger. "Margaret, you're the love of my life. I've wanted to ask you for a long time, but I've waited until you were feeling stronger. I want to marry you, if you'll have me."

Margaret smiled. "I was wondering when you were going to get around to asking me. Yes! You are the love of my life as well." She looked down at her ring. "Where did you find this beautiful Claddagh?"

Avoiding the question, James said, "We can get married in Saint Joseph's and move to a nice apartment in Orange. It's cheaper, and the air is cleaner there. You won't have to work, as my salary will cover things."

"Well, that all sounds grand. I'd like to sing again, but I know I'm a long way from being able to do that."

Knowing that day would probably never come, James nodded in agreement. The doctor had told James that he suspected Margaret had caught tuberculosis in the theater. It was miracle enough that she'd recovered at all—there was almost no chance she'd be able to sustain singing for any length of time.

‡

Wearing his police uniform, James walked into Miller's Pharmacy on Central Avenue right across from Orange Park. He was there to inquire about the apartment upstairs, as advertised in the front window. The pharmacist, Herbert Miller, an older gentleman with spectacles and fuzzy mutton chop sideburns, greeted James and took him upstairs through the back of the store.

When he saw the apartment, James thought it was perfect. The building was on the corner, so there were windows on the front, back, and side, allowing lots of sunlight into all of the rooms. There was plumbing, heat, and some odd bits of furniture they could put to immediate use. Most of all, there was plenty of room to start a family.

"How much do you want for the place?"

"Mr. O'Mara, I'm extending you a special offer of twenty dollars a month because you're a policeman. I expect you to spend some time in the store when you're wearing a uniform. If you hear anything in the evening, I want you to chase the thieves out."

"So, Mr. Miller, you're asking me to do my job and then help protect the store when I'm off duty?"

"Precisely. I hope they see you around and decide my pharmacy may not be the best place to steal morphine."

"You've got a deal. I'm getting married on Saturday, and we'll move in on Monday, if that's okay."

‡

It was a cold winter morning in January of 1888, two weeks after the wedding. Margaret and James were sitting comfortably at their kitchen table, enjoying a cup of tea and discussing plans for furnishing the apartment. Their conversation was interrupted by a knock at the door and the delivery of a telegram. Once she was done reading, Margaret handed it to James and started to cry. James went over to console her, and after some time sobbing, she looked up into his eyes and said, "I know this is a lot to ask, but I—"

James interrupted her before she could finish. "I was going to suggest it myself. Our apartment is big enough. There's no reason for your mom to be alone. Please, invite her to come to America and live with us."

Ellen Keane was grateful for the invitation and accepted immediately. James and Margaret made the trip to Castle Gardens to meet her. "I'm so happy to be here," she said upon arrival. "I can't thank you enough. I'm no charity case and will contribute to the household."

Ellen was a short, slightly plump woman of forty-five, with graying dark brown hair that she wore in a bun. She always looked concerned about something, and her hands revealed a long history of hard work. True to her word, she found cleaning jobs in the well-to-do Vailsburg area of Newark, about a thirty-minute walk from James and Margaret's apartment. On her way home, she would buy fresh groceries to make supper. Because his beat was so close to home, even when James was working evening hours, he could return to a have dinner at six thirty sharp.

Now that her mother was here, Margaret could focus more on improving her health and building her stamina. After long walks around the neighborhood, she would take books and newspapers to Orange Park and read for hours in the fresh air, occasionally feeding the ducks in the pond with some stale bread. As she grew stronger, she tried singing her favorite songs at the level she used to when singing professionally. After a full month of serenading the ducks and passersby in the park, she gave up.

Their first child, John, was born later that year. Margaret did exceptionally well with the pregnancy and childbirth, considering her slight frame and her recent illness. Three more pregnancies and three more healthy children followed. The apartment became a bit crowded, but they made things work. As much as Margaret had enjoyed her brief career as a singer, she adored being a wife and mother. By the time her children were ready to go to the parish school, they knew how to read and some basic catechism.

James became a respected officer of the law in the community. He could be hard-nosed when he needed to be, but only with those he felt deserved it. Indeed, enforcing the law was quite a different matter from keeping the peace. There would be no support from anyone on the police force if he fully enforced the law. Organized crime networks paid policemen to look the other way when it came to gambling and prostitution. James too would accept money, but he intervened if he thought people were being victimized. On occasion, he'd pay a visit to a bookie or madam and threaten to shut them down if he heard about anyone getting roughed up.

The people in the area he patrolled were of a mix of races and nationalities. Over time, he learned how to relate to all of them. He would lend a helping hand to a battered colored woman the same way he would help a white one. Because of his reputation for fairness, he had information coming to him from all directions, allowing him to step into many situations and intervene before they escalated. However, as respected as he was by the community, many of his fellow police officers did not appreciate his methods and called him a "nigger lover" behind his back.

The beat he covered encompassed just over 20 percent of the land area of the city, and it had the lowest crime rate within the two square miles of Orange. The police captain praised him for his work and gave him full autonomy to continue, but confided in James that he would never make sergeant.

‡

During her fifth pregnancy, Margaret struggled with morning sickness. There were many occasions during the nine months when she thought she might lose the baby. Unable to go to early morning mass, she prayed for the life of her unborn child every day upon waking and then said a rosary in the afternoon. "James, this has to be the last one for us," she told her husband. "I don't think I can go through this again."

In the last month of the pregnancy, Margaret's mother stayed home to take care of her during the days. When Margaret's water broke early in the morning on March 21, 1898, Ellen scurried to get the midwife. By the time she got back, Margaret had gone into heavy labor and was about to deliver the baby.

The hissing steam radiators and loud clanging pipes in the second floor apartment went unnoticed by the participants in the birthing room on that frigid but bright spring day. Despite the protests of the midwife, James insisted on being present. He stood next to Margaret, squeezing her hand and telling her that everything was going to be fine while worrying profusely that he would lose her.

James left the room for a moment to check on their young daughter Ellen, who was down the hall. He had left the little girl to amuse herself by looking at a slew of picture books he'd scattered on her bed. As soon as he entered the room, she ran to him and begged him to pick her up and hold her. Ellen was upset by her mother's screams, and James consoled her despite the incredible apprehension he felt. An hour later, the cries of a healthy infant eventually replaced the woman's shrieks. Ellen was not the baby of the family anymore.

The tension that had been pulsing through the bodies of every-one who had taken part in the birth dissipated. Smiles and tears of joy appeared on their faces. Margaret called out to her youngest daughter, "Ellie, please come in to meet your wee brother."

Looking down at her newborn son in her arms, with her daughter by her side, Margaret exclaimed, "I'm surely blessed to have such a beautiful boy! I want to name him Sebastian, after the saint who has his feast day on my birthday."

"Wait a second, dear." James said. "We named our other kids John, Mary, Thomas, and Ellen. They're all good *American*-sounding names. I'm not saying I don't like Sebastian, but it sounds a bit too fancy for our town." This was the first James had heard about his wife's wishes, and he felt that her choice of name would get his third son off to a terrible start.

Margaret's mother Ellen, never shy about stating her opinions, chimed in. "If I might make a suggestion, why don't you name him after the brilliant opera tenor, Joseph O'Mara? You could give him Sebastian as a middle name."

Summoning up a bit of strength, Margaret replied, "Mother, I had my heart set on Sebastian if it was a boy. If I didn't know better, I'd think you're in cahoots with my husband."

Looking down at her son's small red face nestled against her breast, she wiped the wet strands of hair away from her face. "Saint Joseph was such a wonderful husband to Our Lord's Mother," she said. "I don't know whether I'm persuaded or too tired to argue. Joseph Sebastian O'Mara it is."

CHAPTER 4
THE LITTLE OPERATOR

Thirteen-year-old Joey was the spitting image of his father, with dirty-blond hair and piercing light blue eyes. This afternoon, he was sporting a big shiner and had dark smears of dried blood caked around his mouth and chin. The wounds from his last fight had barely even healed.

As he walked into the kitchen, his grandmother, who was seated at the table, gasped and called out to her daughter. "Your young ruffian is home and needs fixing up. You'd think he'd have learned his lesson by now, but he keeps on fighting. He must not have the smarts of his older brothers, who never got into any scrapes."

Margaret raced into the kitchen and first addressed her son. "Joey, come here and let me clean you up. You're all bruised." Then she looked sternly at her mother and said, "If you don't have positive things to say to Joey, I'd prefer you say nothing. Joey is plenty smart. He's just very different from his brothers."

As Joe sat down at the table, his grandmother hurried up from the table and left, mumbling something under her breath. Margaret cleaned her son's wounds with soap and water and asked, "What happened?"

"Mom, I couldn't let them be mean to Teddy. They were throwing stones at him, and I had to stop 'em." Teddy was one of the local stray dogs Joey had befriended. He was a fifty-pound mixed breed, mostly black, with floppy ears. Over the last few months, Joey had been feeding the dog with scraps left over from their family meals. He'd named him after the last president, whom his father always talked about in the most positive of terms.

"Wouldn't it have been smarter to call for Teddy and run away? That dog follows you everywhere."

"I didn't think about that. I got so mad when they—" Joey stopped speaking as he heard the creaking of the back steps, alerting them that someone was coming upstairs.

James, in his blue police uniform, entered the kitchen. He took one look at his son and said, "Again?"

"I'm sorry, Pop. I was just explaining to Mom these kids were trying to hurt Teddy, and I couldn't let 'em get away with it."

James looked his son directly in the eyes and addressed him calmly. "I know what the problem is, and I'm going to help you fix things. The simple fact of the matter is you don't know how to fight. If these kids knew they were in for a battle, they'd leave you alone and go pick on somebody else. I'm going to teach you how so you can put an end to this nonsense."

"Is that really the answer?" asked Margaret. "You never had to teach your other sons to fight, and they have been able to avoid getting hurt."

"My dear, Joey's got a quick temper and will stick his nose into things the other boys wouldn't want any part of. If I teach him and he proves he's not someone to be messed around with, the fighting will stop. Joey, what do you think?"

"Pop, there's only one boy who beats me up. The others just follow him around. He's a lot bigger than me, though."

"I don't like this one bit," Margaret interjected, "but I think your father may be right. You'll face bullies all your life. Maybe it's best to learn to deal with them now."

‡

The lessons began. Joey was of average height but had a sturdy, almost stocky frame for a boy his age. James taught him the finer points of street fighting as he had learned them in his youth—techniques for punching, kicking, headbutting, and using your body to gain an advantage. Joey impressed his father with the physical strength he exhibited during the lessons. However, James constantly pushed the boy to punch harder by taunting him.

"Hit me with everything you've got," he'd say. "Right in the stomach—show me you're stronger than your sister." After Joey snuck a punch through to his father's gut, making him wince, James would follow it up with, "Let's go to the dressmaker today. I want to get you fitted for a nice new white dress to wear on Easter Sunday."

After two weeks of almost daily thirty-minute lessons, James addressed his son. "Do you remember the whole point of why I've been teaching you to fight?"

"So I can fight back and win and not get beat up."

"Yes, that's true, but there's more. You don't want to fight. You want the other boys to leave you alone. They need to fear you." He looked his son in the eye. "Remember three things."

"Okay."

"Stare at your opponent with confidence before things start. Let 'em know you think you'll win. You're not the biggest kid in the neighborhood, but I bet you're strong enough to take on that bully."

"Really, Pop? Do you think so?"

"I know so. I've got the bruises to prove it! With your strength, mix in the unexpected. Anything goes. Surprise them, then you have the advantage," James told him.

"Okay, I understand. What's the third thing?"

"Remember this one most of all. Think speed. Do everything fast. You want this to be as short a fight as possible. So, what are the three s's?"

"Stare, surprise, speed," Joey recited.

‡

Most days, Teddy would wait for Joe under the steps to their apartment. He would then walk with him to school. He would reappear right before Joey began his walk home, as if he were carrying a timepiece.

On his walk to Our Lady of the Valley Parish School, Joey imagined the next confrontation and planned what he would do. He wasn't sure when it would happen, because the boys who were giving him trouble went to the Park Avenue School. His chief aggressor, Tommy Hailey, was your typical childhood bully, endowed with both physical size and strength and always looking to be the center of attention. Because he was a good three inches taller than most of his peers—and built like an ox—he felt very comfortable imposing his will in a loud and insulting way. There were a few boys who would always be in his company, laughing and encouraging him to be even meaner than he was naturally inclined to be.

That September day, when Teddy and Joey got within a few blocks of the O'Mara apartment, the dog became quite agitated and started barking. As this was unusual behavior for him, Joey took heed and prepared himself. He took a few cautious steps forward, and as he passed by a vacant lot, Tommy Hailey and two of his gang jumped out and planted themselves right in front of him. Teddy continued to bark.

"If it isn't little Joey and his fleabag dog." Tommy leered. "They could both use a good beating today, unless they pay the tax. Pay up or get beat up."

Looking him straight in the eyes, Joey said confidently, "I'm not afraid of you."

As soon as the three youths began laughing, Joey reared back with his right foot and kicked Tommy as hard as he could in the groin. When the bully doubled over from the pain, Joey leaped toward him and started pummeling his face—right, left, right—until the bloodied boy fell to the ground in shock.

One of Tommy's friends reached out and grabbed Joey's arm. Teddy stopped barking and began biting his leg and ripping his trousers. That forced the boy to release his hold on Joey and concentrate on getting the dog off his leg, and Joey seized the opportunity to attack. He started pummeling the boy's face, dropping him to the ground. Afterward, he stopped and stared at the remaining boy, who had backed up considerably and appeared reluctant to get involved.

Feeling quite proud of himself, Joey called Teddy to his side and yelled over to Tommy, who was sitting on the ground, bleeding and quite embarrassed. "Do you say uncle, or am I going to come back over there?"

No response. Joey walked toward Tommy, fully prepared to start things again.

"Uncle." Tommy forced himself to his feet, summoning his buddies, and the trio made haste to leave the scene of the fight behind them.

Other than his bruised hands, Joey didn't have a mark on him. He took a knee next to Teddy and addressed his friend. "I wouldn't have won this fight if it wasn't for you." The dog lovingly licked his face.

Joe strutted the distance home. His father had taught him well. Stare. Surprise. Speed.

His mother greeted him as he opened the door. "How was your day, Joey?" She looked him over, clearly pleased to see no evidence of fighting or bruises. The inspection when Joey returned home had become a daily ritual.

"Good . . . Mom, I was thinking—you know how Teddy has become my dog? With winter coming, he'd be a whole lot happier if he didn't have to sleep outside. If I don't get into any more fights, can he spend the night inside?"

"Well, I'm inclined to say yes, if this is an incentive for you. You know how I hate this fighting," she said. "I'll have to make sure it's fine with your father."

They granted Joey his wish, and Teddy got to spend his first night indoors with the family.

‡

As James and Margaret retired to bed, James remarked, "You know that son of yours, Joseph Sebastian, is quite a little operator."

"What makes you say that?"

"You know how I've got eyes all over this town. Well, I caught wind of this fight that happened today over in the vacant lot a few blocks away on Central Avenue. Three boys got the tar whipped out of them by a smaller boy and a medium-sized black dog. Only took a couple of minutes. From the description of what went on, I'm positive this was our Joey. Rather than coming home telling the tale, he figures his fighting problem is over, and why not use that to get his dog indoors?"

"Well, I feel like going down the hall and waking up my mother and telling her this story," Margaret said. "When she implied the reason Joey was getting into fights was because he wasn't smart enough, I got angry. She's always comparing him to John and Tom, and that's just not fair. They're both older and very studious and have never gotten into any trouble. Joey shows very advanced reasoning for a boy his age."

"Margaret, my love, I see a lot of me in Joey. But he catches on to things quicker than I ever did. I had to learn everything the hard way, and I'm hoping he can avoid some of my mistakes."

CHAPTER 5

AN EXPERIENCE TO REMEMBER

The fight was a transformational event for Joe. Afterward, he exuded self-confidence and began carrying himself differently. It didn't hurt that an exaggerated version of the confrontation had traveled around the school and neighborhood, giving Joe celebrity status with the kids in the area. Everyone wanted to be his friend now. However, Joe's interests differed from those of others his age, and he gravitated toward some of the older boys. He became friends with a couple who were members of a local street gang called the "Orange Boys."

The Orange Boys members ranged from fourteen to about twenty. They were involved in petty crimes such as pickpocketing and purse snatching, but their primary activity was fighting and protecting their "turf" from other gangs. They'd claimed Orange Park.

Rituals were a key element of being in a gang. To gain admission to the Orange Boys, the youth had to undergo a series of trials to show their worthiness. First, they had to endure verbal, then physical, abuse. The last trial involved doing something illegal, usually theft of some kind. Once inducted, the older members introduced the newcomers to cigarettes, alcohol, and gambling and regaled them with stories of street fights and female conquests.

As the son of a cop, Joe was persona non grata when it came to joining the Orange Boys, despite his friendships with the members. He'd started hanging out with Toby "Freckles" Moore and Jimmy "Blackie" Walters, sixteen-year-olds who were in the gang. Despite his ineligibility, they felt compelled to "school" Joe on some of the finer points of gang membership. It gave them not only amusement but a sense of status to watch Joe cough incessantly after his first cigarette or throw up after drinking a large glass of whiskey. Gambling was a different matter—Joe would regularly take their money and smokes when they played dice or cards.

There was also a gang ritual where the leadership arranged for new members to lose their virginity at a local brothel as a rite of passage.

"Freckles," said Blackie one day, "our buddy Joe is fourteen and still has his cherry. I'm gonna ask my sister Molly to fix that for him. She'll do it. She's as easy as they come."

‡

Joe took a final drag on his hand-rolled cigarette and stamped it out in the grass before knocking. He had been to the Walters' basement apartment on Pierson Street to meet up with Blackie several times, so he was quite familiar with the place.

"Who's there?"

"It's Joe."

"C'mon in, it's open."

Joe opened the heavy wooden door and stepped inside the dimly lit parlor. A sweet smell of smoke laced with perfume overwhelmed the room.

Turning to his left, he saw Molly standing, dressed in a loosely draped black robe that barely covered her breasts, smoking a small pipe.

"Joe, turn around and bolt the door." Once he'd done so, Molly asked, "Like what you see?"

His heart was racing with excitement. He struggled to give her a simple "yes."

"Get over here and help me finish smoking this."

Without hesitation, Joe moved toward Molly and took the pipe from her hand. He drew on it slowly, watching the small ball of opium glow and feeling the burn from the smoke filling his lungs. As he exhaled, he became lightheaded.

Taking the pipe back, Molly took a deep draw, then reached down between Joe's legs. Gently stroking the area, she mumbled to herself, "Gonna enjoy this" as she exhaled, blowing smoke in his face. "Finish this."

Joe obeyed, taking two more deep drags before the small ember turned dark.

"Follow me," she commanded.

He walked behind her, feeling like he was floating at least a foot above the floorboards. Once they entered the bedroom, Molly made quick work of taking off Joe's clothes and then reclined on her bed, the black robe still draped over her body. She summoned Joe to her.

"Don't worry darlin', Molly'll show you everything you need to know."

‡

Joe's head was in a complete fog on the walk back home. He had been with Molly for almost five hours and had missed family dinner. He had mixed feelings about what had just happened—despite having enjoyed all these new sensations, Joe now felt incredibly self-conscious about reeking of perfume and having makeup smeared on his face. He didn't like the fact he had lost all control and submitted to Molly's commands.

Would he go back to see her? She had offered to teach him all the ways to bring pleasure to a woman. His heart still felt like it was racing as he remembered what her body had looked like draped in that silky black robe.

In front of his home, he stopped for a moment and tried to clear his head. If he was fortunate, he would get through to the bathroom, encountering no one at this late hour. With his luck, however, his grandmother would probably be sitting at the kitchen table and immediately begin questioning in her usual brusque manner.

After walking up the back steps and opening the door, Joe found himself greeted by Teddy. He bent over and patted him on the head. The dog was a welcome encounter, at least. But then Tom walked into the kitchen just as Joe was trying to make his way down the hall to the bath. Before his brother could open his mouth, Joe looked at him and whispered, "Say nothing. Leave it alone."

As Joe furtively made his way down the hall, Margaret opened the door to her bedroom and stood face-to-face with him. Skilled at sizing up her son, she seemingly decided not to probe, asking simply, "Joey, is everything all right?"

His mother had probably made quite a good guess of what had happened, judging by the look on her face. Joey chose not to insult her intelligence by concocting some elaborate story to explain why he was late.

"I'm okay, but I'm really tired. Gonna take a bath and then go to bed," he said.

"Well, you have a good night's sleep. Tomorrow, I'm going to Saturday-afternoon confession. I'd like some company. Then we could take communion together on Sunday."

"Okay, Mom, I'll join you."

‡

On Saturday afternoon, Joe escorted his mother to church for confession. He knew why she'd made the request. This was her way of telling him she knew what had happened and did not approve. In her eyes, confession was a fresh start and an opportunity to do better. By agreeing to go, Joe could admit wrongdoing without getting into the details. He would make her happy, show he was at least listening to her and trying. He'd go through the motions of confessing to a priest, but at heart, he felt like a hypocrite.

The previous evening, after his bath, he'd gone to bed and slept soundly until about eight. Upon waking, the memory of his sexual encounter with Molly consumed his total consciousness. He had a hard time thinking of anything else. Joe could not resist the desire to go back to her. He wanted more.

As they walked, his mother was making conversation and talking about some parishioners whom she was helping. Then, out of the blue, she asked Joe, "Have you given any thought to what you are going to do with your life? I am so proud of John for considering the priesthood, and Tom seems headed toward being an undertaker. I know how smart you are, even if your marks at school don't show it. It makes me sad to think of you at some factory job. You read so many books—perhaps a career as a writer or journalist would be a good one to consider."

"Mom, I've never thought about that. I haven't tried to write anything, but it may be something I could look at. Right now, I'm thinking I would join the navy when I'm old enough. I'd like to see more of the world. In the meantime, I could get a job and save up some money."

"Going to high school would be an opportunity to learn and maybe explore writing as a possibility. It's a better idea to further your education rather than go to work at your age. It will give you more options later."

"I'll give it some thought," Joe replied as they walked into the church, blessed themselves with holy water, and made their way to the pews near the confessional.

His mother went first. As Joe waited for her to finish, he decided he would confess to his "impure" thoughts only, rather than shocking the priest with the full disclosure of what had happened yesterday. That should keep him in the booth awhile and give him significant penance to pray, which would be a good thing for his mother to see.

Joe had been right. After confessing his "impure" thoughts, he listened while the priest went on about how such thoughts led to self-mutilation, then adultery, followed by eternal damnation. He gave Joe quite a heavy penance, about an hour's worth of prayers.

Joe walked out of the confessional and told his mother, "Mom, I've quite a lot of praying to do, about an hour before I can leave."

"Not a problem for me. I've brought my rosary beads, and I'll keep busy praying while you do your penance."

As Joe kneeled to start his litany, he thought about what his mom had said about high school. School wasn't difficult for him. He just wasn't interested in learning algebra or Latin, and he found it hard to even try in classes he hated. However, he found it even more difficult to ignore his mother when she made a strong suggestion. He decided he would at least try for her. He began mentally reciting the string of Hail Marys.

After the session of prayers, they started the walk home. "Mom, I'm giving serious thought to starting high school and seeing how things go," Joe told her.

"I'm so proud of you, Joey. Thank you for listening."

He stayed in and read for the rest of the day. At the kitchen table, with his book in front of him and Teddy under his feet, his thoughts drifted back to Molly. She'd mentioned wanting to see him again on Sunday afternoon. That night, he went to bed at nine and tossed restlessly, thinking about how he was going to manage everything.

The next day, the O'Mara family all went to mass at 10 a.m. and had Holy Communion. Margaret knew that not everyone in the house shared her religious fervor, but it made her feel good to have her husband and children with her at church. Joey's positive direction inspired her to sing joyously during mass.

‡

Molly opened the door, this time with no makeup to hide her red blemishes and her long black hair uncombed and matted. She welcomed Joe by saying, "I thought you'd be back."

"I can only stay an hour. Is that okay for you?"

"I guess. You should be able to fuck me at least twice. Let's share a pipe first."

"I'll wait on the bed for you while you smoke it in here."

"Suit yourself."

After Molly finished smoking the opium, she met Joe in the bedroom. He couldn't wait to take her clothes off so he could replay their initial encounter. He soon realized that this wouldn't be possible. After an hour, Joe was out of bed, dressed, and out the door.

On the walk home, he began reflecting on what had transpired over the last few days. Friday had been an experience to remember. What he had just done was something to forget. Trying to duplicate that night had felt more like a chore than anything else. What had been different this time? He'd wanted to be in total control and declined to smoke her pipe. Despite enjoying all the sensations of the act itself, he couldn't get past the fact that he didn't feel any attraction toward Molly. It was all he could think of during sex. The first night, under the influence of opium, he really hadn't been thinking about anything. It just happened.

Was that intense pleasure possible without the high? It wasn't going to be with Molly. It needed to be with someone whom he was deeply attracted to. Relieved for a moment that he had things figured out, his next thought was, *how is that going to happen?*

CHAPTER 6

THE TESTY OLD SCOT

Joe attended Our Lady of the Valley High School for one year to please his mother. From the start, though, he butted heads with his teachers and hated the subjects he was taught. By the end of the year, he was frequently skipping school, and Margaret was called in many times to hear Sister Mary Therese lament about how lazy and stupid a child Joe was compared to her other boys. At first, Margaret would try to challenge him to work harder and do better, but she finally realized that high school wasn't for him after all. It was holding him back.

After Margaret gave James the latest news, he exclaimed, "I'm glad you finally agree with me about him attending high school. I believe if he enjoys what he does and keeps busy, he'll work hard and be a solid citizen. You know what they say about idle hands. If our Joe isn't busy, he'll invent trouble to get into. Harry Hannah, who owns a shop that fixes cars, was telling me how good business is, but he can't find help smart enough to work with him. He's a testy old Scot, but I think Joe could learn the trade working for him. Besides, Harry owes me more than one favor."

"I think that sounds like a good idea. Joey needs to be challenged, but he has to like what he is doing," said Margaret.

‡

Joe stood next to his dad in the small, cluttered office of Hannah's Garage. Even though he was looking directly at his father while he sold Harry on his son's smarts, Joe could feel the eyes of the proprietor looking him up and down.

"Aye, Jimmy, I'll put him on. I will agree to a three-month trial only, though. The boy better be smarter than you," said Harry, with a twinkle in his eye.

"The boy's more clever than his old man. I know he's fifteen, but treat him like a man. He learns quickly, and he'll work hard for you. If not, you let me know."

"I'll have my foot up his ass if he doesn't work hard. If that doesn't get him going, then I'll be looking for you."

On the walk back to their apartment, Joe's father told him not to take Harry too seriously—his bark was much worse than his bite. However, he needed to work hard and prove himself before Harry would ever consider giving him a paying job.

Harry Hannah had built his mechanical knowledge working on the steam turbines for the shipping industry in Glasgow. When work became scarce, he made his way to the States and had no trouble finding a job as the head of maintenance for Hudson Hat Company. Harry began fixing cars during his off shifts and eventually saved enough to buy a filling station with a garage on South Center Street, close to where many expensive cars were housed in the Vailsburg section of Newark. He hired two colored men, Leroy and Jim, to work at the pump and help with some of the heavy work in the shop. When business increased to a volume he couldn't handle himself, he hired a number of mechanics that didn't work out for one reason or another.

‡

It was day one of the internship. Joe made sure he reported for work a few minutes before his starting time of eight o'clock. He walked into the office and saw that Harry was sitting at the desk smoking his pipe, a blueprint spread out in front of him. With a welcoming smile, he beckoned Joe to come inside.

"Good morning, lad. You passed your first test. You're early. Before I teach you the basics of how to work with tools, I want to see what you think of this 1912 Model T drivetrain on my desk. Look them over and tell me how the car moves."

"How much time do I have?"

"I'll give you an hour."

Joe hadn't done anything quite like this before, but looking at the drawings did not intimidate him. His favorite author was Jules Verne, and he always paid attention to the detailed descriptions of the equipment in books like *Journey to the Center of the Earth* and *20,000 Leagues under the Sea*, even making some sketches based on the author's specifications. He'd also built an understanding of the temperamental coal-fired steam boiler in the basement of their building and knew how to get it back in operation when temperatures in their apartment dropped.

"Joe, you have a lot to learn, but I like that you can make sense of these drawings. I think you'll do pretty well."

Given his first impression of Harry and his father's comments, Joe took the words as high praise.

Later that day, Joe learned Harry had fired the mechanic who'd worked at the garage just short of a year. He made a point of telling Joe his rationale. "I can't tolerate someone being stupid *and* lazy!"

Harry invested time instructing Joe on how to think through car problems. Sometimes this involved changing broken parts or fabricating new ones by working with Harry's network of friends, who had access to metalworking shops. When Harry learned that Joe had a dog, he suggested, "why don't you bring Teddy to work? It'd do my heart good to have a dog around here," Joe obliged and enjoyed having his faithful dog near his side throughout the day.

‡

Three months flew by. Harry could be a little gruff, but he was an excellent teacher, the kind who balanced instruction with leaving Joe alone to work things out on his own. Solving problems independently built his confidence and made the job enjoyable. He would always laugh to himself when Harry would preach the fundamental tenet of his management philosophy: "If you're not making some mistakes, you're not trying hard enough. Just don't make the same mistakes over and fucking over again."

Harry called Joe into the office just before he was ready to leave for the day. He was sitting at his desk and leaning back in his chair. "It's September, Joe. Your three months are up. Do you think I should hire you to work with me full-time?"

A good mechanic was worth at least twelve dollars a week in the area. The worker whom Harry had fired when Joe started had been making ten.

"Mr. Hannah, you'd be silly not to hire me. I can do the work of a mechanic, and you can pay me less because I'm only fifteen."

"Aye, that's true, boy. What d'you think I should pay you?"

"Seven dollars a week is fair. My birthday is in March, though, and I want a two-dollar raise then."

"What would you do if I told you all I could pay you was five?"

Joe was a bit surprised Harry hadn't agreed already and was still negotiating. He also knew that, if he walked out the door, the shop wouldn't be able handle the volume of business that they were currently doing. It was time to call Harry's bluff.

"I'd thank you for all you've taught me, Mr. Hannah, and find a shop that'd pay me seven."

Harry packed his pipe, lit it, and drew heavily, releasing the smoke slowly from his mouth and nose. He stared at Joe, who was waiting anxiously for his response. "Aye, seven it is then. And nine in March. This is all on the condition your work continues to be satisfactory. If it slips, you know I'll sack you."

"Thank you, Mr. Hannah. You won't be sorry."

‡

The months passed quickly for Joe as he worked in the garage. The hard work built his strength and transformed his sixteen-year-old body into solid muscle. While he still retained some of his boyish features, most people assumed he was much older than his age.

Business was booming because of the garage's reputation for quality work, and Harry and his four employees regularly spent at least ten hours a day there Monday through Friday, with a half day on Saturday. When the doors closed at one, Harry would pull out a bottle of whiskey and offer his employees a drink before they went their separate ways. At first, Joe declined, but stayed for the conversation and laughs as they recapped the week's events. As his affection for his colleagues grew, he started joining them in drinking to be social.

Saturday nights were the only time Joe let loose. He found it was best to venture away from home. He would take the trolley down to Broad and Market in Newark and walk to Mulberry Street, to Morphy's Pool Hall. There were usually various forms of gambling going in the back rooms. Whether it was cards, craps, dice, or pool, Joe would bring his weekly earnings to bet, and most nights walked away with two or three times that amount. Joe would nurse one beer the entire time, giving himself an edge over his opponents, who knocked back drink after drink.

Poker was his standard, but if it wasn't his night for cards, he'd switch to craps. When he didn't feel like thinking too hard, he shot pool. He became a recognized face at Morphy's, but because of the low profile he maintained, few noticed just how successful he was. He would usually leave with his winnings around ten, then stop by one of the two brothels in the vicinity. This would give him ample time to take care of "business," freshen up, and make the last trolley home at midnight. He would be in bed by one and ready for morning mass on Sunday.

It had been a good night for Joe at Morphy's. Leaving the pool hall just before ten, he thought of the three working girls whom he saw regularly. He hoped Daphne was available, because he enjoyed being with her the most. She was only a few years older than him, and not only was she an exceptionally cute blond, but she had a great sense of humor. Being with her was fun.

Later that night, Joe was lying on the bed next to her. "You know I enjoy seeing you, but for the life of me, I can't understand why you're paying for it," Daphne said while lighting a cigarette.

Taking the cigarette from her, Joe took a drag and then handed it back. "It's complicated."

"Screwing is not complicated," Daphne said with a giggle.

"I don't have any time for courting a girl. This way, there are no hurt feelings. One day, I might want to settle down, or . . . maybe I won't." Joe rolled over, positioning himself on top of her. "Since you're the one who brought it up, though, I want to make sure I get my money's worth tonight."

CHAPTER 7
LA MANO NERO

The ethnic makeup of the Newark area had changed dramatically begin-ning in the 1890s. Because of poor economic conditions in their home countries, wave after wave of immigrants passed through Ellis Island, and with its high level of industrialization fueling growth industries, Newark was a natural place for them to settle. Most were from Southern Italy and Sicily, with the next largest cohort coming from Eastern Europe. The city became distinctly divided along those ethnic lines.

And as customs and cuisines migrated across the Atlantic, organized crime did as well.

‡

It was November 1915. Joe had become an experienced auto mechanic during his two-and-a-half-year tenure working for Harry Hannah. His specialty was working on General Motors cars, which were quite a bit more technically sophisticated than the popular Ford Model T series that many mechanics learned on. Harry had recently increased Joe's wages to match what experienced mechanics were making around town.

"Joe, how many Cadillacs have we worked on in the last three weeks? Every one of them driven by those greaseballs from North Newark. Don't they have anyone to fix them out that way?" said Harry.

"I remember four. All were very easy fixes—hardly anything wrong," Joe said.

No sooner had he answered the question than he noticed that a black 1914 Cadillac Thirty had pulled off South Center Street and skidded a bit on the wet leaves covering the hard-packed dirt by the gas pumps. Two men in dark pin-striped suits swaggered into the garage, leaving their associate in the car. Jim was at the pump, while Leroy, Harry, and Joe were hard at work trying to straighten an axle on an old Model T.

When he saw the men walk in, Joe got up and approached the one who was obviously in charge. "What's wrong with your Cadillac?"

The man waited to speak until Harry had left the Model T and joined Joe. With a thick Italian accent and a condescending tone, he introduced himself. "Mr. Hannah, my name is Antonio Romano. I am quite impressed with the work you do on our cars. You have a nice business here. We don't want to see bad things happen to it. If you pay me twenty-five dollars a week, I will make sure that nothing does. It is my promise to you." He stood there with a smug expression, arms crossed, and began tapping his feet, waiting for a response.

Joe noticed Harry had become extremely agitated. Joe thought about the twenty-five dollars a week and wondered what they could possibly do for that amount. He was making a good buck now, working over fifty hours a week, and he wasn't making anywhere near that kind of money.

Harry finally gave his answer. "Get your guinea ass the fuck out of my garage. I don't want to see you around here again. The police don't want your kind around here either."

"Ah, Mr. Hannah, my offer next week will be thirty-five dollars. I will forget what you just called me if you agree to the twenty-five dollars today."

"Get out—now!" the red-faced Scot yelled at the top of his lungs. Veins bulged on the side of his neck from the strain. "Don't come back. My answer will always be no."

Antonio Romano beckoned for his associate to follow him to the car, and they quickly took off in the black Cadillac.

"Joe, I'll be damned if I'm gonna pay these thugs," Harry said once they had left. "I worked too hard to build this business just to hand it over because of some idle threat."

"That guy said next week it'll be thirty-five dollars. What are they doing for the money?"

"Do me a favor—tell your father what happened. Let him know I won't pay these bastards. I've got no problem standing up to them."

‡

Joe intercepted his father before he made it home for dinner to avoid having the conversation in front of his mother. He explained what had happened earlier that day.

"Son, I knew these gangsters would make their way to Orange sooner or later. I'm pretty sure Harry was paid a visit by the Black Hand. That bunch is dangerous. I've heard stories from my friends on the force in Newark. Their specialty is kidnapping and protection rackets. They started in North Newark, milking money from hardworking Italians who live next door. Now, they've expanded."

Things were finally making sense to Joe. The bad things which Antonio Romano had been referring to were actually the work of the Black Hand. Harry would be paying them to do nothing. Joe asked his father, "What do you mean by dangerous?"

"They'll circle in on a business that's doing well and make an offer for their services. If the owner resists, they throw a brick through a window to show they're serious. If the owner is still stubborn and doesn't pay, he usually winds up getting roughed up and then agrees. They're ruthless when they go into a new territory to build their reputation, so the next targets part with their money easier. The way Harry talked to them, they might go straight for the beating."

Joe was worried now. "Can't the police stop them?"

"They'll only get involved if something bad happens. They'd prefer that Harry just paid. The Irish bosses here in town might be of more help. I'll give them the lowdown. In the meantime, I want you to be on your guard, and whatever you do, don't take these fellas on. You run if you see them coming. I'll see what I can find out and pay Harry a visit."

‡

The whistling of the wind and the scraping of the barren sycamore tree against the window of their apartment awakened Joe. It was still dark in his room, but he knew it would be pointless to try to get back to sleep. The more he thought about the situation at the garage, the tighter the knot in his stomach twisted.

As quietly as he could, he dressed, tiptoed down the hall to the kitchen, grabbed a coat, and opened the door to the darkness of early morning. Crossing the street with Teddy at his side, he ventured into Orange Park and found a bench not too far from the entrance. He reclined, looking upward at the heavens as the very first signs of daylight appeared, occasionally interrupted by fallen leaves that swirled past his field of view in the gusting winds. Four cigarettes later, the only truth he'd found was that paying Antonio Romano was the only thing Harry could do for now.

Realizing he must get to the garage early and try to reason with his employer, he summoned Teddy and went back home for some coffee and a quick breakfast.

"Teddy, won't you stay here and keep Mom company?"

"Joe, is everything all right? Teddy always goes to work with you."

"Mom, we've got quite a lot of work the next few days, and Teddy has been getting in the way. It's a good idea for him to stay home until we're done."

Joe rushed to the garage, hoping to catch Harry before work started at eight. The gas station opened at seven, and Leroy and Jim alternated weeks when they came in early. As Joe approached the station from Harrison Street, from about fifty yards away, he saw a black Cadillac pull in for a fill-up. He saw Jim leave the office area, engage with the driver, and then gas up the car. The driver, sporting a long overcoat, stepped away out and acted as if he were stretching his legs. Then he circled back to Jim, who was bent over the car, cleaning the windshield. The man pulled a handgun.

With one shot to the back of the head, Jim fell backward and hit the ground. The driver stopped refueling, replaced the pump, got in the car, and drove away. Joe raced to the scene.

When he got to Jim, the last remnants of life were flowing out of the wound into the puddle of blood forming on the ground. Joe kneeled over him and held his hand, feeling the softest of touches back, affirming that the man was still alive. Unsure what to say or do, Joe repeated "I'm sorry" over and over, as if he were chanting prayers at a requiem. Tears were rolling down his face. Even though he saw Jim's blank stare and noticed he had stopped breathing, he refused to release his hold on the man's hand until Harry arrived.

Back in the office, Joe told his employer the story of what had happened. With a wild-eyed look, Harry pulled an old Colt revolver from his desk drawer. "When those bastards paid us a visit yesterday, I never dreamed it'd come to this. I'll be shooting first and asking questions later if those fuckers come back."

The police arrived about an hour later. They had the body taken to the city morgue. Harry told the officer what had transpired in the garage the previous day and said Joe had witnessed the shooting that morning.

"Are you certain it was the same car that came yesterday?" The officer directed the question at Joe.

"Pretty certain. It was the same color, model, and year Cadillac. I didn't notice the license plate yesterday, but I did today. It was NJ 55703, from this year. "

"Can you identify the shooter as the man who was here yesterday?"

"I think it was the fella who came out with Antonio Romano to talk to Harry. I didn't get a good look today."

"The license is very helpful, but without more certainty around the shooter, it'll be difficult to proceed. We'll look into this and get back to you."

As the police drove away, Harry asked Joe and Leroy to join him in the office. He got the bottle of whiskey out and put it on the table. "I'm closing the filling station today, but there's a backlog of cars. We'll finish early, and I'm going to give money to Jim's wife so he can have a proper funeral and find out what else they may need." He poured a round of shots for the three of them, leaving one glass empty. "To Jim. You were a good man and didn't deserve this end." Pausing for a moment before knocking back his shot, Harry proclaimed, "As God is my witness, I'll be ready."

The whiskey warmed Joe's throat as it went down. A few minutes later, he noticed that his hands had stopped trembling.

That day, working was a remedy for the sadness the three men felt. The hours passed, and soon the afternoon light was fading to darkness. "Let's get things straightened up, and we'll make a fresh start tomorrow. I need to wash up a bit before I head over." Harry walked out of the garage and around the back, to the toilet and washroom.

Joe noticed the Colt revolver his boss had left on the floor near where he was working in the shop. Hearing a bit of a commotion outside, he instinctively went for the gun, putting it in his trouser pocket, and walked toward the noise. Leroy followed a few steps behind him.

The mobster who'd visited the garage that morning had Harry by the neck. He kicked in the door to the office open and flung him forward. Knocking his head against a file drawer, Harry tumbled onto the floor. Antonio Romano followed him in while the third associate, the one who'd been driving the day before, waited outside, keeping watch.

"I'm so sorry about what happened to your colored man, Mr. Hannah. If you'd been paying us, this tragedy would not have happened. Don't be a fool. The next one to die could be you, old man," Romano said, hovering over Harry, who was still slumped on the floor.

"You are a murdering guinea pig!" Harry cried out.

Antonio Romano started kicking the defenseless man, once, then twice, then again, with increasing intensity. When he stopped to adjust his body to prepare for an even harder kick, he finally noticed Joe, who was standing quietly about eight feet away. His expression, with his pencil-thin mustache outlining his gritted teeth, changed to a sneer, daring the young man to stop him.

Without hesitation, Joe took the revolver from his pocket, aimed, and squeezed the trigger. The clap from the shot was deafening in the small space. A nickel-sized red mark appeared in the center of Antonio Romano's forehead, and blood mixed with pink and gray brain matter sprayed from the back of his head onto the wall. He appeared to be staring at Joe in disbelief for a split second, then crumpled to the floor.

Joe turned and fired two more shots into the torso of the other mobster, propelling the man's body backward. He slammed against the wall and slid down. Blood oozed from the two bullet wounds in his chest as he sat dying on the floor. Joe immediately ducked below the desk, expecting the third man waiting outside to return fire.

"He's still out there, Joe. I can see his reflection in the window," said Leroy. A few moments later, he added, "He's movin' now, real slow. Probably headed for his car."

Adrenaline pulsed through Joe's body as he lay on the floor. He was having difficulty concentrating and could barely hear Leroy, his ears ringing from the three gunshots. Looking under the desk, he saw the death mask of Antonio Romano, its lifeless eyes staring directly back at him. Joe's mind went blank, and he started to shiver uncontrollably.

"I don't see him no more."

Harry got up off the floor and took the gun from Joe's hand. "I'll be proud to tell the police I killed these bastards. Leroy, you'll back up my story, won't you?"

"I surely will. Way I see it, Joe did the only thing he could do. He didn't want to watch them kill you."

Joe opened the desk drawer and took out the bottle. He needed two shots of Harry's whiskey to calm his nerves and think clearly. He wanted to find his father before he arrived home for dinner, so he left, racing through Orange Park. Once he got to Central Avenue, he frantically walked up and down the streets his dad patrolled.

When Joe finally found him, he was out of breath and unable to speak. His father put his arms around him and told him to take his time. Once Joe could talk, they moved off the walkway and into a storefront that had closed for the day. Occasionally gasping for breath, Joe recounted the day's events exactly as he remembered them.

"I won't second-guess what you did, son. Sounds to me like it was self-defense and you had every right to shoot. Harry'll cover for you. He's a man of his word. Your big problem comes from the fella who got away. He's going to tell the big boss what happened, and they'll come looking for you and kill you if they find you. You need to be out of this area—tomorrow."

PART TWO

CHAPTER 8

FORT BLISS

Joe left Fort Hamilton in Brooklyn on a frigid January morning, the temperature warming as the train made its way toward St. Louis. He could not make himself comfortable on the firm wicker seats, despite having the row to himself. He'd only been able to catch a few hours of continuous sleep here and there since he left his family in Orange two months ago, and he had persisting nightmares of the surviving mobster from the Black Hand finding and strangling him as he lay in his army bunk. Waking in a panic with his heart racing, he was rarely able to fall back asleep before morning revelry. His thoughts would then drift to his mother and the tears that had been running down her face when his father told her Joe had to leave early the next morning.

"Margaret, the boy's not leaving forever. He's going to come home to us after his three-year enlistment. I'll escort him to the ferry in Hoboken, and he'll join in New York City rather than downtown Newark. Joe, you must change your birthday to October 15, 1897, on the form. No one'll question it—I'm positive. You'll sleep in Fort Hamilton tonight," said James as he tried to comfort his wife.

"President Wilson claims he's going to keep the country out of this European War. I don't see how he's going to do it," Margaret shot back. "I don't want our son in one of those trenches, wondering when it's going to be his turn to die. My friends back home are writing to me about how Irish boys are getting slaughtered, fighting in this awful war for no good reason."

It was difficult for Joe to watch his mother being so emotional. He was trying his best to just listen to his parents' discussion without displaying his feelings. When it was time to leave, his mom stood in front of him and took off the sterling silver Celtic cross she wore underneath her blouse. She said, "My father gave me this when I was leaving for America. It's brought me good luck and kept me from harm. Promise me you'll always wear it so the good Lord will watch over you."

"I promise, Mom. I'll be writing letters to let you know I'm okay."

Back in present thought, Joe recalled the last letter he'd written his mother, which he sent just before leaving. Hopefully, his news would calm her. He had received his orders and was being assigned to the 8th Brigade in Fort Bliss, near El Paso, Texas, before he'd even finished his basic training. His sergeant explained that they had an urgent need for soldiers who could fix motorized vehicles there. Joe had impressed the brass at Fort Hamilton shortly after arriving by fixing the commander's car when the mechanics on the base were at a loss for what to do.

‡

Tensions at the border between Mexico and the US were high in early 1916. A band of Pancho Villa's men stopped a train outside of Santa Ysabel, Mexico, on January 8 and executed eighteen American miners on their way to work. For several years, Mexico had been in a state of civil war, where rebel leaders like Pancho Villa and Emiliano Zapata were battling government forces, under the leadership of the US-recognized head of state, José Carranza, for control of the country. In the US, there were affluent investors, including members of Congress, who had a hefty financial interest in maintaining stability near the border.

Sparked by the recent incident in Santa Ysabel, there was talk at the highest level in the military about preparing for an incursion into Mexico. Fort Bliss was a key military base, whose principal mission was to protect the wide expanse of the border between Mexico and the US. Its commander, General John Pershing—an old cavalryman—made a special request for soldiers with experience fixing motorized vehicles. Pershing knew these vehicles and motorized weapons were useless if they couldn't stay running. He also believed it was critical for the US to move away from its dependence on horses and gain experience with the weaponry that was currently being deployed on the battlefields of Europe.

‡

Joe exited the train at Union Station in Saint Louis with a small suitcase stuffed with things from home. He was still getting used to the stiffness and weight of his olive-drab uniform and the way the collar would irritate the sensitive skin on his neck. He let out an enormous yawn as he stepped down onto the platform.

"Where ya heading to, private?" a conductor asked him.

"Sir, I'm looking for the 7:15 to Dallas."

"Since you have over an hour to kill before you head over to track four, just mosey outside that door over yonder, and you'll see a small shop called Pete's. You'll get yourself a mighty fine breakfast—by the looks of you, could sorely use. Tell them Ned from the railroad sent you."

Joe took the conductor's advice and walked to the small diner. The sign out front proclaimed that Pete's served Maxwell House coffee, which immediately conjured up memories of the blue tin sitting on the counter in the kitchen back in Orange. As he opened the door, the aromatic smell of it brewing hit him in the face. He sat down at the counter, taking in the concerto of cooking sounds—breakfast meat and eggs spattering on the griddle—that greeted him and made his appetite increase exponentially.

A matronly waitress came over to take his order. "What you are having, hon?"

"Ned from the railroad said I'd get myself a good breakfast here. I'll start by having a big cup of that coffee, black. I'd like two eggs, sunny side up, and some rashers."

"Ain't got none of those. We got bacon, ham, and sausage links if you want meat."

"Sorry, I mean bacon. My mom calls bacon rashers."

"Okay, be right up, sweetie. I'll bring some toast and grits with that."

"Grits?"

"Just put some butter, salt, and pepper on them. Some folks like to mix 'em with their eggs and put 'em on toast."

The coffee was steaming hot but too weak for Joe's taste. He finished the first cup quickly and asked for a second. By the time his breakfast was served, he was working on cup three and was wide awake. His eyes fixed on the big plate of food, and he noted the eggs were runny and the bacon was not overly crisp, just the way he liked them at home. Midway through the meal, he tried the grits and decided he wasn't hungry enough to eat them.

The same waitress came back as Joe was finishing up. "Bein' that Ned sent you this way, and you're a soldier, how 'bout we settle for fifteen cents?"

"Thank you, ma'am." Joe left a nickel tip, paying the bill with coins from his pocket. The full feeling in his stomach did wonders for his mood. As he boarded the train to Dallas, Joe realized that this was the first time since he'd left home that he really felt like himself.

‡

At the time of Joe's arrival in late January 1916, Fort Bliss was predominately being used to house cavalry troops who protected the border. These troops comprised one battalion of about six hundred infantrymen, divided into three companies.

They assigned Joe to Alpha Company, led by Captain Thomas Franks. Franks was a career soldier who had seen combat duty in Cuba during the Spanish–American War. He believed in pushing his men to their physical and mental limits with rigorous daily drills and maneuvers to prepare them to properly handle combat. Five brand new 1915 GMC 15 trucks had recently arrived and been set up as troop transports. These trucks could carry twelve soldiers fully loaded, including the driver. Their top speed was twenty-five miles per hour. Franks was responsible for evaluating their performance compared to the army's current standard of troop transport: wagons driven by horses or mules.

Joe was part of the four-man mechanic team that Captain Franks had charged with driving, maintaining, and evaluating the GMC trucks. Like the other mechanics, he was assigned a vehicle and would leave early to take the troops to the training grounds. They would take the long way there to put the trucks through their paces on the local terrain. Joe and the other mechanics would drive back to the base using the same tortuous route after completing the drills. Unlike the rest of the squad, who had to take part in drills, the mechanic crew stayed back on base Saturdays to work on their vehicles. Franks also wanted them to completely disassemble the fifth vehicle and put it back together while making note of any special procedures or tools required.

‡

Driving the vehicles to the training grounds and back proved to be the biggest challenge for Joe. He had spent very limited time behind the wheel working at the garage. Winters in the El Paso area were normally quite dry, but February 1916 proved to be a bit of an exception. Frequent short cloudbursts of rain in the early afternoons created mud on the rutted road back to camp. After a grueling day of drills, the last thing the infantrymen wanted to do was get out of the truck and help push while Joe tried to maneuver the transmission properly to rock the vehicle out of the ditch. Frustration would set in when the scenario repeated itself a short while later. As the month progressed, the conditions improved, and Joe became more skilled at avoiding trouble spots. The other soldier mechanics had similar experiences.

Two of them, Will Berry and Stan Bley, both strapping, six-foot-tall nineteen-year-olds, had gained their experience working with motorized farm equipment on their large family farms outside of Indianapolis. They were both low in the pecking order in their respective families and had grown tired of taking orders from their older siblings. By the time they were sixteen, they'd planned to get out of town and enlist on the same day.

Donnie Walsh, meanwhile, was a short, red-haired, freckled hell-raiser of twenty from Boston. Afraid the boy would bring shame on the family by being arrested, his parents had given him an ultimatum: either enlist, or they would turn him in to the police. He'd gained experience working at a small garage close to home before his enlistment. He was by far the least skilled mechanic of the group and was always looking for the easiest assignment, if not avoiding work altogether.

The Saturday maintenance day was light duty. The GMC trucks were mechanically very simple machines and easy to work on. Pulling the fifth truck apart and putting it back together wouldn't take as long as Franks had expected.

"Would you guys fucking slow down? If we play our cards right, we can stretch this out and maybe avoid Saturday drills in March," suggested a very annoyed Donnie in his thick Boston accent.

"These trucks are being over-maintained. In the beginning, I could see why, as they wanted to make sure we all knew how to fix them. I'm sure they'll back down on this schedule soon. When they ask me, I'll set them straight," replied Stan.

"Stan, don't be a fucking hayseed. Would you rather be pulling cactus needles out of your ass on Saturday, too? What d'you think about this, Joe?"

"Donnie, leave Stan alone. You barely know your ass from a hole in the ground when it comes to being a mechanic. You're mighty lucky to have the three of us covering for you and have no right to tell Stan what to do," Joe replied. He stood up, turned away from Donnie, and pulled a crumpled pack of cigarettes from his pocket.

"You're not going to give me the fucking high hat," Donnie shouted as he leaped at Joe's back, putting his arm around his neck and pulling him to the ground.

Caught completely off guard, Joe took a few seconds to regain his composure. Lying on his back while Donnie hovered over him, he said, "What the fuck do you think you're doing?"

"Why you sidin' with the farm boys? I thought we was friends."

"If you pull that shit again, I'm gonna be your worst enemy."

"You know, you really pissed me off."

"Jeez, Donnie. I thought I had a temper. You're gonna get yourself hurt going after somebody like that. Stan is right. You're a lazy bastard, and we won't let you get us in trouble."

"I hate the drills. I thought you'd definitely see it my way. I'm sorry, Joe. I shouldn't have tackled you. Are we okay?" Donnie took a knee and extended his hand to Joe, who was still on the ground.

Taking it, Joe replied, "Yeah, we're okay."

CHAPTER 9

FIVE QUEENS

El Paso had recently undergone significant change. Once known as "Six Shooter Heaven," it had been a hub for gambling and prostitution. At the beginning of the twentieth century, progressive groups began fighting to change things, and had successfully transformed it into a more respectable and industry-focused city.

Then, when the Mexican Revolution started in 1910, many middle-class Mexican families, fearing for their lives, migrated to El Paso, shifting the population toward a slight Hispanic majority. Just a short walk across the Rio Grande into Juarez, it was easy to find games of chance, prostitutes, alcohol, and drugs, as the Mexican police force protected these businesses because of payments from organized crime.

‡

Sunday, March 5, was the first day since Joe's arrival at Fort Bliss that platoon brass gave his squad a pass to leave camp. They set a schedule of passes for the soldiers to limit the numbers descending on El Paso and Juarez at once.

"You were not here for the lieutenant's speech yesterday, so I'll give you the short version." Sergeant Williams directed his comments at Joe, who had just finished making his bunk and was getting ready to leave. "Think twice before going into Juarez. Remember, the Mexicans hate us. They'll take your money and cut your throat if they get a chance. That includes the women, who're meaner than the men. Stay in El Paso, and don't get too drunk."

After walking the streets of El Paso for about two hours, Joe found that even the gambling places he had been told about were closed on Sundays. While he knew Juarez could be dangerous, he rationalized that the victims were mostly out-of-control, drunk soldiers. Eager to get into a card game, he told himself that he was going to be careful as he started the mile walk to the bridge that would take him into Juarez. American soldiers in uniform had free access to cross, provided they stayed within the city limits.

As he made his way across the bridge, Joe found that the landscape was the same as it was in Texas, but the view across the Rio Grande surprised him. Adobe structures in various stages of disrepair and wooden shacks with tin roofs adorned the hillside next to the river there.

After crossing, he walked toward a set of buildings he thought could be the beginning of the city. Barely fifty yards in, a half dozen Mexican girls accosted him. While he couldn't understand their Spanish, he fully understood that each of them was making a case for why he would be the happiest man in Ciudad Juarez if he spent an hour with them. As one girl backed up into him and ground her backside into his groin, he felt a very slight movement in his back pocket, prompting him to grab the wrist of the young lady who was picking his pocket. While twisting it ever so slightly, Joe yelled to the others, "Get out of here!"

"No me hagas daño!" the girl cried, while Joe continued to hold her as the others watched from a safe distance. He could see the look of terror on her face. Reaching into the front pocket of his trousers, he grabbed a dollar bill and gave it to her, then released her. The young girl quickly ran away, then stopped about twenty feet from him. Grinning ear to ear, she offered a polite "Gracias." With a tip of his hat, Joe started walking toward the buildings again.

From the collection of establishments intentionally set up to take advantage of soldiers making their way across the border, Joe chose the Cowboy Saloon, a bar that tried to mimic a nineteenth-century American Western establishment.

Walking through the swinging wooden doors, he noticed a woman wearing a tight floral dress. She was a real beauty, with medium-length dark brown hair. Sitting at a high-top table, she was speaking with two men, both dressed in dark gray suits. She met Joe's gaze and acknowledged him by drawing her ruby-red lips into the slightest of smiles.

There were soldiers standing at the long bar in the back, four card games going, and some working girls who were making the rounds. Joe picked a seat at the bar close to one of the games, so he could nurse a drink and try to look in on the action without being too obvious. He couldn't help but notice the beautiful brunette occasionally glancing his way, though.

After a few hands, it became obvious to Joe that two of the players were working together. The game was seven-card stud, with six players. After card five or six, one of the two players would bet aggressively, as if they had a dominant hand. This would chase the other players at the table a good portion of the time. Since Joe had started watching, these two men had been the last players standing in six of eight total hands. He observed that one of them always folded before the last bet, so they never fully revealed their cards.

A middle-aged American businessman was clearly losing his patience as he lost the last of his chips. He got up from the table and muttered, "This is not my day."

"Would you mind if I take his spot?" Joe asked.

"Be warned, young man—we don't want to take a soldier's money, but if you insist . . . at least we know you have a place to sleep," said one of the cheating players. He was a fortyish, well-dressed Hispanic man who spoke English with only a slight accent.

"I've been warned."

This game had higher stakes than Joe was used to, so he knew he needed to win a hand early in order to be able to wager freely. If he didn't hold a respectable hand when the bets started increasing, it would force him to fold.

The player to Joe's left dealt the cards, the first two down and the third up. Joe saw that he had drawn two queens as his hole cards, with a deuce showing. On the fifth card, Joe was dealt a third queen. That put him in a powerful betting position.

The cheating player who'd addressed Joe earlier had a pair of tens showing and raised the stakes. On the sixth card, Joe picked up an eight, while the cheat drew another ten. On the last card, he drew another queen, face down. Hoping his opponent was holding four tens, Joe bet aggressively, chasing everyone else.

"Private, I sure hope you have a good hand that can beat four of a kind. I see your next bet will clean you out."

"Yes, sir, I call." Joe flipped over the cards, revealing his four queens.

"Well, that might just be the luckiest hand I've ever seen. Take your winnings."

Joe calmly rose from his chair and moved all the money from the center to his side. This was the biggest pot he had ever won, well over a hundred dollars. As he sat back down, he noticed that the brunette had moved closer to the table, taking the seat at the bar he'd recently vacated.

Joe played for another two hours, drawing good cards and adding to his winnings.

Best to go to the base in daylight with all this money, he thought as he turned to go to the bar to recruit some soldiers to head back with him. Most of them were doing shots of tequila and talking obnoxiously to the prostitutes. Joe then spotted the woman in the floral dress, who motioned with her head for him to stand next to her. She lit the cigarette in her black holder and continued to look at the card game while speaking slightly above a whisper, in perfect English.

"Soldier, please continue to look at the bartender and not at me. I'm afraid you've made some people furious with your skill at poker. The owner tolerates this cheating ruse because they share their take with the house. You can see—the man you beat is quite upset and talking to the bouncers, who I was sitting with earlier. They won't let you get back to El Paso without taking your money and causing you harm."

"Okay, thanks for the tip. Why are you telling me this?"

"Let's just say I'm impressed with the way you carry yourself. You figured out their scheme, won fairly, and deserve to go home with your money without being hurt. I also have a solution. I live in El Paso, and my driver can take us back to my apartment, a mile from your base. When we arrive, you can decide if you want to join me for a drink or not."

Joe surveyed the bar and noticed that both the cheating card players and one gray-suited bouncer had left. Weighing his options, he became certain he'd get bushwhacked even if he was in the company of some drunk soldiers. "Okay, I'll ride with you," he said.

"I'm going to leave now. I'll be in a green car with my driver. Stay here and smoke a cigarette. When you're done, go to the toilet in the back and out the door directly opposite. Turn right and proceed slowly until you see the car. I'm sure they'll be out there but expecting you to leave through the front door."

After Joe finished the smoke, he proceeded down the hallway as instructed. As he opened the door to the outside, he looked left and saw the back of the bouncer, who was waiting at the end of the alley. Cautiously, he made his way in the opposite direction, walking about fifty feet before he saw the car, the brunette waiting for him in the back seat. Joe ran to the vehicle, opened the rear door, and took a seat next to her. He put his head down below the window.

"Pedro, llévame a mi apartamento." The car took off at normal speed. The woman took Joe's hand in hers and pressed her finger to her lips, motioning for him to be quiet.

After a few minutes, they arrived at the bridge crossing, where she showed her papers. They entered El Paso, and Pedro dropped them off at her building. It was just getting dark when they arrived.

"Well, soldier, won't you join me for a drink? My apartment is small, but very comfortable. My name is Lilly, Lilly Álvarez."

"A beautiful woman saves my hide and invites me to have a drink. I don't think that's an offer I can turn down. My name is Joe."

Lilly acknowledged the compliment with a full, ruby-lipped smile. She took his hand and said, "Please, follow me."

The apartment was on the second floor. They took the back stairs rather than engage with the doorman. When Joe entered the room, he was met with modern-style furniture—seemingly newly purchased—against a backdrop of large, vividly colored paintings portraying strangely shaped individuals and animals. The atmosphere it created was both sophisticated and surreal.

"I will call you Joseph. It's better for me. What would you like to drink?"

"How about something strong? I need to settle my nerves a bit."

"Oh my, I completely understand. I'll pour you some mezcal when I return."

Joe took a seat on the couch while he waited, and as promised, Lilly soon served him mezcal in a shot glass with some orange slices. On her plate, along with the liquor and fruit, were cigarette papers and a lump of marijuana. Joe remained quiet, eating a piece of orange as she rolled a cigarette.

"Did you know El Paso was the first city in the US that made marijuana illegal? This came to pass last year, and it makes me want to smoke it more, you know? It makes me relax and forget for a short time all the troubles in this crazy world. Will you join me?" Lilly lit the cigarette and inhaled deeply.

Feeling relaxed, safe, and thoroughly fixated on the woman's beauty, Joe took the smoke from her outstretched hand and mimicked her motions. He paused, then exhaled, feeling a strong burning sensation in his throat from the marijuana, which was harsher than what he was used to smoking.

"My husband owns the Cowboy Saloon, and several other establishments in Juarez. He is a very wealthy man, much older than me, and has quite a lot of influence in this area. We have what you call . . . an understanding. I am at his side when he needs to be seen with a wife, and I leave him alone when he is off playing with his young matadors. In turn, I can do what excites me, as long as I'm discrete with my actions. I normally stay away from soldiers, since most of them act like children. However, there is something different about you. You are young, but I truly appreciate your manner."

Lilly rolled another cigarette and lit it. After they'd finished that one, they both leaned back on the couch and stared into each other's eyes.

"You're right about marijuana," he said. "It takes your mind off everything. All I can think of is that I'm looking at the most beautiful woman I've ever seen."

Lilly moved in closer. "Kiss me, Joseph."

Joe slowly shifted his head toward hers, and the pair kissed, lightly and slowly at first and then increasingly with more passion. She unbuttoned his uniform, then got up and stepped into the bedroom. She brought back a black satin robe and handed it to Joe. "I'm going to change, and I suggest you do the same."

Lilly left her jewelry on but changed into a long white satin robe, the sash tightly drawn to cover her body. "Joseph, you look Irish. My father was Irish. My mother is from Mexico. Tell me your story."

He began talking about his mother and father, his family, and then himself. She listened intently, staring directly into his eyes, urging him to tell her more. When talking about his work, he decided to recount the story of that tragic day at the garage and why he'd had to enlist.

Lilly lit another marijuana cigarette, inhaled deeply, and passed it to Joe. He politely declined this time in order to keep some level of control.

"Marijuana is like truth serum for me," she said. "Listening to your story makes me want to share mine. I hope you don't think less of me. Perhaps you think I am this strong woman. It's just an illusion."

She drew in a deep breath before starting. "Joseph, I wish I was brave like you. I'm a coward. My surname is Álvarez now, but it used to be McConnell. I watched my father abuse my beautiful mother for years when he drank. He started looking at me strangely when I turned sixteen, so I ran away to be safe and married a man I didn't love. My father continued to abuse my mother. I should've ended his life, but I didn't have the courage. Thank God he died three years after I left. My rich husband now takes care of my mother. I have educated myself in these twelve years because I want to be more than just a kept woman. It's too comfortable here for me. If I was brave, I would leave and be the woman I really want to be."

By the time Lilly finished, she was sobbing. Joe took the sleeve of his robe and wiped the tears from her face. He kissed her forehead to reassure her.

"Joseph, I'm so glad we have gotten to know each other. You've shared your secrets, and I've shared mine. Now, I want you to share my bed."

They spoke very few words over the next hours. At 11:30 p.m., Lilly looked at the clock and cried. "I don't want you to leave. You have made me so happy. When will I be able to see you again?"

"You know a soldier can't answer that. What I can tell you is, I'll find a way back to you as soon as I can."

‡

The following morning, Joe woke up in his bunk with a feeling of exhilaration. After revelry and roll call, he appeared to be the only one in his squad who had any life in him, as most of the other soldiers were sporting vicious hangovers. He was looking forward to the drills today, as he felt like he had to burn off some energy.

Yesterday had been quite a day. He always expected to win when he was gambling, but at the Cowboy Saloon, he had won a small fortune. Then, Lilly had rescued him. Thoughts of her beautiful face raced through his head. For hours, their enjoined bodies had thrashed, then rested, then thrashed again, like wild animals in a forest of silk sheets and fluffy goose feather pillows. They'd gone together, hand in hand, to the shower. Water splashed on his face as he gently pressed his lips against hers. He had never felt such emotions before.

CHAPTER 10

PANCHO VILLA

Around dawn on the morning of March 9, Pancho Villa and his band of about five hundred men on horseback raided the town of Columbus, New Mexico, and the nearby military installation of Camp Furlong. They killed ten civilians and eight soldiers during the raid, which lasted for two hours. Villa's intention in attacking the small town and army installation on American soil was to provoke a response by the US, so as to destabilize his adversary Carranza's regime. He knew he was forcing President Wilson to authorize an expedition into Mexico. If Carranza opposed the expedition, the US would cut off diplomatic relations. If Carranza supported the invasion, he would lose the support of patriotic citizens, who would be violently opposed to having US soldiers on Mexican soil.

While the country supported him for keeping the US out of the European war, President Wilson had to act swiftly in this matter to keep the public with him in this election year. He ordered General John Pershing to capture and disband Villa's units and then withdraw from Mexico as soon as possible. Wilson gave the orders before discussions even began with the Carranza government. When negotiations started with the

US, Carranza stopped short of approving the Pershing expedition, only approving entry if another incident like the raid on Columbus were to take place in the future. The US ignored that technicality and proceeded with the troop movements.

The "Punitive Expedition" began with 4,800 US Army regulars who were based at Fort Bliss and Camp Furlong. It would be a considerable logistical challenge to support Pershing in the pursuit of Villa into the Mexican state of Chihuahua. A lack of decent roads, reliable rail, and any genuine sense of cooperation from local Mexican officials would impede his forces. In addition, the Chihuahua region experienced high winds and frequent dust storms, which could appear with very little warning.

‡

There had been a buzz at Fort Bliss when news broke of the raid at Columbus. The general consensus was that soldiers stationed there would play a role in pursuing Pancho Villa. Captain Franks confirmed that to Alpha Company on the afternoon of March 10.

"You will be part of a mission to bring this murdering bastard to justice. We must stop him before he comes back over the border to kill more innocent Americans. Alpha Company will leave by rail at 0700 tomorrow for Columbus. We'll set up camp there and wait for orders on our next steps."

Sergeant Williams informed Joe that he would accompany the cavalry and convoy of supply wagons, which were also leaving at 0700 tomorrow. They would fill the five GMC trucks, which were at Bliss, with crates of rifles. He would help pack his truck and then receive additional instructions.

Joe's state of euphoria ended abruptly with these orders. He thought of his mother and how upset she would be to learn that he was going to be involved in fighting. His thoughts then drifted to Lilly. He would not have an opportunity to see her and say goodbye.

Joe met the original crew of drivers—Will, Stan, and Donnie—at the supply magazine. There was a new soldier named Rudy who would drive the fifth truck. Five members of the Quartermasters Corps would ride shotgun with them and gain some experience with the operation of the trucks. The road to Columbus was mostly in a satisfactory state, allowing motorized vehicles to travel much faster than either the wagons or riders on horseback. The drivers would need to maintain a slow pace to stick with the convoy for the duration of the trip, thus enabling the protection of their cargo.

The plan was to break camp at the halfway point and reach Columbus the following day. Pershing was eager to pursue Villa soon after arriving and did not want to push the horses in the first leg of the expedition.

The first three hours of the trip were uneventful. The trucks outpaced the horses and needed to be slowed down several times. Separation from the cavalry group would spell disaster. Even though one could see for miles across the dusty brown desert prairie, Pershing was taking nothing for granted and kept the caravan tightly packed, keeping the motorized units moving at little more than a crawl.

Next to Joe, the private from the Quartermaster Corps quickly put his M1903 Springfield bolt-action rifle on the floor between his seat and the door. He fell asleep about ten minutes into the trip, so Joe had to seek diversion elsewhere as he drove at this painfully slow speed. He began looking for the occasional rut on the hard-packed dirt. For entertainment, Joe would speed up and hit the holes with the tire on the passenger side, hoping to wake up the sleeping soldier by jarring him in his seat. He hit the fourth one hard enough that both passenger and the cargo of rifles jumped a good inch. The private briefly opened his eyes, then resumed his sleep. That last rut also knocked some common sense back into Joe, prompting him to take a more cautious approach.

The boring drive continued until they were ordered to stop after three hours to stretch and rest the horses. They had traveled, in total, just under twenty-five miles. Donnie Walsh, who had been following Joe's truck in the convoy, went over to Joe to bum a cigarette. With his thick accent, he asked Joe, "What the fuck were you doin' back there? I was followin' you and wound up hittin' these holes really hard. The guy next to me asked if I'd been drinking."

"Just trying to have some fun." Joe pointed to the large-framed, almost oafish-looking Quartermaster Corps private, who was now sitting and leaning against the tire of his truck, sleeping once again. "I don't know how this guy does it, but he stayed asleep the whole time. He hasn't said a word to me the entire ride."

"Are you up for playing some cards later on, maybe after mess?" Donnie suggested.

"Sure, let's round up some guys and play."

Overhearing the conversation, the groggy-eyed Quartermaster Corps private woke fully and extended his oversized hands to both men. "Count me in. By the way, my name is Eugene, from Asheville, North Carolina." He had a substantial Southern drawl.

"Sure, love to have ya. My name is Donnie from Boston. My shanty Irish friend here from New Jersey's named Joe."

Joe shot back, "If I'm shanty Irish, I'm not so sure what that makes you, Donnie." He sensed Donnie had sized Eugene up as an easy mark. After the hours in the car sleeping and his very slow pace of speech, Joe agreed with that assessment.

He attempted to make small talk during the next leg of the journey with Eugene, asking him some questions about himself and North Carolina. After a few minutes of curt responses and one-word answers, though, Joe realized a conversation with him was impossible.

"You're not one for doing much talking, are you?"

"Got that right."

"Well, we have another three hours of driving. I'll try to keep this truck on the road. You keep watch for any horses. This next stretch, they told us to be careful, as we'll be less than a mile from the Mexican border."

The caravan continued uneventfully until just around three. The line of trucks, cavalry, and wagons then ventured off the main road for a short distance to a rise in elevation. This afforded them an excellent view of the surroundings and made any type of attack on the convoy much more challenging.

The soldiers moved the trucks and wagons carrying weapons and ammunition, the most coveted cargo, to the center of the camp. Two-man tents encircled the trucks, almost covering the small plateau. They assigned a considerable number of sentries to be on guard for a raid.

After dinner, Joe, Donnie, Eugene, and two of the other Quartermaster Corps privates settled down near the campfire to play cards—five- and seven-card stud and draw poker. Joe preferred the stud games, where most of the cards were visible to all players. Draw poker was strictly about demeanor and reading your opponent's intentions.

He had played cards with Donnie before and had a healthy respect for his skill. Donnie started out winning the first three hands with relatively small pots, and when it was Eugene's turn to deal, he selected draw poker. Eugene bet foolishly in the first three hands and folded early, confirming what both Donnie and Joe thought about his playing abilities.

Joe drew a pair of tens and requested three cards. He picked up another ten. Two of the other players requested four cards, Donnie requested three cards—suggesting that he was holding a pair—and Eugene requested one. After looking at the cards, the two other privates folded. Donnie bet a dollar. Joe saw his bet and raised him two dollars, which chased Donnie.

"Three dollars to you, Eugene, to stay around."

"I see your three dollars and raise you ten."

That made Joe angry, but he tried not to show it. While there were no discussions on betting limits, this was a friendly game that usually confined betting to an absolute maximum of five dollars on a single bet. The smart thing to do would be to not call Eugene's bet and let him take the hand. Yet Joe's temper and ego got the better of him.

"I'll see your ten, and raise you ten," he said defiantly.

"Well, I'm betting you don't have four of a kind. I see your ten and kick in ten more."

Sensing he had been had, Joe also knew he had to see this to the end. While throwing in ten dollars, he responded, "I call."

With no expression, Eugene laid down his cards, revealing a queen-high straight. Joe was having a hard time keeping his emotions in check. He was mostly angry at himself for falling for the hustle. He had underestimated Eugene. Joe stayed silent as the man took the pot, built mostly with his money. His blood was at full boil.

The pattern continued for a few more hands. All the other players chose the stud games, and Eugene always dealt draw poker. Joe won back some of his money playing those games and played conservatively with draw poker. It seemed a bit more than coincidental to Joe, though, that Eugene had his best hands and won all his money when he dealt the cards. Joe sensed that Eugene was cheating, but he couldn't see exactly how he was doing it.

At 2100, the order was given to suspend activity and go to sleep.

Joe hated to lose when he gambled. However, he was most upset by being outsmarted. Now it was his turn to give the silent treatment. Falling asleep was not easy as he thought about spending five hours with Eugene on the road tomorrow.

CHAPTER 11

COLUMBUS

There was a whirlwind of activity in Columbus when the cavalry and supplies converged there a day after the infantry had arrived. The small western town was still reeling from the raid and devastation that had taken place less than two weeks before. Pershing was eager to set out in search of Pancho Villa as soon as possible. His plan was to split his cavalry forces in half and take two routes south across the border, then establish a base of operations in Mexico.

Eight Curtis JN-3 biplanes had just arrived in Columbus. Pershing had heard about how the aeroplane was being used extensively in the European theater for reconnaissance, strafing, and some very limited bombing. Stories of "dogfights" between fighter planes filled the headlines of American newspapers. Pershing was now in command of the entire fledgling 1st Aero Squadron, which comprised those eight planes and just under a hundred enlisted men and officers to support operations. Captain Benjamin Foulois, commander of the squadron, advised Pershing that these eight planes were only suitable for reconnaissance. This frustrated

Pershing, who was being pressured by the administration to apprehend Villa quickly without "raising a ruckus."

A few days after their arrival on March 15, Pershing and his cavalry troops headed west to Culberson's Ranch, then south into Mexico. Major Frank Tompkins led the cavalry, which headed directly south from Columbus. The plan was to meet about 110 miles south at a mostly abandoned Mormon enclave called Colonia Dublán, which had the potential to be their base of operations in Mexico because of its ideal location in a valley of the Sierra Madre mountain range. To successfully conduct operations from there, a supply chain had to be established for about four thousand soldiers and horses, with infantry to be added later.

The US Army purchased an additional fifty trucks from a variety of manufacturers to build the supply chain. They sent them unassembled to Columbus by rail. The eight Curtis Jenny biplanes had come the same way and had just finished being assembled by the 1st Aero mechanics. Because they used Nash Quad trucks as support vehicles for the biplanes, they were very familiar with trucks. They were given the leadership role and tasked with assembling the fifty unassembled vehicles with the support of mechanics from the regular army, forming eight two-man teams. They paired Joe with an affable Californian, Corporal Eddy Hernandez.

"Well I tell you, Joe, I service 'em, I fix 'em, but I will be goddamned if I would ever get in one," Eddy said during a smoke break.

"I was thinking how exciting it'd be to go up in one of those, or maybe even learn how to fly it," Joe replied, looking at the fleet of Jenny biplanes right outside of the building where the two men were working on a Nash Quad.

"Well, if you have a long runway to take off and no wind and only want to fly in a straight line, the Jenny is okay. Anything else, forget it. The wind down here is bad. I don't think the Jenny can handle it."

"Okay, so they're not built tough enough. Well, I can't say that about this Nash Quad. It ain't fancy, but I haven't seen anything like it. There's four-wheel drive and steering, and the build's so solid."

"From what I have heard, four Quads are going to be handed over to the Quartermaster Corps to establish the supply chain into Mexico," said Eddy.

‡

On March 16 at 0900, the first truck convoy in US Army history set out from Columbus for Dublán, carrying soldiers, food, gasoline, and General Pershing's belongings. Four Dodge Touring cars also made the trip. The Quartermaster Corps borrowed seven mechanics from the 1st Aero to drive and potentially service the Nash Quads. Joe was the only regular army soldier to be part of that team. An early-morning reconnaissance mission by two Jenny biplanes established that there were no bands of horsemen large enough in the area to attack the convoy on their way south.

Eddy and Joe rode together. Their cargo was a variety of food items, making the load on the Quad relatively light. Eddy proved to be the exact opposite of Joe's previous travel companion. Joe enjoyed his talkative nature and learning more about California and San Francisco, Eddy's hometown. The first two hours flew by with Eddy driving. At the first stop, they estimated the convoy had covered forty-five miles, putting them ahead of schedule. All the drivers switched places.

Joe got the hang of driving the Nash after the first few miles. However, the terrain became more treacherous after that, with large, sharp-edged rocks jutting out from the packed dirt. The order to stop soon came, because one of the Dodge Tourings had gotten a flat tire.

Eddy and Joe used the time to have another cigarette and look out on the vast desert prairie—dried dirt with the occasional scrub. To the south, they noticed that there was some dust kicking up, and eventually they saw four horsemen galloping toward the small caravan. Lieutenant Gorney ordered them to be ready, with rifles in hand, but not to engage unless there was an obvious threat.

"I suspect these riders are Carranza's men just coming to check on us. I was told we might meet some opposition at the border, but we rode through without a peep."

In fact, the four horsemen were government soldiers. They were dressed in a mix of white uniforms and non-matching clothing. Approaching the caravan slowly, they trotted around it, peering at each of the soldiers, who stood watching them in silence. Eventually, they stopped in front of Eddy and Joe. The lead rider looked down at Eddy and sneered. "Que haces con los gringos?"

Eddy answered while looking the horseman in the eyes. "Soy Americano."

The four Mexican soldiers found that to be a funny response and started laughing. They all peered at Eddy as they completed the loop around the caravan. Just before they began their gallop away, they yelled, "Gringos se van a casa."

Lieutenant Gorney approached Eddy. "What was that all about?"

"Sir, they don't want us here. They told us to go home."

"Do you think they'll do anything about it?"

"Sir," said Eddy, "my guess is they'll try to make life difficult for us, if they can. I wouldn't expect them to confront us directly."

"Thank you, Corporal. All right, men, let's get things moving."

The road got progressively worse for the next three hours. All the vehicles had to slow down to handle the uneven terrain and avoid the hazardous rocks. It was 1300 when the caravan stopped for a break. Joe noticed that Lieutenant Gorney had a concerned look on his face and asked, "Sir, how much longer, do you reckon?"

"Private, I estimate about an hour and a half. We're going to have to get unloaded quickly so we can be past the rough spots before nightfall."

The caravan then set out toward their destination. Joe was happy that Eddy took the last leg of the driving, because this proved to be the most troublesome part of the journey yet. Upon their arrival at the camp, Joe was taken aback by the considerable level of organization already in place. Even more surprising were the several local merchants set up with wagons and tents, presumably there to take advantage of the new military presence in the area. The caravan proceeded down the hard-packed road to the center of the camp, where they stored all the supplies.

Lieutenant Gorney requested extra help to unload and refuel the trucks quickly. He also requested four of the Apache Indian Scouts make the return trip to Columbus, riding in the empty trucks. They left behind the Dodge Touring cars, as they would have slowed the trip down on the bad roads.

"Men, my goal is to get moving so we're on the better road by nightfall. That is about three hours from now. I want our best driver behind the wheel. I want the riders to have their weapons easily accessible. They've given me strict orders not to shoot unless attacked."

Joe preferred to have his Colt M911 with its seven-shot cartridge at the ready, as he was a much better shot with the pistol than with his rifle.

Sticking his head out the window, he introduced himself to the Apache soldier in the back of the truck. He had read so much about Indians in books, and now he was with the real thing. The scout was wearing a cavalry uniform. His sunbaked face showed many lines and creases when he smiled at Joe. He was wearing a white bandana over his shaggy medium-length black hair. Some strands of gray poked out.

"I am Kuruk, great nephew of Geronimo. We hate Mexicans because of what they did to his wife and child. We are happy to fight with you. I will be your eyes and ears on this journey." Some of Joe's trepidations about riding back in the dark were eased upon hearing the scout speak with such calmness.

The four trucks were on the road shortly before 1600. Nightfall was just after 1900. About an hour into the journey, Eddy remarked, "I hear it. I hear a Jenny. Look up guys, and wave."

It took a couple of minutes for the plane to come into view. All the soldiers with free hands waved, and the observer in the back seat of the plane waved back and gave them a thumbs-up.

After three hours of driving, Lieutenant Gorney stopped the caravan for a brief break. "We've made good progress to get here. We'll finish the challenging part in less than thirty minutes."

Addressing the lieutenant, Kuruk spoke. "Sir, I hear horses in the distance, not more than six. They are approaching and will be here in ten minutes if we stay." The three other scouts nodded in agreement.

"Let's try to pick up the pace. They won't be able to keep up with us on the good road."

Eddy suggested he take the wheel, and Joe readily agreed. Within twenty minutes, the riders had caught up to the caravan. There were still about five miles of rough terrain to negotiate, so the quads could not increase their speed. The riders were now pacing the trucks, about fifty feet to the right. Darkness hid the men; the soldiers could only hear horses galloping and the Mexicans shouting. Joe gripped his pistol tightly. They were starting to unnerve him. He asked Eddy, "What are they yellin' about?"

"More of the same from this afternoon," said Eddy. "They're calling us pigs and telling us to go home."

At last, the terrain leveled out and the caravan could pick up speed. The four trucks now outran the horses. A few moments later, the Americans heard shots from behind them. A bullet hit the rear end of the last vehicle in the line but did no damage. Lieutenant Gorney shouted for them to go to maximum speed and not return fire.

After about five minutes, when they were far enough from the Mexican horsemen, they slowed down, then maintained a steady pace toward Columbus. After an hour of driving without incident, signal flares broke the darkness of the night sky in the northeast.

"Men, that's a US Army flare, and we need to see what's going on over there. Reduce your speed, and follow the lead car carefully!" ordered Lieutenant Gorney, shouting so they all could hear him over the engine noise of the four quads.

The caravan moved carefully off-road and into the desert, illuminating a rather bright but narrow section of the way forward. Another signal flare went off, helping the lead driver to better orient the following vehicles. Within ten minutes, the lead truck's headlights revealed a biplane down on the dirt of the desert floor. The left wing and landing gear had been ripped from the fuselage. Shredded fabric, wire, and wood struts were littered everywhere.

Gorney and the soldiers from the caravan got out of the vehicles to check on the pilots. Joe commented to Eddy, "now I know what you are talking about with the Jennys. I'm surprised the crew is still alive."

The pilot, spoke first. "Ol' Buzz and me was wondering when you boys were going to make it out this way. We crashed a while ago but just started shooting those flares. We was hoping you would be the ones to join our party and not those damn banditos we saw riding around."

"Are you injured?" Lieutenant Gorney inquired.

The copilot replied, "Nothing a few shots of good bourbon couldn't cure." He added, "The wind picked up, and we both decided that we needed to land. Crosswind gusted just as we were about to touch down and damn near flipped us over, ripping the wing and wheels off. We then just hit the ground quite hard. We both were plenty shook up, but not hurt."

"Well, I can't offer you that shot of bourbon. I can offer you a ride back to base."

"Sounds good. Why don't y'all help us gather our shit and put it in the trucks. I suspect we'll have to come back tomorrow and see if we can salvage this plane," said the pilot.

Gorney asked Joe to move into the back of the truck, so the copilot, a lieutenant, could ride on the more comfortable seat. Joe began talking with Kuruk, who had a kind nature, and they bantered back and forth. After two and a half hours, the caravan crossed the border back into the US. The four quads reached the base at around 2230. All were happy to get back after a long day.

Temperatures had dropped considerably over the last two hours. Joe was shivering and hurried to get into his bunk to warm himself up. He knew he needed to unwind a bit before he could sleep, and he thought back to what Kuruk had advised: "Keep your memories but forget the past."

Upon hearing the words the first time, Joe thought they made little sense. Able to concentrate now, he thought hard about what the wise Indian man could've meant. He believed Kuruk had been telling him to cherish the good moments and let go of everything else. That made perfect sense to him. Just before he went to sleep, he grabbed his notebook from under his bunk so he would remember to make some notes in the morning.

CHAPTER 12
DUBLÁN

Joe was sweating profusely in the Mexican early-afternoon sun as he unloaded all the boxes that he'd been carrying in his Nash Quad. He took the red bandana from around his neck and wrung the water from it.

Yesterday, he'd had to stay the night in Dublán because of an afternoon windstorm. The wind had come whipping into the valley, blowing sand into eyes, noses, and mouths. Many soldiers had stumbled over each other, trying to walk backward into the wind to their bunkhouses. During evening guard duty, a few shots were fired at the sentry, who was fortunate enough to find cover and evaded getting hurt.

Over the past few months, the camp had swelled to produce a little city of tents and more permanent adobe structures. Outside the confines of the base, another little city cropped up, this one consisting of Chinese and local merchants, as well as some Americans, selling a variety of wares. A brothel had also been set up in this little community of sellers. The US Army sanctioned the enterprise and provided doctors to ensure the prostitutes were as healthy as they could be.

After lights out, Joe lay in his army cot, thinking about how he'd gotten the better end of things compared to the other army regulars. They'd assigned him to the Quartermaster Corps, which ended up managing the supply line from El Paso to Columbus and on to Dublán. Joe would only have to take part in drills and exercises—which took place in the scorching summer sun in full uniform—for two days a week. The rest of the time, he would usually drive three days and spend one full day working as a mechanic and performing maintenance and repairs to the trucks, cars, and motorcycles that were in use.

After the skirmish with Villa's troops at Carrizal in mid-May, efforts to catch him had slowed down. The cavalry had advanced as far south as Parral, about four hundred miles past the border, only to be chased by Mexican government forces northward. Pershing had proposed more aggressive measures to control the situation in that region of Chihuahua, but President Wilson rejected them. Pershing realized it was impossible to achieve the original mission objectives from this position, instead taking a defensive posture at the base in Dublán.

With the National Guard reserve forces summoned to guard the border stateside, Pershing could bring ten thousand men as part of the expedition's forces in Mexico. Daily drills were intense and focused on hand-to-hand combat, grenade throwing, and the proper use of the bayonet as a weapon.

"Next!" yelled the sergeant, starting a combat pairing. Soldiers in line, twenty yards apart, raced toward one another with rifles sporting wood bayonets. The goal of the engagement was to land a hit with the wooden bayonet to any part of the body. Blows to the head and back were not allowed. The victor of the match was determined by the officiating sergeant, and returned to the end of the line to fight again. The loser left and had to take part in marching drills with his company.

Donnie was particularly annoying that day. He stood behind Joe in the combat drill line and was talking nonstop about how quick his fighting moves were and how he fully expected to beat all opponents. Joe was trying to concentrate on some lessons he'd learned when his father taught him how to street fight. Watching the initial matches, he noticed that all these guys were doing the same thing.

In his thick Boston accent, Donnie cried out, "Joe, well look over there. I'm going to be fighting our old friend, Eugene." Joe had just noticed Eugene in line. From a distance, he looked unusually large compared to the soldiers around him, and the weapon he was carrying looked more like a child's toy.

"Let's trade places," Joe said. "I've some unfinished business with that fucking cheat."

"What's it worth to ya?"

"A buck."

"He's all yours. Make sure you beat the cocksucker."

After taking Donnie's place, and remembering his father's advice, Joe stared at his first opponent. Eugene returned the stare with the same level of intensity. Joe decided to take a different approach—he stuck out his tongue and laughed. He mouthed, *Fuck you, cracker* repeatedly, knowing the southerner would eventually be able to read his lips.

Almost before the sergeant finished shouting "Next," Eugene, his face filled with rage, raced toward Joe at full throttle with his rifle out-stretched. He generated a cloud of dust, reminiscent of a galloping horse on the prairie. Joe took a defensive position, squatting and waiting for the approaching soldier to come closer.

When Eugene got to within six feet of him, Joe thrust his rifle like a sword between the legs of his hefty opponent, causing him to stumble and struggle to regain his balance. Then, Joe propelled himself upward with everything he had at the wavering soldier, hitting him hard with his raised elbow directly below the collarbone, finally knocking him to the ground.

Joe raced over and hovered above his opponent with the wooden bayonet pointed downward, pressing just slightly into the base of Eugene's neck. Staring down into the beaten man's eyes, Joe did not utter a word as he waited to be declared the victor. When that happened, the crowd erupted with cheers. Joe reached down and helped Eugene to his feet. Staring up into the man's eyes, he said, "We're even, asshole."

Joe made it to the final round. His uniform was soaked with sweat, which had left his body in abundance during the matches. He felt slow afoot, and he struggled to come up with a strategy for his last opponent, who was considerably taller and easily weighed thirty pounds more than he did. Joe lacked the energy to do anything creative and decided he would proceed cautiously and try to gain an advantage only if his adversary made a mistake.

A game of cat and mouse ensued between the two soldiers. They both used their rifles to thrust and joust, but neither committed to a maneuver for victory. The crowd, expecting a brilliant match between the two foes, started to boo and catcall. Time eventually ran out, the two soldiers obviously exhausted and happy that the match was over. The sergeant declared a draw and, upon seeing the condition of both men, decided not to comment on this last bout. Instead, he congratulated them both for outstanding performances in all their matches.

As a tall, slender lieutenant approached, it was impossible for Joe not to notice the two ivory-handled Colt revolvers he wore Western style. Underneath the wide-brimmed hat casting shadows on his face, Joe detected a big smile. He came to attention and saluted.

"At ease, Private. Where'd you learn how to fight like that?"

"Sir, my father taught me how to defend myself when I was a kid back in New Jersey."

"So, an East Coast lad. Your dad taught you well. I saw you thoroughly thump your opponents in each match until the last one. What happened there?"

"Sir, to be honest, I was so tired, I didn't think I had the strength to attempt anything. I fought, hoping he'd make a mistake that I could take advantage of. From the look of things, he was thinking the same as me."

"Private, that was a wise decision. You only go hard if you think you can win." The lieutenant packed his long goose neck pipe and lit it with a match.

It finally dawned on Joe who this man was. He had heard stories about Lieutenant Patton, Pershing's aide in Mexico, walking around camp like a gunslinging cowboy, acting as if he were running the entire operation.

"What's your name, and who is your commanding officer?"

"Sir, Private Joseph O'Mara. Technically, my commanding officer is Captain Benjamin Foulois of the 1st Aero. However, I'm on indefinite loan to the Quartermaster Corps to support supply chain operations from Columbus to Dublán. Part of the time I'm a mechanic, driving the Nash Quads down here to deliver supplies, and then a regular soldier on days like today."

"Are you a good mechanic?"

"Sir, that was my job before I enlisted. Since I joined the army, I've been involved with all kinds of vehicles. Fixing cars and trucks is second nature to me."

"Thank you, Private O'Mara. That'll be all."

Lieutenant George S. Patton had been aide to General Pershing since the Punitive Expedition began. Because of the lull in action, Pershing had given Patton the assignment of familiarizing himself with newer armored car prototypes, which were driven to the camp in Dublán. The earlier design of the White Armored Car No. 2 had not met the requirements for speed and firepower, leading to its rejection during the evaluation at Fort Sill in Oklahoma. Patton was a trained cavalryman and did not feel comfortable with the details of motorized weaponry at this time. He wanted to evaluate these vehicles firsthand but could not do that without support. He saw an opportunity to have his own man provide this assistance rather than using soldiers who were not in his command. Patton had many conversations with General Pershing about the future of warfare. They both agreed it was not a question of *if* motorized weapons would replace the horse, but *when*. Patton did not have a hard time convincing Pershing to formally transfer Joe to the 11th Cavalry and promote him to corporal.

‡

"Corporal, can't you make this goddamn thing go any faster?" bellowed Lieutenant Patton.

Joe was riding alone with Patton early in the morning to evaluate the armored car before the scorching sun beat down and baked everything in its path. "Sir, unfortunately, I cannot. The armor cladding weighs down this car and prevents me from accelerating unless I'm on a level road." The White Armored Car No.2 continued to lumber along on one of the maneuver fields. Joe had to ignore the lieutenant's orders to speed up, as the terrain was uneven and the top-heavy vehicle could tip over.

Peering out the front window, the lieutenant ordered, "We've straight-level land coming up. Take it up to top speed. I'm going to see if I can hit something with this machine gun."

Joe inspected the terrain to make sure he could safely drive the vehicle faster. The lieutenant cranked the wheel to turn the turret manually and survey the surroundings. He spotted a small cactus, about half the size of a soldier, roughly thirty degrees to the right.

"Turn right slowly and head straight for that cactus. I'm going to see if I can hit it with the machine gun. Keep your current speed."

Joe knew the lieutenant would not be able to hit the cactus at their cruising speed because slight bumps in the terrain would cause the mounted gun to bounce around too much. He decided he would keep going and let him find that out for himself.

Patton fired the machine gun in bursts, missing his target every time. "Loop around and let's try this again, but at half the speed."

"Yes, sir. I'll get her down to twelve miles an hour."

At the slower speed, Patton could compensate for the vehicle's movements and, after a few errant shots, hit the cactus six times, ripping into its main trunk.

"Let's take a break, Corporal. I want to get your thoughts on what we just did."

The two got out of the car and leaned against it. Patton packed his pipe and lit it while Joe took out his pack of cigarettes and joined him for a smoke.

"Corporal, how would you feel about driving this contraption towards an enemy line of fire? Your honest opinion here."

"Sir, I wouldn't want to get too close. The tires are exposed, and if they were shot out on this ground, they'd dig in, and you'd get stuck and be a sitting duck. I think the trick is being able to fire the machine gun continuously while you're approaching, working with other cars to attack."

"Corporal, I think you're spot on. If most of the moons aligned, this vehicle might do well on a battlefield. It has too many limitations to be useful there. Better for patrolling and recon missions, I think."

CHAPTER 13

TWO MARES

Lieutenant George Patton had six of the armored cars under his command, along with twenty-five soldiers and a combination of drivers, mechanics, and gunners. Patton wanted to create an *esprit de corps* among this group, so he had them all moved into some of the adobe huts that Mexican natives had helped the soldiers build shortly after arriving. He demanded absolute discipline while they were engaged in what he called "soldiering activities," including coming to attention and saluting. However, he made sure his men had some of the best conditions in the camp and enjoyed better rations. While he did not billet with them, he would frequently make his way over to join them for dinner, tell and listen to stories, and have a good laugh.

Patton heard from one of the other lieutenants that about twenty-five miles south of camp—near San Miguel, at Rubio Ranch—fresh poultry and vegetables were for sale. He decided he would take an armored car patrol of four vehicles there to pick up provisions. Three of the cars had the full complement of soldiers with a driver, a gunner, and a mechanic, who fed ammunition into the machine gun when the vehicle was moving. Joe drove with Patton in the last car, forgoing the third man to leave sufficient storage room for the food.

Patton's intensity quite intimidated most of his fellow soldiers. Joe was one of the few who didn't feel that way. In fact, he found the lieutenant had quite a good sense of humor. On the ride to the ranch that day, he asked Joe if he'd ever caught the clap. Joe broke a smile, and with his eyes on the road ahead, he calmly answered, "No, sir. I've been very lucky that way."

After negotiating a pass through a low point in the mountains just outside of camp, it was smooth sailing south, with the mountains to the west and stretches of flat prairie to the east. The four vehicles were in "open" mode with all the hatches clasped, allowing for better visibility and some airflow in the cars.

After about an hour and a half of driving, the ranch appeared before them in the distance, with the town of San Miguel in the mountains over-looking it. Patton ordered the vehicles to stop about two hundred yards from what looked like the main barn. The hacienda was a fair distance from the structure, on the other side of the road. Joe wondered how the lieutenant would handle the situation, because walking the two hundred yards with no appreciable cover was far too risky.

"Men, I'm not looking to scare the rancher, but I'll be damned if I'll waltz up there on foot," said Patton. He chose Donnie as the gunner because he'd showed excellent marksmanship with the Browning in drills. He ordered the other cars and soldiers to observe in place and wait for his command before joining.

"Corporal, drive slowly straight toward the barn. Private, keep the machine gun pointed away from the building as we approach. I think my Spanish is good enough to let them know we're here just to buy food."

Following the lieutenant's orders, Joe drove less than ten miles per hour, approaching the barn. Patton yelled out several times in Spanish, but no one appeared.

"Lower all hatches. Point the machine gun straight ahead and drive forward," ordered the lieutenant. With that order, Joe became concerned. He sensed Patton was highly suspicious of the situation. Following the order, he got the vehicle moving. Shooting came from the barn, with bullets ricocheting off the front hatch just as it was being lowered.

"Private, spray the barn with bullets. I am going to get out of the car and shoot the bastards if they try to run away."

Donnie aimed the Colt-Browning M1895 and fired, shattering glass and splintering wood on the old barn, allowing the lieutenant to take cover behind the vehicle. The shooting from the armored car stopped while the return fire from the barn kept coming at them. Although Joe knew that the bullets bouncing off the car's reinforced surface posed no threat, he still was afraid for his life. This was live combat, and the enemy was trying to kill him.

Patton beckoned with his arm for the other armored cars to make their way up to his position. "Fire another volley into the barn while we wait for the others." Donnie obliged and fired a round into the building.

The shooters quickly realized they were outgunned and tried to make a run for it. Six horses and riders came racing out of the barn. Coolly, while taking cover, Patton took aim with his ivory-handled Colt revolver, fired, and dropped one rider. He got in the car, looked at Joe and said, "Corporal, top speed after them."

Because the hatch was down, Joe's vision of the dirt road was very limited. He was concerned about hitting a rut too fast, so he proceeded cautiously at first. The remaining five riders headed up a rather steep hill toward San Miguel. This road was well-traveled and had a hard-packed surface, allowing Joe to pick up speed and gain on them. The other armored cars lagged well behind them.

"Private, do you have a shot at the riders? I'd prefer you didn't take out the horses, as that gets ugly."

"Yes, sir."

"Fire when ready."

Donnie aimed and fired about six shots at the fleeing horsemen. One dropped from his saddle and hit the ground. The others realized they had to get off the road and galloped into the prairie, where they could take advantage of the terrain. Patton realized the pursuit was futile and ordered Joe to drive back. The fallen rider was lying face down in the dirt, his horse waiting beside him.

Patton checked the man for a pulse. "Good shot, Private! You killed him. Corporal, help him drape the body over the hood of the car and head back to the ranch. I'm going to ride this mare back." The lieutenant proceeded slowly, trying to get a feel for the horse.

After they finished their task, Joe said, "Donnie, get back in the car fast, and man the machine gun. I think I see a gunman on the ridge, right where the lieutenant is headed." Then he yelled for Patton. "Lieutenant, enemy shooter at two o'clock!"

Patton swerved to the left and broke out into a full gallop as bullets came down from the hillside, hitting the ground he had just occupied. With Joe driving back along the road, Donnie fired a constant barrage into the area where the enemy gunfire had originated.

The shooting from the ridge stopped. Joe increased their speed and caught up with Patton and the other armored cars about a mile from the ranch.

The rancher, Francisco Rubio, spoke English well and explained the circumstances of what had happened. "This man dead on the ground is Julio Cardenas. He's one of Pancho Villa's top men. Both Villa and Carranza's men come to my farm and take what they want. They're no friends of mine. Cardenas and five men were here today, and they saw those vehicles coming and assumed that you would stop here. He told me to get in the house and be quiet. If we made a sound, he promised he would come back and kill me and my family. I could not risk warning you."

Joe studied Patton while the man conversed with the rancher. Despite feeling safe now, tension still consumed his entire body. In contrast, the lieutenant acted as if nothing out of the ordinary had transpired. His actions resembled those of someone casually visiting a grocer in his neighborhood. Then, while looking at the corpse on the ground, Joe remembered the difficulty he'd encountered with Donnie, swinging his dead comrade onto the hood less than a half hour ago.

Patton said, "Senôr Rubio, we shot up your barn. Please accept these two beautiful mares as payment for the damage that Villa's men caused. We came here to buy some food and would like to continue to do so. I understand you have chickens, corn, and other vegetables."

"I just had twenty chickens killed for Cardenas. As he was going to take them, please accept them with my compliments. I also have some bushels of corn and squash."

"Senôr, the US Army will pay its way. What do you prefer, dollars or pesos?"

Rubio accepted the ten US dollars and was visibly pleased.

"Drape this son of a bitch Cardenas on the hood next to his friend. Secure both bodies with some rope. We are going to drive back through San Miguel this time, a display of US Army force. Tonight, we're going to have a celebration dinner. Men, you made history today. This was the first motorized vehicle attack in US military history," declared the lieutenant.

Joe was glad Patton had directed two other soldiers to take care of the second body. Driving was excellent therapy for him. With every mile, he felt a bit more like himself.

As they finished climbing the hill to San Miguel, Patton ordered, "Corporal, slow down through this little town. I want to make sure word gets around."

Finally, having the bodies strapped to the hood of a car like hunted animals made sense to Joe. Patton was trying to make a powerful statement to the locals who might wish harm on the forces stationed in their home-land. Then another thought popped into his mind. Perhaps that wasn't all of it. Maybe Patton's message was to his troops as well. War is ugly and you need to be mentally tougher than your adversary. Forget they're human beings. They're the enemy, nothing more.

The four armored vehicles wormed their way through the narrow streets with the two dead Villistas displayed in plain sight. The residents took notice, and word spread through the village as the caravan exited the town and descended into the valley. Leaving the confines of the built-up area and gaining a clear view of their surroundings allowed them to open their hatches, letting the air rush in to cool down the soldiers, who were sweltering from the sun.

After about an hour without incident, the cars rolled into camp. "Corporal, let's first drive to HQ and drop the bodies off," Patton told Joe. "I need to tell General Pershing what happened. We will then get this food over to the mess tent."

Several news-starved correspondents were staying nearby. When they saw the armored cars with the bodies stopping at HQ, they scurried over to find out more.

"Lieutenant, can you please tell us what happened?"

"Gentlemen, I certainly will after I brief General Pershing. Let's just say I have a great story for your papers."

‡

That night, the armored car company of the 11th Cavalry had a delicious dinner of chicken, biscuits, squash, and corn. All the men had quite their fill of food and were in a loquacious mood.

The comradery with his fellow soldiers did wonders to help Joe reconcile his thoughts about the incident. He realized he had little con-trol over the situations he would find himself in, and a clear head was a requirement for survival in the army. He began telling his version of the day in a spirited fashion.

"Without hesitation, Patton gets out of the armored car, takes out his gun, and shoots the fucking guy off his horse. I tell ya, he's got ice water running through his veins. Then, we chase the horses, and I push the gas pedal to the floor to catch them. As we're gaining on them, Donnie here fires off some shots from the turret and hits one!"

"Quite an accurate summary of the day's events, corporal." The men were so absorbed in Joe's storytelling, they hadn't seen Lieutenant Patton coming up from behind. The entire company of twenty-five stood at attention and saluted.

"At ease, men. While we have strict rules in camp that forbid drinking, I think we can bend these rules because of this special occasion." The colored orderly who accompanied Patton, carrying four bottles of Buffalo Trace bourbon, started filling the soldiers' cups.

"This is a historic day. I'm proud of how you behaved under fire. We've set the enemy back by killing one of Villa's top men. Let's drink to our success." Patton raised his glass. "As an old cavalryman, I have to say initially I had my doubts about these armored cars. Today, I realize armored cars and tanks are the future of warfare. Private Walsh, you registered the first kill using a motorized vehicle in US Army history. I say that calls for a cheer."

Donnie smiled ear to ear as the other soldiers yelled, "Hip, hip, hooray!"

Patton stayed for about an hour and chatted with his men. When Joe was coming back from the latrine, Patton made a special point of going over to him, patting him on the back, and telling him, "Corporal, some might think *you* have ice water running through your veins. I wanted to thank you personally for saving my hide when I was riding back. When I spoke to Private Walsh at the ranch, he told me you're the one I should be thanking. He said he didn't see the shooter and wouldn't have fired without your direction."

"You're welcome, Lieutenant. Just doing what the army trained me to do."

"Joe, that's what a good soldier says. I don't have a crystal ball, but I suspect things are going to be ending here in Mexico soon, and we'll eventually make it to Europe. I want to be where the action is, and I want to be surrounded by men like you. You have a bright future and will become an officer if you decide to make the army your career."

"Thanks, sir. It means a lot for you to tell me that. I'll keep it in mind."

‡

Joe slept soundly all the way through to revelry. Upon waking up, all he could think of was how much he wanted a cup of coffee. Leaving the tent, he couldn't help but notice how hot it was for this time in the morning. Regardless of what was planned, it would be a tough day.

Donnie was waiting for Joe to come out of his tent, and when he saw him, he whistled to get his attention. "Got a minute?"

"Yeah, sure, Donnie. You look like your dog just died. What's wrong?" The two men started walking to the mess tent, where breakfast was being served.

"Yesterday, I was on top of the world, being that I was the first to record a kill in an armored car and all. Last night, it finally hit me that I killed a guy. When I closed my eyes, all I could see was the two bullets I shot ripping into his back and him falling from the horse. Then you and me throw his body on the fucking hood of the car like he's some animal."

This revelation surprised Joe. Yesterday, killing a man hadn't appeared to even phase his friend. It took a moment for him to decide how to respond.

"You feel bad because killing somebody don't come natural to you. I'm betting if that same guy had a chance to kill you, he would've taken it and not thought twice."

"Yeah, I guess. You ever kill anybody?"

"I did. Two bad guys who would've killed a friend of mine. I didn't plan on doing it. Things happened so fast. I felt like I didn't have a choice."

"So, you didn't get spooked by it."

Joe immediately remembered the sleepless nights and nightmares after the incident. Truthfully, he didn't think much about it anymore. The army left little time for thinking. Maybe this had been a part of his past that he had left behind.

"Oh, I didn't say that. I still think about it, but I guess I'm okay with it now."

"Well, that Mexican I killed would've rode off back to his camp. And like you were saying, if he'd had a chance, he would've put a bullet in me."

"Yeah, and there's no telling how much blood was on his hands. Pancho's men aren't known for being saints."

"So, probably I did a good thing, right?"

"Donnie, you followed orders and did your job. Way, I figure it, the guys that sent us down her and are giving orders are more responsible for the killing than we are. All we're trying to do is stay alive."

CHAPTER 14

BACK TO ORANGE

"My goodness, Joey, you look like you're thirty years old," exclaimed Margaret O'Mara as she stared at her son, who had just walked in the door dressed in full uniform. The Mexican sun had changed Joe's pale complexion to a ruddy shade of tan and covered any trace of his former boyish features.

It was February 1917, and Joe would turn nineteen the following month. He looked at his mother and saw the same vibrant woman he had left sixteen months ago. However, it was also true she had aged, with streaks of gray appearing in her long, chestnut-brown hair. Joe felt some pangs of guilt as he imagined her saying extra rosaries at church, worrying about her youngest boy.

Running into Joe's outstretched arms, his mother cried tears of joy. "I've prayed every day for your safe return. I know you can take care of yourself, but a mother will still worry."

Teddy, who had been asleep in the living room, ran up to see Joe, tail wagging. Joe got down on one knee to greet the dog, who jumped him, knocking him to the floor, and began licking his face. "I missed you too, Teddy."

"You know that dog of yours has been waiting every day for you to walk through the door. He's been good company for me since Grandma died."

Joe had heard about his grandmother in one of his mother's letters. He certainly wasn't going to tell his mom, but he cared more about his old friend still being alive than he did about this woman he felt absolutely no emotion for.

Joe took his mother's hand. "I'm sorry, Mom."

"Let me put a kettle on, and let's have a cup of tea together. I appreciate your letters so much, but I want to find out more. I'm afraid this country will enter the war in Europe, and you'll be on a boat headed to join the slaughter."

"Mom, I have a six-week leave because the expedition ended. My orders are to return to Fort Bliss in El Paso. The reserve units that guarded the border are being sent home in waves. The regular soldiers like me who started the expedition must go back and protect the border. Pancho Villa is still out there. I don't see me leaving there before I'm discharged—that's November of next year."

"Weren't you in danger?"

"If you're a soldier on active duty, there's always going to be some danger. I wrote to you about the incident in the papers with Lieutenant Patton."

"I can only imagine some of the things you've seen. I know you, Joey; you'll not be telling me things that might scare me. You're just like your father that way."

Joe did not respond, his silence an acknowledgement of his mother's words.

The door opened, and in walked James in his police uniform. "Well, my local spies let me know a soldier had paid a visit to the house, and I quickly figured things out." He saluted his son. "Nice work, Corporal—come over and give your old man a hug." Joe obliged his father, and the men embraced. "Son, we have plenty of things to talk about."

Joe had always thought his father could impose his will on most anyone. Since he had left, James had developed a bit of a gut, grayed considerably, and started to wear spectacles. Joe found himself surprised at how his dad looked, but it went beyond the physical changes. He couldn't put his finger on it, but the once-commanding man projected a level of vulnerability now—and that made Joe worry about his safety.

‡

"Well, if it isn't big Jim O'Mara, escorted by a soldier."

George McMahon, proprietor of a small local tavern, was a short, stocky man. He was wearing a bar keep's apron and had a stubby unlit cigar wedged in the corner of his mouth. He gave James a familiar pat on the back as the two sat down at the bar. Joe, meanwhile, put down a five-dollar bill. McMahon picked it up and promptly gave it back.

"If you're sittin' with big Jim, your money's no good at my bar." He brought them two draft beers and two shots of Bushmills and then went to tend to the other patrons.

"Son, I'm proud of you. Making corporal in just a short time at your age is quite an achievement."

"Dad, I made corporal for two reasons: I'm a good mechanic, and they needed me to work on lots of different vehicles. The second is that you taught me how to fight smart."

"Well, glad to pass on something useful," James said. "Your mother knows some of the details of why you had to leave, but I don't want to talk much about it in front of her. That's why I wanted to take you here."

Joe took out a pack of cigarettes, lit one, and focused on his father.

"God bless Harry, he's a man of his word. He told the story to the police when they came. And he told them he did the shooting. That night, he went back and purged his shop of any written mention of you, anticipating a break-in. That happened two days later. He shut down the shop and continued paying Leroy, so he'd have him when he reopened. This business really shook up Harry and got him thinking sensibly."

As his father spoke, Joe thought about what his life would have been like if Harry hadn't been so stubborn and just paid the twenty-five dollars a week. Jim would still be alive. Joe would probably still be working in the garage and never have traveled outside the Newark area. He never would've met Lilly, Patton, or Donnie.

"There's been a lot more discussion at the station about what we're going to do about those 'guinea bastards' coming to Orange than what to do about this case. Since there was no one pushing —and with Harry being a solid member of the community with no priors—they closed the investigation. Harry reopened the shop after a few months, and there hasn't been any trouble."

Joe was relieved to hear the case had been closed. However, he was still worried about the Black Hand. He asked his father, "Should I be at all concerned about the Italians still looking for me?"

"I don't think so. Since you left, a truce seems to have developed between the Irish mob here in Orange and the Italians set up near Branch Brook Park. Don't take any chances, though. I think it is okay for you to visit Harry to say hello, but I don't want you helping or working there during your leave. Wear your uniform when you visit. No one will recognize you. "

"Okay, Dad." Perhaps his father was being overly cautious, but Joe decided he would follow his advice to the letter.

"Oh, the other thing I wanted to tell you is about your saintly mother." A big smile flashed on James's face as he took the second half of his shot and washed it down with the beer. "You know I had to pull a few strings, but I was able to get her out of jail."

Joe's eyes widened. He knew his father was being playful, but he was never one to make things up out of the blue. "How'd Mom wind up in the can?"

Apparently, since Joe's departure, his mother had become very active in the local women's suffrage movement. Being outspoken about women's rights, she'd joined the cause for a more concentrated push to amend the constitution.

"You wouldn't know it by looking at her, but your mother's as tough as Teddy Roosevelt. A bunch of lady suffragettes gathered at city hall in Newark and marched, carrying signs and chanting. Mayor Gillen apparently told the police chief to get the crowd to disperse. Well, these ladies were having none of it, telling the officers they had every right to protest. When they wouldn't listen, the cops formed a line and walked slowly forward, trying to move them along. Your mother wouldn't budge and wound up knocking a cop down with her sign to stand her ground. She was one of the first ones in the paddy wagon and spent a few hours in jail."

Joe knocked back his shot and waited for the alcohol burn to stop. The only part of the story that surprised him was that his mom had struck a policeman. She was always so vocal about how violence solved nothing in the end. She must have been really mad. Joe asked, "How'd you get her out?"

"Newark police called the station, and I went down and got her. Before they released her, they told me I needed to do a better job controlling my wife. I thought, 'I'll be damned.'"

"How did mom take all of this? What did you tell her?"

"I told her, 'I completely understand why you were steamed about not being able to vote.' But, she better be more careful, and most of all, keep that Irish temper of hers under control."

Joe and his father had a hearty laugh. After a few more drinks, they walked home together.

‡

That night, Joe was having a difficult time falling asleep, thinking about his mother and listening to Teddy snoring from his place next to the bed. His mom had firm beliefs. She was a deeply religious Catholic and talked with fervor about her home country and the fight against the British Empire. Now, she was involved in the women's suffrage movement. Despite detesting violence of any kind, she'd still gotten so riled up that she'd assaulted a police officer.

Then he thought about his father. Outside of his admiration for Teddy Roosevelt, he never talked about causes and rarely shared his opinions on current events. However, it was no secret what he cared about or how he would act. It was obvious he loved his wife and family and would protect them above all else. Whenever Joe observed members of the community interacting with his father, it seemed as if they considered him part of their extended family. He lived by this set of rules, a code which he set himself.

Then Joe thought about himself and concluded quickly he was more like his father than his mother. He wasn't religious or particularly patriotic. He struggled to understand why so many of his fellow soldiers had an intense hatred for Mexicans. Since he had come home, there'd been all this talk about how the Germans were monsters and how that country needed to be punished. As a soldier, he would put a bullet in a Mexican or a German if they ordered him. It was about duty, not hatred. He had a quick flashback to Antonio Romano's face right before he'd pulled the trigger. He still felt hatred toward that man today.

Moving on, Joe's thoughts drifted to Lilly and the night he had spent with her before the expedition left. When he left, he would get to El Paso a few days early and try to see her again.

‡

It was a strange feeling for Joe to walk the streets of Orange and go through Orange Park dressed in his uniform. Memories flooded his consciousness from all directions as he retraced his steps to Harry's garage. Remembering his naivete regarding the Black Hands extortion racket, he realized he really had been a boy before he left for the army. He was so different today and concluded this was what it felt like to be a man.

Walking to the gasoline pumps, Joe saw his old colleague Leroy, who ran over and gave him a bearhug. "Mister Harry, come right out here, there's someone to see you."

Harry's eyes were wet as he approached them. "Joe, I can't believe it's you. Your father didn't tell me where you went, but I think it was a smart idea to get out of here."

"Harry, I wanted to come and thank you for taking responsibility for what I did."

"Jesus, Joe. I wouldn't be standing here if you hadn't acted. It was the right thing to do. You've got your whole life to live. And I have to say, you certainly fill out that uniform nicely. By that tan of yours, I suspect you may've been involved down in Mexico."

"That's true. I got to work on a range of cars and trucks the army used. I even worked on the aeroplanes."

"I made some decisions right after that day. Your father stopped by after the break-in here and we talked. He convinced me that unless I wanted to wind up dead, I should shut the shop down until things calmed down. Instead of being a stubborn arse, I heeded what he said."

Joe listened patiently to his mentor, although he couldn't help feeling the slightest bit angry. Did all of this really have to happen for Harry to wise up?

Harry continued, "I also vowed that when I opened back up, I'd employ whoever I wanted in the shop. I've two of Jim's sons helping with pumping gas and the heavy work, and I've been teaching Leroy all I know about being a mechanic. It's taken some time, but he's catching on and doing well. I know there are plenty of people who won't bring their car in anymore because I've a colored man working on cars these days. I say, good for them. Business is booming. When Leroy is up to speed, I'll break in one of Jim's sons to do mechanic work so we can take on more business."

Joe acknowledged Harry's comments, but had a nagging question. As big of a heart as Harry could display, he also knew that he could be downright mean and pinch pennies unnecessarily. Joe knew it would irk Harry, but he just had to ask, "Being that Leroy's doing such a good job, I hope you've raised his pay to what is fair for an apprentice mechanic."

"Joe, don't go stickin' that nose of yours where it don't belong. I pay them better than most would pay a colored worker. I've gone above and beyond to take care of them."

Joe waited to respond, taking a cigarette out of his pack, lighting it, drawing in deeply, and exhaling. "I know you've been good to them, better than almost any boss around here. Why would you risk losing Leroy by not paying him enough? Maybe some smart guy in another garage figures out what you're doing and makes him an offer that doubles his salary. He couldn't turn that down."

"Aye, Joe. I wasn't thinking that way. You've got a point."

"If Leroy feels he's making decent money and taking care of his family, he doesn't even bother talking to anybody."

A sense of satisfaction came to Joe at having broken through Harry's stubborn streak, appealing to his common sense. Staying with Harry was also in Leroy's best interest, as Joe knew the old Scot would treat him with respect.

"Aye, Joe. That makes good business sense. I think I'll look at gradually taking his wages up to keep him with me. You know you've a job here when you come back, and I'll pay you what you're worth."

Joe hadn't decided what exactly he was going to do in the future. However, the idea of going back into the same work situation that he'd left did not appeal to him. He politely said, "Thanks, Harry. I'm not sure what I want to do when I'm back."

"Well, I hope you don't get shipped over there to fight the bloody Germans. I think it's just a matter of time before this country gets involved. I believe nothing Wilson says."

Joe responded, "People in Texas and New Mexico are scared that there could be an invasion because things aren't too stable down there. There's a rumor about the Germans urging the Mexicans to invade the US to keep us occupied and out of the European war. I'm betting I'll serve out my time right down there."

Harry nodded. "Take care of yourself, Joe, wherever they send you."

"Thanks, Harry. I have gotten pretty good at that."

CHAPTER 15
MARTHA OR ELLA

Tom O'Mara was four years older than Joe and could not have been more different in appearance. He was several inches taller than his brother, with dark hair and a lanky build, and wore spectacles. At first glance, he appeared studious and quiet, but by nature, he was very gregarious. People warmed up to Tom quickly. The two brothers had always been close despite the age difference.

Tom started as an undertaker's apprentice at Hannifin's Funeral Home, near the Bridge Street Bridge that connected the city of Newark to Harrison, while he was still in high school. He worked his way up and was being groomed to eventually take over as funeral director. When he mentioned that some of the older vehicles at the home needed maintenance, Joe jumped at the opportunity to work with his brother on a per diem basis for the duration of his leave.

While having lunch together in the small garage of the funeral home, Tom asked his brother, "Joe, I love listening to your stories. One thing I notice, though, is you never talk about yourself. You're always playing poker, aren't you?"

"Not always, brother. What do you want to know?"

"I need some advice on how to approach a very special young lady. Think you can help?"

Rather than confess to his brother that he had no experience actually courting girls, Joe said, "Just be yourself. Everyone likes you. Think of something fun to do and ask her out."

"This girl's really special. You may have met her already. Remember Martha, the greeter and organ player who works with Hannifin during the wakes?"

"Not really. I've just seen her from a distance. I noticed she dressed to the nines—looked like she was ready to star in the moving pictures."

"Why don't we go on a double date? Martha's so outgoing—I'm sure she has tons of pretty friends you'd like to meet. It just seems more relaxed if we do it together."

"Okay, I'm game. I know the weather is a little chilly, but we could go down to Asbury Park, stroll the boardwalk and eat some taffy."

Joe thought it was crazy that Tom was asking for his advice. He was so outgoing. Did he really lack confidence to ask a girl out? Joe was looking forward to spending the day with his brother. Despite being close, they never really did things together outside of family activities.

Later that afternoon, Tom came back to Joe, who was working on a Model T hearse in the garage. "You were right. I suggested Asbury Park this Sunday, and she said yes. Additionally, she promised to invite her friend Ella. Said she's beautiful and loads of fun. We'll meet to take the 10:15 a.m. train from Broad Street Station."

"Hm . . . beautiful and fun. We'll see."

"There's one thing I want you to know, but I want you to keep it under your hat. Martha's German. Hannifin wasn't going to hire her, but she convinced him that she's a natural for the job. Her real name is Wolff, but Hannifin got her to agree to introduce herself as Martha White at the home."

"Tom, you know I couldn't give a shit about that sort of thing."

"I wasn't worried about you. There's so much buzz about Germany these days. Mom gets quite a few letters from her old friends back in Ireland, and after she reads one, she'll go on a bit of a rant about the Germans from time to time. I just don't know how she'd react."

"Tommy, I don't think you're going to be proposing to Martha on Sunday. Stop being so damn nervous. I promise not to bring up the Kaiser."

Once Tom confirmed the date, Joe felt a level of anticipation. Additionally, Martha had come down to the garage the next day and introduced herself to him and said she was looking forward to Sunday. Joe liked her immediately. He would be ecstatic if Ella was half as nice as Martha.

‡

When Joe saw how Tom had dressed for the date, he became quite self-conscious. He was wearing his army uniform, the only decent clothes he owned. Tom was the picture of fashion dressed in a dark blue suit, white spats, a red tie, and a straw hat.

They all met at the station in Newark with plenty of time before the train left. As promised, Martha's friend Ella O'Connor was a real beauty. A faux fur hat sat atop her wavy strawberry-blond hair, and she was wearing a stylish pleated dress, which accentuated her womanly figure, underneath her long wool coat. Ella had applied makeup to make herself look much older than her eighteen years.

In contrast, Martha dressed more conservatively, in a long green dress and black wool coat. She was tall, had a girlish figure, and wore no makeup, her curly dark brown hair hidden by a wide-brimmed hat. Martha had enchanting green eyes and a beautiful smile that could warm a room.

After boarding, the couples flipped the wicker seats on the Long Branch line coach so they could face each other, with the women sitting by to the window. The train took off, and bright sunshine came through the windows, helping to warm up the coach.

Twenty minutes into the trip, Joe noticed his brother fidgeting in his seat. He knew Tom well. There was something bothering him, but he couldn't put his finger on what. Both girls were absolutely wonderful, and they really seemed to enjoy Joe's tales about the army. Martha loved his imitation of Lieutenant Patton and Donnie and asked to hear more stories.

Soon, Joe asked, "You ladies mind if I smoke a cigarette?"

"No problem at all, soldier boy," Martha replied, "as long as you offer Ella and me one to join you."

While taking out the pack, Joe joked, "I thought *respectable* ladies weren't supposed to smoke cigarettes."

Feigning offense as she reached for the smoke, Martha said, "These respectable women don't like to be told what's good for them."

Joe lit all the cigarettes and proclaimed, "Tom and I are very used to strong women. Although our mother doesn't smoke, she's got an iron will and is the clear head of our family. Don't you think, brother?"

"Absolutely. Our father'd be the first to agree."

Martha started coughing as if it was her first cigarette. She whispered in response, "Well, I like her already." Once she regained her breath, she could restart the conversation. "Truth be told, my parents would have a fit if they saw me smoking and if they knew I was out with boys today. They're very strict. My mother is a strong woman and runs the household, but my father makes all the decisions. My older sisters are strong women and make choices for themselves. I want to be like them."

It finally hit Joe—as he regaled the group with his army stories, Martha fixated on his every word. When she responded, he realized he was doing the very same thing. She captivated him. *Tom is upset because it seems that Martha likes me.*

After spending time with her, it became obvious why Tom had been so nervous about asking her on a date. Other than the fact that she was German, she would be the perfect girl to bring home to their mother. Joe imagined Martha playing the piano and singing along with Margaret. In time, she would probably even join her at demonstrations in the fight for women's suffrage!

While there were definite similarities between the two women, there were also some distinct differences. Martha exuded a lightness of spirit with her wit and humor. Mom could be so serious, and there was always the specter of their Roman Catholic God that she would frequently bring up, which made Joe feel guilty about some action or thought.

As the train slowed down at their station, Joe decided that, for the sake of his relationship with Tom, he would let the girls decide on which brother they wanted to be with.

It was a beautiful, sunny, and unusually warm early spring day in Asbury Park. The two couples made their way off the train, and Martha grabbed both O'Mara boys' hands and squeezed them. "You know, my good friends call me Marty. I consider you both to be my good friends. Give us girls a few minutes in the ladies' room." Without waiting for a response, the two women went off together.

Tom spoke first. "I have only one request. Can I be the godfather of your firstborn child? Five minutes into the damn train ride, I knew I had no chance of courting Martha. It's clear she's only interested in you. Go for her, Joe, with my blessing. I think I'll try to warm up to Ella, but I don't think I'm her type, either."

"Believe me," Joe said. "I'd no intention of stealin' your girl or showin' you up. Ella's a beauty. I'd have thought she'd be the type I'd go for. But there's something truly special about Marty that's got me thinking a different way."

‡

The couples separated from each other as they walked down the boardwalk, taking in the sun and the fresh sea breeze. Things were quiet except for the crashing of the waves and the croaking of seagulls. Joe looked over at Tom and Ella. They seemed to be getting along well. Ella practically hadn't stopped laughing since the pair had gone off together. That made Joe feel better about what was happening.

"Joe, would you mind giving me my second cigarette?" Martha said with a giggle. "I want to decide whether I enjoy smoking. I think it makes me look older and perhaps a bit more sophisticated. What do you think?"

"Marty, you're beautiful with or without the cigarette."

She gave Joe a friendly kiss on the cheek. "You're sweet. I haven't met any boys like you. You're so confident and interesting. I could listen to you talk all day. I think I'll have that smoke."

Fighting the breeze that was picking up, Joe could finally light the cigarettes, and they found a bench to sit on and faced the ocean.

"I don't know if Tom told you," she said, "but I think you should know—my parents are from Germany. They speak very little English. They came over in 1885 and have been good, hardworking citizens. I'm worried our neighbors will be angry with us if this country goes to war against Germany."

"Marty, I grew up around Irish in Orange. Little by little, I have met all kinds of people. Just because people are different from you don't mean they're bad. And just because people are the same as you don't mean they're good."

"Joe, I'm so happy to hear you say that. I know you're only working at Hannifin's for a short time. When do you have to go back?"

"I head out on Monday, April 2, to go back down to Texas. I'll finish my enlistment for good in November 1918, a long time from now."

"I want to get to know you before you head back."

"I'd like that very much."

‡

Joe ended up planning all his available time around Marty's schedule. They would spend any spare moments they had together at Hannifin's. Joe thought of Marty constantly. Even though he was attracted to her and wanted her as a lover, he knew it was not the right thing to do, given the short time they had together before he left. He decided he would be the perfect gentleman. His sense of honor and responsibility took precedence over his urges.

"Tom," Joe began, "after Sunday mass, Mom is planning a farewell dinner for me with the family. I'd like to ask her—if it's all right—if I could invite Marty." He felt comfortable asking his brother, since Tom and Ella had gotten along so well and had seen each other again.

"You sure don't waste any time. Thanks for checking, but I'm okay. I can see how happy you are. "

‡

Pleased that Tom was fine with his plan, Joe now needed to present his question to his mother. They were sitting at the kitchen table right before breakfast. The rest of the family hadn't joined yet. Joe felt a touch of apprehension as he spoke, because he wasn't quite sure how she would react.

His mom smiled. "Joey, I'd love to have your friend join us for dinner. She could come to mass and then have dinner with us."

"That sounds good. I'll get her in the morning." Joe didn't have the courage to tell his mother his friend was Lutheran. He also knew Marty wouldn't mind going to a Roman Catholic service.

When he invited her, Marty thought it was an excellent idea. She also decided it was time her parents knew she was interested in boys. "I've been telling my sister Minnie about you. She's eager to meet you. Please wear your uniform. You look so handsome in it, and I want to show you off."

That Sunday was the first day of April. The morning was chilly and gray. Tom let Joe borrow his 1910 Model T, which he had purchased a few months earlier, to pick up Marty. The family was planning on attending eleven-o'clock mass at St. Johns in Orange, so Joe set out early to get to the Wolff's home on South Second Street by ten.

He pulled up in front of the gate and let himself in, walking toward the front steps, only to hear the warning barks of a small dog. The door opened, and a tall woman in her mid-twenties stepped out. "C'mon in, Joe. Don't mind Toodles—she's all bark. I'm so happy to meet you. Marty has told me so much about you. I'm Minnie."

You could tell the two women were sisters, but there was a toughness, almost a masculinity, to Minnie that contrasted with Marty's very feminine appearance.

Soon, Marty appeared, wearing a long black velvet dress with a white Victorian-style collared blouse and flashing a big smile. "I see that you've met Minnie, and Toodles hasn't bitten you, so we're off to a good start." She took Joe's arm and escorted him downstairs to the kitchen to meet her parents. "Joe, this is my mother, father, and my younger brother, Fred."

Joe stepped forward to greet her father first. "I'm pleased to meet you, Mr. Wolff."

Wilhelm Wolff rose from his chair and took Joe's extended hand, shaking it without saying a word. Mr. Wolff was not much taller than Joe's five feet ten inches, but every ounce of him suggested enormous physical strength and power.

Mrs. Wilhelmina Wolff standing by the oven wearing an apron, baking bread. She was a small woman with very plain features. She walked toward Joe and, doing her best to be pleasant, cracked a half smile, extending her thin bony hand and speaking with a thick accent. "Nice to meet you."

Joe had imagined what Marty's parents might be like, and this certainly wasn't it. After what seemed like an exceptionally long pause, Marty said, "Ich werde zu Hause bis ein und zwanzig Uhr."

Minnie looked at Joe with a smile and crowed, "Which translates to you, Joe, that we'll come out looking for you if you don't have her back here by nine o'clock sharp."

‡

Joe held the door open for Marty, gave the Model T a couple of cranks to get it running, and hopped inside. "Marty, I must tell you, I've kept to myself regarding anything personal with my family. My mom's overjoyed to meet you. She knows nothing about you other than your name. Just be yourself. I can't imagine her not liking you."

The entire O'Mara clan, including all the brothers and sisters, gathered in front of the imposing structure of St. John's Church in Orange. Joe went down the line, introducing his friend as Martha. When it was Tom's turn, Martha walked over and gave him a kiss on the cheek. Joe saved his parents for last, and James had a big smile on his face as he clasped Martha's hand in both of his and welcomed her.

Martha turned to Margaret and extended her hand, and before she could speak, the older woman approached her and said, "Let's get things started with a hug. I'm so happy to meet you." She took Martha into her arms. "It's not too early to take a seat," she then told the group, ushering everyone into the church.

It was Palm Sunday, and the altar boys gave everyone a small piece of palm as they entered the narthex. Once they were all seated, Joe's mother caught his eye. He was pretty certain that was a look of approval he saw. Marty made a great first impression.

As the congregation bellowed back their responses to the priest in Latin, Martha did not take part, but she joined in singing some hymns. As she left the church, Margaret told her what a pretty voice that she had.

When the family got back home, James thought it appropriate to say a few words. "This is a special celebration today, and we're having our Easter Dinner a week early. We're thankful to have Joe home for a visit and wish him a safe return to Texas tomorrow. We also want to welcome Joe's guest, Martha, to our home. Let's enjoy each other's company today and give thanks for this wonderful food."

Once James had finished, Martha approached Margaret. "I'm a good cook and would love to help you prepare the food," she offered.

"Are you sure, Martha? My two girls can help, although neither would claim they'd enjoy doing it. Since Joe is leaving tomorrow, I would think you'd want to spend the time with him."

"I'm sure, Mrs. O'Mara. I thought we could chat a bit while we got everything ready."

"I'd love your help."

‡

Even though it was chilly, Joe turned into Orange Park to enjoy the twilight with Marty before he brought her home. The wonderful dinner of turkey, stuffing, vegetables, and soda bread with fresh butter had induced everyone to eat a little more than they really wanted to.

"Joe, I really like your family, especially your mother. I sensed she wanted to know more about me when she asked about where my people were from, so I just opened up and told her everything when we were preparing dinner."

Joe couldn't imagine that their first meeting could've gone any better. Everything had happened so fast, but he couldn't see himself being with another girl.

"My mother has her ways. When I was chatting with the rest of the family while you were in the kitchen, I was checking on you. I sensed everything was going well because of the nonstop talking."

"Your mom told me how hard it was to leave her home and everything she knew to come here, and she knows what it feels like to be treated poorly and has nothing but sympathy for my parents with all this talk about how evil Germans are these days. She said she would enjoy having me over again while you're gone and has already asked Tom to be my chauffeur."

"Marty, I'm so happy my mom likes you, but I suspected you'd be like two peas in a pod once you got to know each other." Joe needed to pause for a moment. He stroked Martha's face gently. He had to leave in the morning, and although their romance was off to a flying start, it had to be put on hold. He knew how he felt but wanted to be fair to the girl he had just fallen in love with, so he took on a more serious tone.

"Since that day in Asbury Park, I've been doing some thinking. I want to court you properly, but that's not possible, because I gotta get back to Texas."

Martha took out her handkerchief to wipe the tear running down her cheek.

"I promise I'll write and let you know what's going on, but . . . I don't want you to be miserable sitting around waiting for me. I want you to enjoy yourself, and if someone better comes along for you, then maybe it wasn't meant to be for us."

Marty choked up, more tears streaming down her face. "Joe O'Mara, you know I'm in love with you. How could you say something so cruel?"

"Marty, I'm in love with you too. I want the best for you. I don't want you just waiting around while I finish out my time. You'll have guys fighting each other to take you out. Don't be miserable. Enjoy their company. Use the time to make sure that I'm the right guy for you."

"It will break my heart to think of you with another girl. I know I'm being selfish, but I don't want you even near anybody else."

Touching her face again, Joe reassured her, "I didn't say it had to go both ways. I've met enough girls to know that you're worth waiting for."

Behind Marty's tears, a small smile emerged. "So let me get this straight. You're promising not to break my heart, but it's okay for me to break yours?"

Joe chuckled. "Well, I wouldn't put it that way, but it sure sums things up."

"Please hold me tight and kiss me forever, soldier boy."

A long, passionate session followed. Martha responded to Joe, but he made sure that things did not progress past the point of no return. He wanted her to be more than just his lover. If he didn't get himself killed, and if she didn't find someone else, he would ask her to be his wife when he returned for good.

Joe drove back to Harrison and said goodbye after one last embrace. On the way home, he thought about his promise to Martha, which brought on a feeling of euphoria that he did not completely understand.

CHAPTER 16

TEMPTATION

The rhythm of the train wheels on the track was hypnotic, lulling Joe into a dream state that was only interrupted by the conductor's piercing voice announcing the next station. The pattern repeated itself all the way to St. Louis, giving him time to reflect on all the events that had occurred since his last train ride westward. It had seemed he'd spent a lifetime away from home when he left the first time, but the harsh reality was that he was only halfway through his commitment to the army.

He opened his small leather case and took out a picture of Martha beaming at the camera with her little dog at her side. His thoughts drifted back to the magical time he'd spent with Lilly a little over a year ago. Joe had promised that the first chance he got, he'd go back and see her. It didn't sit right with him that this had never happened.

He felt the stark contrast between the chilly spring weather he'd left behind in New Jersey and the hot afternoon sun of El Paso as he finally disembarked the train. Walking the streets looking for a place to stay before reporting for duty the next day, his eyes were drawn to a boarding house sign that read, *Room, Board and Bath - $2*. Seeing this as a great opportunity to eat and clean up before trying to find a card game, he checked in.

Relaxing in a tub of hot water at the boarding house, washing off the journey's sweat, Joe gazed at a small painting beside the door of the bathroom. It was of a beautiful woman, wearing a traditional white Mexican dress with a red trim, hands on hips, waiting for her partner to begin a dance.

‡

Joe dressed in civilian attire. His intentions were innocent as he walked the short distance to Lilly's apartment. She needed to hear from him directly why he had not come back and why they could not see each other again. He proceeded to the front door and engaged with the doorman. "I was hoping to see Lilly Álvarez. I'm a friend, Joseph O'Mara. Could you check if she's available to see me?"

About five minutes passed before the man came back and told Joe he could go upstairs. Wearing the same white satin robe, Lilly opened the door and said, "Please come in, Joseph. It's nice to see you. You're looking well."

Immediately, Joe noticed that there was something different about her. She was speaking fast, her face looked drawn, and her makeup seemed carelessly applied. "Sit down on the couch, and I'll bring us something to drink," she told him. She came back with a tray with mezcal, oranges, and a small vial.

Joe took a glass and an orange. "I feel like a heel that it's taken me so long to come back to see you. That day we met was really special for me. I wanted to come back, but couldn't until now."

Taking the vial and tapping it carefully against the underside of a long nail, Lilly put her finger to her nose and took one quick sniff. "Would you like some cocaine? It's refined from coca leaves that the Indians in South America have used for centuries. It gives me so much energy."

"No, thanks." He shook his head. "Just days after we met, they sent me on the chase for Pancho Villa."

"No apologies, please. I knew the fort cleared out, and I read the papers."

"I wanted you to know I thought about you often. I started thinking differently about a lot of things after that night. Before I met you, I never thought I would settle down with a girl." Joe sensed Lilly was hearing his words but barely listening to him. She'd been so loving when they first met. Tonight, she was cold. Most of all, she was distant, far away from this moment.

He continued, "After the expedition ended, I went home for a month and met a swell girl that I plan to marry when I go back for good."

"I am happy for the both of you. I'm sure she's special. My circumstances have changed considerably as well." Lily paused, took a sip of her drink, and snorted more cocaine. Some white powder remained on the outside of her nostrils. "Please don't ask me why, Joseph, but you must never come back here again."

She stood up in front of him, untied the sash from her robe, and let it drop to the floor. "I want to make love before we say goodbye."

At the sight of her naked body, Joe stood. Lilly took his hand, and he took one step toward the bedroom, then said, "I can't."

"What do you mean? Don't you want me?"

"It's not that. I'd feel rotten about it. If Marty ever found out, it would break her heart."

"Don't be silly. She will never find out. She'll never know."

"Yeah, I guess . . . but I'll know. As much as I want to be with you, in my heart, I know it's not right."

"Joseph, you met me before this girl. If you hadn't left, we would have been lovers—we would've enjoyed so many nights together." Lilly moved closer, put her arms around his neck, and put her face directly in front of his. "I want you in my bed. Then, we say goodbye."

Joe put his arms around her waist and pulled her close. He kissed her forehead and looked into her eyes. "Thank you. I'll always remember you." Then he walked out the door without looking back.

‡

On the way back to his room, Joe felt he needed to calm down, so he went into the first drinking establishment he passed. Sitting down at the bar, he ordered a beer and a shot of whiskey. The beer was refreshing, and he quickly finished it and ordered another.

While waiting for his second drink, he questioned what his real motive had been in going to see Lilly. He was happy things had turned out the way they did, because he couldn't imagine coping with his guilt. He felt ashamed. While his better angels had eventually prevailed, he'd been so close to following Lilly into the bedroom. Perhaps it was her manner that had helped him make the right choice.

Lilly had claimed that smoking marijuana helped her escape from this "crazy world." Now she was snorting cocaine to give her energy. What had changed? Why did she refuse to talk about it?

Over the course of the next four drinks, Joe tried to deduce what was going on In Lilly's life. His father once told him that hopheads who needed money to support their habit were responsible for a high percentage of the robberies and assaults in Orange. It hurt him too much to think about what Lilly might do to afford drugs like cocaine.

Joe acknowledged he was drunk, but he still thought it was import- ant to sort through his feelings before he returned to his room. Lilly opened his eyes to what was possible with women, but at most, she would have been an occasional lover. Marty was his girl. If she found somebody better before he got back, it would break his heart. Head spinning, Joe figured it was time to go to bed, and he made his way back to the boarding house.

CHAPTER 17

THE WAR AT HOME

April 12, 1917

My Dearest Joe,

Your mother and I have been praying you will not be sent to Europe. You seemed confident that you would stay near the border, but now war has been declared and our worry has increased. Since they published the Zimmerman Letter in the newspapers in March, so many people have been doing terrible things to German Americans. Two men attacked my father coming back home from work. Luckily, he fought them off and only had some small bruises. My mother is afraid to leave the house. Your sweet brother Tom has been picking me up and bringing me back home every day for work. Your mother has given me that picture of you in Mexico with the donkey. I love it and look at it every morning and wish you were here making me laugh. I love and miss you.

Your girl forever,

Marty

April 28, 1917

My Dear, Sweet Marty:

First, I want you to know how much I miss you. Second, I wanted to share the good news: they have assigned me to the Quartermaster Corps and are transferring me to Columbus, New Mexico. They have given me responsibility to run the shop there for supply vehicles and armored cars. I will support the 24th Infantry, which will use Camp Furlong in Columbus as their camp to protect the border. I am happy to have these orders, because I know I will be much safer than I would be in the trenches of Europe. Some of my friends have told me they would rather fight in Europe than work with a bunch of niggers, because the 24th is an all-colored regiment. I told them they were crazy. I am sorry to hear about your parents. Please ask Tom and my dad for help if you need it.

I am happy that you and my mother don't have to worry so much. I look at your picture every morning to start my day. I love and miss you.

Your guy forever,

Joe

Despite running on a platform in the 1916 presidential election of keeping the US out of the "Great War" raging in Europe, President Wilson convinced congress to declare war against Germany on April 7, 1917, because of increased submarine activity in the Atlantic and the sinking of American merchant vessels. However, the US was poorly prepared to take part in the conflict. Congress approved a sum of $3 billion to build an army of one million men that would act as an independent force in the European theater. Because of the lesser size of the standing army and the relatively small quantity of national guard troops, camps were hurriedly set up across the country to build this force. The 24th Infantry Regiment, formed after the Civil War and made up exclusively of negroes known as Buffalo Soldiers—though led by white officers—had a distinguished track record in the Western US during the Indian campaigns, the Spanish–American War, and Philippine Insurrection. Following the declaration of war, the regiment transferred to Columbus to guard the border.

‡

It was May 1917. Joe had been working in the repair shop at Camp Furlong in New Mexico for a month. Excluding the officers, he was one of just a handful white soldiers at the base. Since the 24th regiment had transferred to Columbus, facilities such as bathrooms and mess halls had become segregated by race. Joe did not fully observe the guidelines.

"Joe, you're one of the few white soldiers who can stand being around us. Why's that?" First Sergeant Ulysses Thompson asked him one day. Thompson was a career soldier in his early forties and had served with distinction in both Cuba and the Philippines. He'd been awarded the purple heart twice and had a large scar on his face, incurred during the famous assault on San Juan Hill in the Spanish–American War.

Joe opened his mouth, but the sergeant interrupted him before he could get a word out. "When we're together, just you and me chewing the fat, rank don't mean nothing. I want you to call me Ulysses."

Joe nodded and offered him a cigarette while lighting his own. "Well, my mom and my girl are afraid that I'd die if I got sent to Europe. I've been on this duty before with Pershing, and it can be boring, but it's not too dangerous, especially if we stay on this side of the border. I've got no problem with colored people. I worked with two colored men back in New Jersey, and we became good friends. Tell me this—why're you all are so eager to get to Europe to join the fight?"

"Joe, when you're walking down the street in your uniform, most folks see the uniform first and give you some respect for being a soldier."

"Yeah, that's true."

"When I walk down the street and white folks see me, they see a nigger first and don't even see the uniform."

"No, that's not true."

"Ha! The hell it ain't. If they see the uniform, then they're mad that a colored man is in the army. Where you're from, up north, most white folks won't say anything to your face. They just think *nigger*. Down south, where I'm from, they'll call you nigger to your face, and if you're not careful, they'll do a lot worse. Us colored soldiers feel we deserve better. We think going to fight in France is an opportunity to do something great that'll make all of us look good, so we get treated better."

Joe thought back to Jim and Leroy at the shop. Really, he didn't know how they felt.

They'd just seemed like they accepted things and were trying to make the best of their situation. Ulysses's anger surprised him. He said, "It ain't worth getting gassed or ripped apart by some machine gun going over the top."

The sergeant shook his head. "Maybe we're less afraid of the Huns and the Turks over there than we are of y'all here."

‡

Because of his familiarity with the White Armored Car Number 2, Joe was given the duty of training soldiers from the Third Battalion on the operation of these vehicles. The plan was to use them, along with the regular cavalry, to patrol the border. He would work with Sergeant Thompson to identify men suitable for this task.

The weeks since the onset of the war had felt like they dragged on for the soldiers stationed in Columbus. The border area between them and the Mexican town of Palomas was exceptionally quiet, and the patrolling soldiers had very little to do. The threat of invasion by marauding bands of Mexicans had seemed like an absolute certainty two months ago. In June, it felt more like a remote possibility. The army brass at Columbus thought this would be a good time to introduce something new to the men and to test the colored soldiers' aptitude for the operation of the armored car.

"It ain't all bad, Ulysses," proclaimed Joe, after the sergeant had expressed his reservations about the vehicle. "On level terrain, you can out-run horses. Keep the M1895 firing at what you're attacking, and you'll be fine. All the armor cladding gives you protection from bullets coming your way. You got to keep the car moving, so it's more difficult to hit."

"This is a big change for us. Most of the men in this unit have never even been in a car, let alone driven one. You're going to teach me every-thing you know about the operation of this vehicle. I'm not the smartest colored man in the company, so it'll be a good test." Ulysses grinned at his own self-deprecating remark.

Over the course of the next week, Joe and Ulysses spent their days taking out the vehicle and testing it, much in the same way Joe had done with Lieutenant Patton. The lessons were discouraging for Ulysses at first, because he had to learn the coordination of shifting gears. Once he'd accomplished that, his next hurdle was to achieve higher speeds and avoid getting stuck.

After the fourth day of practice, as the sun beat down while the pair took a smoke break, Joe addressed Ulysses directly as his superior. "Sergeant, you know you can drive this thing as good as I can."

"Corporal, I wouldn't say that. I'd say I can drive this good enough for now. You're a fine teacher. Three more men need to learn how to drive. I've four gunners picked out, and then we need four ammo men to drive and shoot as backup. The brass might say something to you, but I think you should have mess with us. Before we get started, I want the men to know that you're not someone to be feared or hated. Breaking bread together is the best way I know to do that."

"Sure," Joe said, "if you think that'll help, I'll do it. I don't think brass will say anything to me about it. We're supposed to be working closely together on this."

Things started out slowly for the new drivers. Sergeant Thompson had picked soldiers he thought had high self-confidence. The first few days were a humbling experience for these men. Joe was very reassuring, telling them that everyone who could drive a car learned the same way. Like with the sergeant, it took about a day for them to learn how to shift and change speeds properly.

Sergeant Thompson selected less accomplished riflemen as gunners. He'd realized when training with Joe that this was less about sharpshooting and more about keeping the weapon continuously spraying bullets. It took a little over a week to build the soldiers' confidence that they could operate the vehicles enough for them to sufficiently to use them.

"Joe, what d'you think? Can my men use these vehicles to patrol the border?" asked Ulysses.

"I'd start out slow and have them get the feel for driving on a good road, like the one toward Palomas. You'll need to manage your fuel when you go on longer runs. I'd plan on going only a hundred miles in a day. If one vehicle breaks down, head back to base. You don't want more than one vehicle out of commission, because two additional men just won't fit in the White. I'll show you a couple of things that can happen with the car on the road and how to get you back on your way."

Ulysses started to laugh. "I'm spending too much time with you, Joe. I already knew pretty much what you'd say."

‡

Lieutenant Hennessey walked into the shop where Joe was working. "Corporal, I'd like to get your honest assessment of where the colored soldiers are with the operation of the armored cars."

"Lieutenant, I think that is a better question for Sergeant Thompson," Joe told him.

Lieutenant Michael Hennessy was a career soldier who also came from northern New Jersey. He had enlisted right after the Spanish–American

War and had worked his way up through the ranks, accepting an assignment to work with the Buffalo Soldiers for a promotion. He was notoriously tough and extremely arbitrary with the colored soldiers.

"Well, if I wanted to get a nigger answer, I would've asked a nigger soldier. I see that you've been having meals and fraternizing with the colored men. You look white, so I'm assuming your mother isn't a nigger. Is that right, Corporal?"

Joe hadn't expected his answer to provoke such a response from Hennessey. Clearly, the lieutenant would take anything other than addressing the questions as insubordination. That would not do him or the colored soldiers a stich of good. In a conciliatory tone, Joe responded, "Sir, that's correct." After a brief pause, he added, "I believe the men are ready to take a next step and begin shorter patrols with the White armored cars with no support from me."

"Thank you, Corporal. Don't get me wrong—Sergeant Thompson is a good soldier, but he's colored, and you know they all stick together. I didn't trust him to give me a truthful answer."

Lieutenant Hennessy reported back to his superiors and recommended the experiment with the armored cars continue. Sergeant Thompson received orders to work toward expanding the patrol operation with the cars to four days a week, covering up to one hundred miles east and west of Camp Furlong in Columbus. Joe was instructed to continue to stay close to the operation but in more of an advisory role.

Sixteen soldiers under Sergeant Thompson from the Third Battalion remained in New Mexico, while the rest were sent to Houston, Texas. Their mission was to guard the construction of Camp Logan, which was to be used for expeditionary forces being sent to fight in Europe.

‡

By the end of the day of August 24, news had spread to Columbus about what had transpired in Houston. The newspapers were calling it a mutiny of

150 colored soldiers and a cold-blooded murder of white civilians, resulting in the deaths of seventeen people, including local police and soldiers. Officials imposed martial law in the city of Houston, arrested the participants in the uprising for court martial, and sent the remaining members of the Third Battalion back to Columbus, deprived of their weapons.

Sergeant Thompson went into the shop where Joe was working. He was upset and on the verge of tears. "It don't make a damn bit of sense to me. Why would these soldiers go off and hunt folks and gun them down without a reason? Unless their lives were in danger, I can't believe they would go off like that. You know, the ones they held back in Texas to stand trial are as good as hung."

"Ulysses, it don't make sense to me either. I've gotten to know the men in this regiment. They're good soldiers. You're not hearing the whole story. The battalion will be back tomorrow. I think you'll get a better idea of what happened speaking to some men who were there."

‡

Private Lester Lewis had been part of the regiment for four years. He had just gotten back from Houston, where he was originally from, when Ulysses brought him into the shop to speak with Joe. "Lester, tell the story to Joe, just like you told me. I want to get a white man's thoughts on this."

Joe noticed Lester was reluctant to get started. He sensed his fear in speaking to him. Joe knew he needed to reassure him. "Lester, it's okay. Ulysses and I are friends. We're just looking to understand what happened."

"Well, I can tell you both, since I come from the town, white folks in Houston seem to hate us more than most places. I sensed there was goin' to be trouble as soon as I heard we was goin' to be stationed there. Hey, we're all used to being called 'nigger' and 'boy.' Our mamas tell us when we's kids, the best thing is to stay away from white folks, especially the women. From the moment that we got there, the men who were building camp were cruel for no reason. They'd pee in our water and spit in our faces. Even Hennessy got mad at how we was being treated and called a meetin' with the police in town to complain. I think that might've made things worse."

Growing up Joe knew colored people mainly worked for rich people, hotels, and restaurants. Right before he left, though, more were coming into Orange to take factory jobs. Outside of work, white people mostly avoided colored people. He'd never heard about anything like this. He probed for more information. "Did they threaten you?"

"Worse. They got in your face and kept jabbering and telling you how a nigger is supposed to act in this town because Jim Crow is the law. They pushed you to raise your hand against them, so they'd be justified in shooting you. Some of us got steamed off and gave them lip right back and got knocked around pretty hard. Most of us got scared and calmed down, but some got angrier and angrier."

"Joe, I told you they don't respect the uniform if a colored soldier wears it," said Sergeant Thompson. Joe nodded in agreement. Ulysses was right.

Lester continued, his pace slowing down. "That afternoon, we heard the police had beaten and killed Charley Baltimore and a mob of white folks was coming to camp. About a hundred or so men went into the magazine to get arms to go into town. Baltimore showed up at camp beaten pretty bad, but wound up joining the others as they left. Bullets started flying as soon as they got into town. That's all I know."

Looking directly at Lester, Ulysses lamented, "I wish I'd been there. Maybe I could've talked some sense into them. What'd they think was going to happen? The goddamn army ain't going to admit they made a mistake sending in colored troops to Houston. The military court ain't gonna say, 'We can see how poorly y'all were treated and we can understand what you did.' Nah! They'll make an example of these soldiers to show all of us what happens when niggers get out of line just like they'll do in East St. Louis. Everyone knows that the white folks did the killing and burning there."

Listening to Ulysses, Joe got the same empty feeling in the pit of his stomach as he'd had the day the Black Hand murdered Jim. Antonio Romano had killed a human being to get Harry's attention, as opposed to throwing a brick through the window of the garage. Now the army was probably going to hang colored soldiers without building an understanding of why they'd acted how they did.

"Ulysses, those soldiers reached their breaking point and didn't care what happened to them. If they killed innocent people, they're wrong, but I won't judge them. Once you're pushed beyond your breaking point, there's no telling what any of us would do. The army shouldn't have put colored soldiers in that position." As Joe finished, he felt some relief, because he could make some sense of this tragedy. As soldiers, they were taught military discipline and how to fight the enemy with reckless abandon at the same time. He had witnessed many soldiers in training drills losing control and taking things too far. When you were serving, there was pressure coming from all sides. By design, the higher-ups kept everyone on the edge.

Joe had joined the army to escape and hide. Compared to his life in Orange, it had been one big adventure. Then Marty came into his life, and he wanted to trade the second part of the adventure to be with her. Still, until this incident, he used to wear his uniform with pride. "Ulysses, if I could, I'd walk right out of this camp and never give the army a second thought. I've had enough."

"Joe, you and me both. I thought they'd bury me in my uniform. I was proud to serve. Now, when it's my time to re-up next year, I'm going to tell them to keep their damn army. Maybe I'll make my way up to your neck of the woods one day."

‡

On December 10, 1917, thirteen colored soldiers who'd been convicted as the ringleaders of the riot were hung and buried in unmarked graves. Empty soda bottles filled with strips of paper with their names were buried along with the bodies. They sentenced sixteen more soldiers to death in two more court martial trials. President Wilson intervened and commuted the sentence of ten of the men to life in prison. In a public statement, he confirmed the fairness of all the trials and said he hoped the proclamation of clemency would inspire colored soldiers to "further zeal and service to the country."

PART THREE

CHAPTER 18

FATHERS

The last year had been a difficult one to get through. Joe had become sick and tired of the intense heat of New Mexico, the repair work he did on army vehicles, hearing the song "Over There" proclaiming how the Yanks were going to be the ones who turned the tide of the war for victory, and all the rumors of his unit being sent overseas for the last push to get Germany to surrender.

The atmosphere at Camp Furlong had been depressing, as it appeared every soldier of the 24th regiment carried the burden of what happened in Houston squarely on their shoulders. The white army brass felt it was their duty to instill a new sense of discipline into the colored troops, which only resulted in increased resentment that frequently came out in outbursts of fist fighting between the soldiers.

Weary of being in the army, once the war ended in November 1918, Joe could not wait to return to New Jersey. On the long train ride home, he'd thought almost exclusively of Martha and very little about what he would do for a living. He had a nice sum of cash—just over two hundred dollars—obtained from the army and lesser card players. In his mind, he had plenty of money to buy an engagement ring and nice Christmas presents. He wasn't thinking past that.

Joe came home to a warm welcome from his family. Also, there was a celebration for him at the Wolff home in Harrison that Martha organized, inviting the O'Mara family. The couple announced their engagement and plans to be married sometime in 1919.

After sleeping until ten one morning in mid-December, Joe made his way into the kitchen and started to reheat the coffee that was left on the stove. He stared at the pot, waiting, and didn't notice his father joining him on the other side of the table. After filling his cup, he returned to his seat and said, "Dad, when did you sit down?" Joe noticed the serious expression on his father's face.

"Son, I know you have been through a lot, but whatever daze you're in, ya gotta start snapping out of it. You asked Martha to marry you and don't have a clue how you're going to support her. You've got two good options for work, and you've already turned them down."

Just then, Joe's mother walked into the kitchen and joined them at the table.

Joe replied curtly, "I need some time to figure things out. One thing that's for certain is I don't want to spend twelve hours a day pulling cars apart and putting them back together."

Margaret stated emphatically, "James, he hasn't been home a month. Give him some time to refresh his spirit. You're always talking about how smart Joe is. Let him think through his options through Christmas."

Joe was happy his mom had come to his defense. Their eyes met. She knew he needed more time.

His father responded, "Okay, a decision on work by the start of the new year. I'll even lay another option on the table. I've got some connections that can get him a job at the county jail in Newark as a guard. I'd rather you stay away from policing, but . . . it's an opportunity to earn your way up, maybe make detective someday."

"Dad, that sounds pretty interesting. I'd like to find out more from you about that."

His mother reached across the table and grabbed her son's arm, saying, "We both wish you'd stay away from policing. For the life of me, I don't know why you wouldn't work for Tom. You boys have always been thick as thieves. When Hannifin retires in a few years, he'll be running the place."

‡

It was a cold, windy January evening in Harrison. Drafts invaded the living room through the large front windows of the Wolff home. Candles taken from the recently scuttled Christmas tree flickered, swayed, and cast small shadows on the white-painted plaster walls. Pots of fragrant lilies surrounded recently deceased fifty-five-year-old Wilhelm Wolff, who lay dressed in his dark Prussian blue German Army uniform. Wilhelm had worked at the Peter Hauck Brewery as the master brewer's assistant and had dropped dead of a massive heart attack on the shop floor.

The family dog took refuge under the coffin, while a dozen onlookers made conversation in hushed tones. "He looks so peaceful lying there, despite wearing that uniform," Minnie whispered to Tom O'Mara, who had prepared the body for the viewing.

Standing next to her husband-to-be, Martha added, "He wanted things this way. He was proud to be a soldier and to own this house in Harrison. He worked so hard every day. It doesn't seem right that God took him before he could retire."

Joe could see Marty was upset and tried to comfort her by pulling her closer to him. She had been so happy upon his return and the announcement of their marriage. The pendulum of her emotions swung the other way upon her father's death. It just didn't seem fair.

Responding to his gesture, she said, "Joe, I know he barely knew you, but he had a lot of respect for you because you were in the army."

"He thought being in the army showed responsibility and jumped to the conclusion that meant you could take care of a wife and children, just like he did," interjected Minnie, scowling at Joe.

Joe had been under the impression that Minnie liked him and was happy for her sister. He didn't know where the comment was coming from, so he let it pass.

Later that evening, when the house cleared out, Martha and Joe had a chance to talk. "My mother has asked us to move in here with her once we get married."

"Marty, I'm not sure how I feel about that."

"She doesn't feel safe without a man in the house. You know my kid brother Fred doesn't qualify. There's plenty of room here, and this'd allow us to get married right away. My mother will adjust in time, and then we'll be in an excellent position to get our own place. I think we could make it work. We used to have a boarder a while ago who was on the third floor, where we would be staying. We hardly knew he was there."

Joe couldn't help himself. He sarcastically asked, "Guessing he wasn't living up there with his new bride, was he?"

"Don't think I haven't thought about that too. I've been putting extra money away so we can have a proper honeymoon."

"Okay, tell her we'll try it for six months. I don't worry about your mom. I'm not sure if Minnie likes me, and I can't stand Fred."

"Well, I guess it's time for you to find out about Minnie. She does like you, but she's angry at *all men* these days. That's the reason for her shitty comment to you tonight. Minnie got herself pregnant by the lawyer she worked for, and when she told him, he fired her. Fred's not going to be a problem, because my mother won't allow it. She wants her youngest daughter to have a happy husband."

"So we'll have a baby crying downstairs who'll distract attention away from our loud, passionate lovemaking!"

Martha smiled for the first time since she'd found out about her father. "Exactly, that's the plan. Baby's due at the end of May."

‡

The ornately decorated dining room at the Knickerbocker was almost empty, which was unusual for a Sunday night. Since opening in 1906, it had been one of the top dining and nightlife destinations for wealthy New Yorkers. Even before the outbreak of the Spanish Flu, patronage had taken a downturn. Now, as things normalized, with fewer people getting sick, it was clear business was not what it had used to be.

Martha O'Mara lit a cigarette and slowly blew the smoke away from the dinner table. She glanced at her husband and remarked with a giggle as she looked around the dining room, "So, this is how rich people live?"

Joe knew his wife was tipsy and was being silly. He just smiled back.

"If I'd known what you were like in bed, I'd have followed you to New Mexico," said Martha, staring seductively at him. He choked on his drink, and the pair laughed hysterically for a solid minute.

Thinking about the marathon session of lovemaking that had ensued as soon as they checked into their room, Joe lovingly looked at his wife and said, "You better stop that talk or we won't make it through dinner. We have plenty of time for that. We're staying another night. Right now, I'm hungry."

"I'm going to order the lobster. Never had it before. Hope I can figure out how to eat it."

"Madame, would you care for some more champagne?" asked the waiter as he came over to take their order.

"Yes, please. I'd like to order the lobster for dinner."

"And I'll have the New York Strip steak," said Joe.

"How would you like that cooked, sir?"

Joe didn't understand the question.

"Most of our patrons order this steak done medium, with sauteed onions and mushrooms."

Realizing the waiter was trying to help, he said, "Thanks, I'll go with your recommendation."

After the man had left, Joe turned to his wife. "Enjoy the champagne, dear. Pretty soon, you won't be able to get a drink."

"Remember, I'm just a silly woman. You know we can't be trusted to vote. I hope that ridiculous amendment doesn't pass. You know we are just put here on this earth for our husbands' pleasure." Martha sighed theatrically and took another big sip from her glass.

"Oh, such a sore point for my mother that they ratified prohibition before women got the right to vote. She's one of the few suffragettes who's not for making booze illegal. I think my dad has convinced her it'll make crime worse. He's talked about retiring before it takes effect in January of 1920."

Their conversation continued until the waiter brought the food out about twenty minutes later. "Madame, I took the liberty of removing the lobster from its shell for you. It'll be much easier for you to eat. Sir, I hope you'll enjoy your steak cooked medium, smothered with onions and mushrooms."

Once the waiter had left, Martha took her small fork and dipped a piece of the lobster into the melted butter, daintily placing the tidbit into her mouth. "This is the most wonderful thing I've ever tasted. I know lobster is expensive, but let's try to have it every year for our anniversary."

Joe nodded. "It'd be nice to celebrate like this every year."

"After dinner, before we go upstairs, let's go to the ballroom for a short time. I'd love to listen to the band and dance with my husband."

"Marty, you know I'm not much of a dancer. I don't want to embarrass you."

"Joseph Sebastian O'Mara, that's not possible. I feel like the luckiest girl in the world to be your wife." She started to gently pet Joe's leg under the table, gradually getting closer to his groin area. In as sultry a voice as possible, she asked, "Do you feel the same way?"

"Of course. I'd do anything for you."

"Then it's settled. We finish dinner and then do a bit of dancing before we go back upstairs."

‡

There was a twelve-piece band all dressed in white dinner jackets and red bow ties in the ballroom. There were only a few couples on the dance floor. About forty other guests were at tables, drinking and smoking and paying very little attention to the music.

"I don't know the name of this song, but it's a waltz. Hold me, look into my eyes, and follow me. Do everything slowly," Marty said.

Joe was doing his best to be patient. All he could think about was her body pressed up against his and his desire for her, which was growing with each passing minute. When was she going to end this torture?

The music stopped, and the bandleader went to the microphone. He was visibly upset and looked as if he were about to cry. "Ladies and gentlemen, that'll be the last song of the evening. I can't go on and finish." He took out his handkerchief and wiped his brow. "Today, I was told I can't work here any longer because they say I'm a Bolshevik. Just because my parents are Jews who came from Russia doesn't mean I'm a Red. I've enjoyed making music and people happy here for five years, but it all ends tonight because someone said they saw me at a Communist Party meeting and reported it to management."

A voice called out from a table in the back. "Good riddance. We don't need your kind here."

Before storming off the stage, the band leader shouted, "Goodbye and good luck, fucking chaser!" Several hotel employees promptly escorted him out of the ballroom.

Joe and Martha were speechless. They walked back to their table, where Joe filled Martha's glass with the last of the champagne. He lit them each a cigarette and then broke the silence. "Since I started at the jail, seems to be a constant stream of people they call Bolsheviks who spend a night or two there and then get released."

"From what I've read in the papers, people are afraid what happened in Russia could take place here. My mom reads the Jersey *Freie Zeitung* on Sunday and thinks it's a genuine threat. The border with Russia was very close to where they lived outside of Konigsberg, and she's got plenty of stories about the Russians."

Joe really didn't want to talk about this. He was eager to get back to the honeymoon and suggested, "Let's not let this spoil the rest of our night at this fancy hotel."

"What ever do you mean, Mr. O'Mara?" Martha said in a tone of forced seriousness. "Let me finish this drink and I'll be ready to go upstairs."

‡

As soon as he'd heard the news from the warden at the county jail, Joe raced home to Harrison, got his wife, and took a taxi to the family apartment in Orange. As he walked in the door, he saw his mother in shock, his four siblings trying to console her. Tom gestured for his brother and sister-in-law to join them in another room where they could discuss matters away from the others.

Speaking in a shaky voice slightly above a whisper, Tom began, "We don't have a lot of the details. Mom asked me to handle speaking to the police because she just couldn't. They found Dad shot dead at the post office in Orange early this morning. One bullet to the back of the head.

The police have already started an investigation and will keep us apprised of what they learn."

Joe didn't know what to do. He needed to relieve his nervous energy somehow. He decided he would go down to the police station and get more details about what had happened. "Marty, I'm going to go out of my mind if I stay here. I gotta get down to the police station and find out more. I'll be back as soon as I can."

"I understand. I'll be here with your mom."

Joe went into the kitchen and got down on one knee, took his mother's hand in his, and looked up into her eyes. No words needed to be spoken. He got up and left for the police station.

‡

Huffing and puffing after the half-mile run to the police station on Park Street, Joe walked through the heavy wood-and-glass doors. He was still wearing his green county jail guard uniform. Luckily, the reception area was empty, so he proceeded to the desk and introduced himself. The policeman on duty offered Joe his condolences and told him to wait a few minutes until the sergeant, who was handling the investigation, could come out and brief him with the latest information.

Joe's head was pounding. He refused to acknowledge his loss until he got more information. He nervously took out his pack of cigarettes and lit one.

A tall, rather portly officer with sergeant stripes on his uniform came out and looked around the waiting area. He had a red, bulbous nose that dominated his face. Joe saw him and got up from his chair. He estimated that the man was about the same age as his father, judging by the gray threaded through his red hair.

"Well, I don't even have to ask who you are. My God, son. I can't tell you how sorry I am for what happened. You're James's youngest boy, Joe, aren't you?"

"Yes, sir."

"I'm Tom Sullivan, the sergeant who is handling the investigation. Your dad and I go way back. He was a credit to the badge—a better man you won't find on this force."

"Thanks, Officer Sullivan."

"Please, son, call me Tom. We were so close, you almost feel like family."

"Okay, Tom. I'd like to get the latest information."

"Surely I can do that, so you can fill in your family. Come back to my desk and I'll tell you everything I know."

Joe's head stopped pounding. He felt relieved. Sullivan gently placed his arm around Joe's shoulder as he led him to his desk, which was the tidiest one in the area.

"Joe, this is my top priority. I won't be working on anything else until we find your dad's murderer. It appears that James was killed in his attempt to prevent the post office from being blown up by anarchists. We've found explosives at the post office near where we found his body. We suspect he saw something funny in his rounds, checked on it, caught the fella red-handed. Another bird comes from behind and shoots him in the head. At this time, we're following up on some leads to confirm. Please, not a word of this outside the family. It will hurt our chances of getting the killer."

Joe appreciated how much the officer had shared. Still, there was one thing that just didn't make sense to him. He needed to ask. "Tom, why didn't they blow up the post office after they killed my dad?"

Sullivan nodded his head up and down many times before answering. "Yup, yup, yup, we were asking ourselves the same question. Ya come to blow up the post office, why not finish the job? Son, one thing you gotta remember—these Reds are crazy people. They do stuff for no reason. They're amateurs. After they got involved with James, we're thinking they were so spooked, they just thought it was best to turn and run."

Joe thought that was a reasonable explanation. He thanked the officer and left the station. As he began the walk to the apartment, the realization that he would never see his father again hit him. He continued to walk, trying to hold back the tears to put on as brave a face as possible for his mother.

‡

"My father was truly the Good Samaritan. Despite the uniform he wore, he practiced what Jesus taught us every day of his life. He was a kind man who would lend a helping hand to those who needed it the most. He lived his life in the service of others. I'm proud to be his son." Father John O'Mara's voice was breaking up as he finished the eulogy for his father. There were three hundred people at the funeral at St. John's Church in Orange, many of the whom James had protected on his patrol. They were in tears as they listened to his son speak.

A small procession of family members and policemen began the short walk down Chapel Street, following the horse-drawn coffin to the entrance of the parish cemetery. Dressed in black with a veil over her head, Margaret walked arm in arm with Joe and Tom. She was still in shock and needed the physical support to keep her upright. Five days ago, she'd kissed her husband goodbye, as she had for over thirty years of marriage. That was the last time she saw him alive.

The police chief pledged to her that the force would stop at nothing to bring the murderer to justice. He would not go into details, but was optimistic that the investigation would bring justice soon.

Standing at the gravesite after the rifle salute to the fallen policeman, Margaret could finally speak. "I can draw comfort knowing your father's in heaven now," she told her sons. "He was a truly good man with a generous heart. He was my best friend."

While the family walked back to their apartment in Orange, Tom made a point of reassuring his mother. "Mom, you know I'll take care of you. You don't have to worry."

Joe had been silent most of the day because he could not find the right words to say to anyone. He believed he was being deprived of the happiness he deserved with Marty after enduring his time in the army. Losing Marty's father was hard enough. What cruel God could have let this happen to his dad, so close to retirement? The sadness in his heart was being transformed to anger.

"Mom, I'm going to stay close to the investigation. I'm not gonna be able to rest until Dad's killer is brought to justice."

"Joey, let the police do their job. Justice won't bring him back to me. Your father would want you to be thinking about that wonderful girl you married and starting a family. Try to let this go."

"Okay, Mom." Joe would not argue with her today. He had no intention of letting this go.

CHAPTER 19

THE BOLSHEVIKS

Two weeks had passed since his father's murder. Upon learning that the Newark Police had apprehended the probable killer and were bringing him to the county jail, Joe rushed to the warden's office and requested permission to be assigned to the cell block where the suspect would be held. The warden explained the Orange Police had witnesses who could confirm Abe Livosky was a member of the communist ring that helped plan the destruction of the post office, and ultimately the triggerman who had killed his father. The warden obliged Joe's request and said he would understand if Joe wanted to give the new resident a "warm welcome," but advised against taking things too far.

Joe was surprised by the prisoner's appearance when they were introduced. Livosky looked like a kid. He was a good two inches shorter than Joe, with a slight build. After escorting him through the long corridor of cells in silence, Joe's anger got a hold of him, and he pushed the handcuffed prisoner's head into the bars of his cell before opening it. Livosky remained silent as blood streamed from his nose. Once Joe was on the other side of the bars and the cell locked, the prisoner said, "Do that again, and I'll make sure you don't make it home. I got connections."

"You're lucky that's all I did, you fucking Red bastard."

A wry smile appeared on the prisoner's face. He said, "Everyone is becoming meshugena with all of this talk about Reds these days. You think all us Jews are Reds? Some of us are just *businessmen* trying to earn a dollar, just like everybody else."

"They brought you in for the murder of a policeman in Orange two weeks ago. That policeman was my father."

"Sorry to hear that. The last thing me or my associates would do is murder a policeman. It's just terrible for business." Livosky paused for a moment to stop the blood with his shirtsleeve. "You can find plenty of Reds in apartments above the stores on Prince Street. The ones I know are very studious and afraid of their own shadows."

"So, you're admitting you're a hood but not a Red?"

Abe responded, "I prefer businessman, but you got it straight."

Joe studied Livosky. Despite his youthful appearance, he gave the impression of being a much older and more experienced man. Though he was clearly a mobster in the making, Joe perceived a level of intelligence that he'd rarely observed in the prisoners he'd come in contact with so far. "If what you say is true, then why'd they bring you in?"

"I guess I'm going to be finding that out real soon."

Three Orange police officers were walking down the hall toward the cell. When they reached Joe, one directed, "Guard, handcuff the prisoner. We're going to take him to the back room for questioning."

Joe did not recognize any of the men. After putting the cuffs on, he watched them take him away.

‡

Before he left for the day, Joe returned to Livosky's cell. The prisoner was slumped over in a chair, sporting two black eyes and bleeding now from his mouth and nose.

"They tried to beat a confession out of me. They said if I confessed, I wouldn't get the chair. I told them I didn't know anything, and they smacked me around. You can see they did a pretty good job."

"What do they have on you?"

"They said they've got plenty of witnesses to pin this on me. The fact is, I was in Orange the day of the murder on an errand for my boss. I had to help a *very good* friend of his with a *big* problem that she had. After I took care of it, I came back to Newark."

Joe looked directly into the prisoner's eyes. Over the years, he had learned that his instincts about people were usually right. There was just something here that wasn't adding up. "When you say errand, what are you talking about?"

"My boss Moishe has an eye for the ladies—got a couple on the side. He knocks up one of them and asks me to help her take care of it because he wants to keep everything hush-hush. Best guy around for that sort of thing is in Orange."

"So Moishe was the only one who knew you were in Orange."

Livosky looked incredulously at Joe, then responded, "I can't believe Moishe would give me up. He's been like a father to me. He'd want no part of taking out a cop, like I said before. Moishe preaches we do business with class—with finesse, as he calls it. He said us Jews need to be smarter than the Irish, who think like cavemen, and the Sicilians, who have a lust for blood. Whenever someone talks about somebody whacking somebody else, he asks, how do we solve the problem with finesse?"

Joe was mentally trying to piece facts together. What Tom Sullivan had told him about the murder hinged on the fact that an anarchist did it.

At this point, the one thing he was pretty sure of was that Livosky was not a Red. He needed to talk with Sullivan and find out more.

"Livosky, I'm not promising anything. You might be guilty as hell, but I don't think so. I gotta do some snooping around to feed my curiosity. I'll give it to you straight either way."

"So you believe me! You're not a schmuck."

"Let's say I'm on the fence for now."

Before leaving the jail, without going into any details, Joe asked for the warden's permission to get the following morning off. His wish was granted.

‡

Taking public transportation, Joe trekked from Harrison to Orange and got to the police station by nine thirty. As he walked through the heavy doors, he immediately recognized Pat Maloney, his father's closest friend on the force, having a heated discussion with Tom Sullivan in the receiving area. When they noticed Joe, they stopped, and Maloney went to greet him.

"Joe, I'm so sorry for your family's loss. I'm ashamed I haven't made it over to see your mom yet. How's she taking it?"

"I won't lie. She's taking it real hard. You should go and see her."

"I will real soon. What brings you into the station today?"

"I want to talk with Tom Sullivan. We've got the suspect in custody at the county jail where I'm working and want to ask him a few questions."

Joe noticed that the expression on Pat's face immediately changed from a look of sympathy to one of discomfort. Then, Tom Sullivan called out for Joe and started walking toward him. Maloney patted Joe on the shoulder and said, "Take care, son," then left quickly.

Sporting an ear-to-ear smile, Sullivan engaged Joe. "Well, I'm no mind reader, but I can guess why you're here. I'm hoping you landed at least one good one on the face of that dirty kike."

It would be important how Joe asked his questions. He believed Sullivan was trying to make quick work of the investigation and get credit for bringing a cop killer to justice. However, it was not clear at all why Livosky had been chosen as the fall guy. "Yeah, I was able to get a good one in," he told the policeman. "Just here to thank you and get a couple more details. My mom is still having a hard time with this, and I'm hoping this good news will help."

"No need to thank me, son. Just doing my job. Sure, ask away. There's so much evidence, it's what they call an open-and-shut case."

Nodding affirmatively, Joe asked, "How did you know Livosky was a Red?"

Sullivan raised his voice considerably. "When news traveled to the big house about them trying to blow up the post office, a couple of cons who don't believe in this anarchist shit came forward and said they know the members of the ring and who planned the bombing. They fingered Livosky."

Joe worked to keep his expression in check and meet Sullivan's hard stare during his explanation, focusing on the tip of the man's enormous nose rather than looking directly into his eyes. He asked, "And you have a witness who saw him pull the trigger?"

"Sure do—private citizen came forward. A passerby that watched what was happening and just had the courage to speak up. Since Livosky has priors, we got a picture from Newark and used it to confirm it was him. Half a dozen other people can put him in the vicinity at the time of the murder. Like I said, open and shut."

"Thanks Tom. My mom asked me to handle speaking with the police. When the time came, she wanted to fully convince herself that you had the right guy. I'll tell her the good news."

Joe thought back to the look on Pat Maloney's face when he brought up Tom Sullivan. He was almost certain now that Livosky was being railroaded to get a conviction.

‡

Before making his way to work, Joe stopped off to see his mother. He wanted to inform her of what was going on before it broke in the newspapers that police had apprehended someone for the murder. When he let himself into the family apartment, the teakettle had just reached a boil and started whistling. Seeing his mother gingerly rising from her seat at the kitchen table, he went over and embraced her. Rather than rush through an explanation to get back to work, he decided he would take some time to visit, have a cup of tea, and then give her the details.

His mother did not appear to be doing much better. The look of sadness she'd worn since learning of her husband's murder had not changed. Joe noticed she was speaking much softer than usual. "Thanks for having a cup of tea with me," she said. "I can tell you got something on your mind that you want to tell me."

While they both took a seat at the table, Joe grabbed her hand and squeezed it slightly. "Is it that obvious?"

Pulling a handkerchief out of her sleeve and wiping her eyes, his mother said, "Although I know I don't look it, I'm doing better. I can handle whatever you need to tell me."

This reassured Joe, and he told the full story without glossing over any parts. He began by giving his impressions of Abe Livosky and why he felt he was innocent. The last thing he mentioned was Tom Sullivan and his potential motivations.

"So, Tom Sullivan is leading the investigation?"

"Yes. do you know him?"

"Now, your father would rarely talk about his work. He didn't want me to worry. But he did tell me about Tom more than once. He said he'd 'rather trust old Satan himself than Tom Sullivan.' He also mentioned that they got in quite the row not so long ago. Some of the other officers had to pull your father off Tom."

"The first time I spoke to Sullivan, right after Dad died, he gave me the impression he was a good friend. Said he was so close that I was like family to him."

"Hardly."

Joe had not been expecting this. While lacking a clear understanding of many facets of the murder, he now was sure that Livosky didn't do it. The so called open-and-shut case was being constructed, not investigated.

"Mom, you know Dad would not want an innocent man to be found guilty of his murder."

"James would turn over in his grave if that happened. See what you can do to make things right. Promise me, though, you'll be careful."

"I will. Please do me a favor when you see Pat Maloney and get his take on this. I need to stay clear of the Orange police station for now."

‡

After leaving his mother, Joe hopped on the trolley, which took him east on Central Avenue into Newark. After the short ride, he hurried to the Essex County Jail on New Street. Upon his arrival, he apologized to the warden for coming back later than he'd expected. Because he'd been able to confirm his suspicions with his mother, he began to map out an elaborate plan in his head to get Livosky off the hook. It depended completely on compelling Livosky's boss, Moishe, to act on the prisoner's behalf.

It was early afternoon. The sun cast light into the dreary six-by-eight-foot cell, spotlighting the prisoner, who lay on his bed. When he saw Joe, Livosky got up and put his face close to the bars, asking in a soft voice, "What'd you find out?"

Joe said, "I don't think you did it, and maybe I can help you."

"Well, thanks . . . but I got a question. Why would ya wanna do anything to help some Jew who can't do anything for you?"

Until this point in time, Joe hadn't taken the time to fully understand his motives. Now, he realized he was getting involved in this for his
father. He responded, "My dad was a great guy and the best cop in Orange.
I'm doing it for him. He'd want me to spring you. Besides, I know you're a
hood, but you don't seem like such a bad guy."

"Well, I'm not so sure—if the shoe were on the other foot—that I'd be
jumping to help you." Offering his hand to shake through the bars, he said,
"My friends call me Ziggy."

"Ziggy, my guess is they're gonna formally charge you soon and try
to get a quick trial. They've got witnesses who'll testify you're a Red, were
in Orange at the time of the murder, and pulled the trigger. The way I see
it, you got one chance at saving yourself."

"I'm all ears."

It took Joe a while to convince Ziggy that Moishe had been involved
in his arrest. As time was of the essence, it was critical that they acted
before there was a full understanding of why. They would use his many
affairs with women to compel him to act. Since the witnesses were put up
to testify against Ziggy, Moishe should be able to get at least some of them
to retract their testimony, blowing up the prosecution's argument.

Joe asked, "Does Moishe's wife know about his running around?"

Ziggy laughed. "Miriam Tabatchnik doesn't even know her husband
has a side business. She believes he earns all of his money at the butcher
shop, where he worked with his father until the old man died. He leads a
double life. To his wife, he's a model husband, father, and Jew. The Moishe
I know has a weakness for the twists. He tells me, 'Ziggy, I've the biggest
circumcised svantz in Newark. It'd be a sin not to share it with more than
one woman.'"

"So, he'd try to prevent this from getting out to his wife?"

"Absolutely. Moishe wants to shield his wife and mother. He's careful not to overspend for fear of raising their suspicion, so he must have a

wad of money hidden somewhere. Of course, he spends freely to keep the dames on the side."

"What would he do if he thought someone was going to give his family the straight story about the abortion?"

"I see where you're going with this. But he's quite the con man and could believe he could talk his way out of it."

"So, if there's hard proof, we could convince him to do something he really didn't want to do."

"Yeah, it would take hard proof. Great idea, Joe. How're we going to get it?"

"Ziggy, leave that to me."

CHAPTER 20

BLACKMAIL

Martha was waiting in the living room, nervously tapping her foot, watching through the window for Joe to come home. She had just read in the *Newark Evening News* about twenty-year-old Abe Livosky, a known communist who was soon to be arraigned for the murder of her late father-in-law. After finishing that article, she put the paper on the floor, unable to read further. It was just after 7 p.m. when she noticed the figure of her husband opening the front gate and bounding up the wooden steps to the house.

Rising from her chair, Marty greeted him at the door. She could tell immediately that something was occupying Joe's thoughts, as he barely had time to kiss her before he began speaking. He turned his head to the living room toward the newspaper on the floor.

Shaking his head, Joe said, "He didn't do it."

"When I saw the story, I thought you'd be coming home relieved. Instead, you look like a crazy man. How do you know he didn't do it?"

"We have so much to talk about. I won't be able to sit through dinner here. Let's go to a tavern nearby, get a table, and talk this through over a couple of beers and sandwiches."

Martha's curiosity could not have been piqued any higher. She readily agreed. Going downstairs to the basement kitchen, she put their dinner into the icebox and explained to her mother that they were going out for a while.

They did not have to walk far to find a tavern that was relatively empty. They found a private table, ordered food, and sat down. Martha, who only smoked when she was away from home, couldn't resist tonight and took one from the pack that Joe lain on the table. Proceeding through a hurried sequence of lighting the cigarette, inhaling, exhaling, and sipping her beer, she said, "Okay, Mr. O'Mara. Spill."

Joe started by taking his wife through a detailed chronological account of the events from the time he left her at his mother's apartment to his last discussion with Ziggy. Usually, Martha only interrupted Joe when he told stories with her laughter. Tonight was different. She grilled him intensively regarding all his assumptions. By the time he reached the discussion he'd had with his mother about Tom Sullivan, Martha rapped her knuckles gently against the table and said, "He didn't do it. You mentioned you had a plan. Tell me about it." She noticed the look of apprehension on his face.

"This is where you come in," Joe said. "I'll need to get my brother and some of his friends to help, too."

After three hours of intense conversation, numerous cigarettes, and a dinner of liverwurst sandwiches and cold draft beer, the couple left arm in arm to head back to their house. Martha's sixteen-year-old brother Fred was on the front porch, sneaking a smoke. He quickly dropped it when he saw his sister and her husband coming up the street.

"Don't worry Fred. I won't tell Mom."

"Okay, thanks. Where'd you guys go?"

Martha couldn't help herself. Giggling, she responded, "I'm getting a chance to be Theda Bara."

"What are you talking about?"

"Oh, nothing, Fred, just being silly."

‡

It took a week for Joe to organize and rehearse the plan. At the jail, he talked through the details with Ziggy to get his thoughts on how Moishe would respond. Then the day finally came to put the operation in motion.

Martha O'Mara was hardly recognizable in her new-fashioned dark gray dress. It accentuated every curve of her slender body while just covering the knees. Her good friend Ella, now Tom's fiancé, had worked for two hours getting her hair and makeup right. She wore an emerald brooch to highlight the color of her green eyes.

Joe was across the street from the Tabatchnick Butcher Shop. When Martha got the signal from him, she went inside and peered into the glass case where various cuts of meat and sausage were displayed. When she was sure the man working behind the counter had noticed her, she went up to him and told him, "I'm looking for a very special cut of meat."

Moishe Tabatchnick answered, "Can you be more specific? I'll do my best to help you."

While staring at the man's crotch to ensure he received the message in full, Martha put as much seduction into her voice as possible. "The recommendation comes from a mutual acquaintance of ours. She said it was a special kosher cut coming from the loins. She told me she'd never had anything like it." Moishe's jaw dropped as he stared back at her.

"Hmmm. I see. Who's the mutual acquaintance?"

Martha had been coached not to respond out of fear that Moishe might actually check with the woman. Instead, she mentioned the alias he used when having these illicit affairs. "She told me your name is Morris."

"Oh, I see. What makes you think I'd be interested?"

Having been warned he might play this hard-to-get game, Martha was prepared. Staring him right in the eyes, she said, "My husband's a rich man, Morris, and there're certain advantages to that. I find him a bore. I need excitement while he's away. If you're not interested, it'll be somebody else."

Looking Martha up and down again, Moishe said, "All right. What d'you propose, miss?"

"Lucy. My name is Lucy. Meet me in Military Park, across from the Robert Treat at three."

‡

Martha was sitting on the bench at Military Park, nervously waiting for Moishe to arrive. She noticed Joe moving about the park, ensuring everyone was ready. Joe's brother Tom was a skilled amateur photographer and had brought two good friends who were members of his camera club to help. He had chosen a precise location for Martha to sit, where he could take advantage of the sunlight for good exposure and snap pictures from his hiding place in the adjacent wooded section.

Joe gave Martha the signal that he saw Moishe approaching. She took out a white pearl cigarette holder, pushed in a cigarette, and quickly lit it, feeling her hands shaking.

Moishe approached, sitting down next to Martha on the bench.

"I'm so happy you came," she said. "My only dilemma is where to start first." Martha felt like an actress, having rehearsed this all before. She put her hand on Moishe's thigh—Tom's cue to take a picture.

"So I see you're no shrinking violet, Lucy. It seems you need to spend some time with a real man."

"I so do need that. From the moment I walked into the store and saw you, I wanted you to take me. I hope the Robert Treat has thick walls.

I can be loud when I'm enjoying myself." Following her next cue, Martha lifted off her hat. Then she raised her head, pressing her lips into his. As she finished and moved away, Moishe pulled her head back toward his and passionately returned the kiss. They both sat silently for a moment. Martha got up from the bench first. He followed, and they walked toward the hotel.

Joe had stationed another of Tom's friends, armed with a small Kodak camera, near the front door of the Robert Treat. Martha grabbed Moishe's arm as they walked under the canopy. When Joe saw everything was going according to plan, he made his way into the lobby. He started walking out as the pair entered.

"Oh, my God! It's my husband!" exclaimed Martha, in as surprised a voice as she could muster.

Joe stormed out and grabbed his wife. "I hired a dick to trail you. I didn't want to believe what he was telling me. Now I see you're nothing but a two-bit whore."

"I hate you!" Martha yelled.

Moishe took a step backward, then ran for about twenty yards. Martha and Joe watched him stop, look around, and then continue at a brisk pace on Park Place.

Martha spoke first. "I'm glad that's over with. I was so nervous. I guess I hid it pretty well."

Joe responded, "I should say so. You had him hook, line, and sinker. It made my blood boil to see you kiss him, but I knew this was the only way to trap him. I always thought you could be in the moving pictures."

"That's the way I got through it. I thought, this is what actresses do all the time.'"

‡

The authorities formally charged Abe Livosky with James's murder. Moishe Tabatchnick asked his attorney, David Steinberg, to represent him in the criminal trial. During one of their meetings, Livosky had shown Steinberg the pictures. He explained that they, along with a letter of explanation detailing Moishe's affairs and proof of the abortion would be given to his wife, Miriam, if the trial proceeded, and gave Steinberg an ultimatum.

Steinberg argued Moishe had nothing to do with Livosky's detention. Furthermore, this threat would make him furious. Livosky shot back, stating that since he knew he was innocent and someone had put up witnesses to lie. Someone as powerful as Moishe could influence them to retract their testimony. Whether Moishe was involved or not was irrelevant to him. He was waiting to go on trial for his life, and this was his chance to beat the rap. If, upon his release from prison, he should die under suspicious circumstances, the pictures and letter of explanation would find their way to Miriam.

One week after Livosky communicated his threat to the attorney, the prosecution got word that two witnesses were having some second thoughts regarding their testimony. They wanted to be absolutely certain they could identify the suspect before they would testify. On two separate days, the prosecution brought them to the Essex County Jail and exposed them to a lineup of four men, including Livosky. The first witness, the private citizen who saw the murder, declared he could not identify the attacker. The second witness, a convict who'd come forward, identified Livosky but said he'd been mistaken in his original testimony and that he did not take part in the planning of the post office bombing.

Considering the witnesses were a key part of their case, the prosecution dropped charges. They released Ziggy on a warm spring morning.

CHAPTER 21

REVENGE

It was an unusually warm April day, and the windows and doors in Ralph's Tavern in Harrison were open. The trio sitting at a table inside laughed so loudly that it could be heard all the way to the street. Joe had suggested to Ziggy that they meet in the tavern where the operation was first planned. Now, after two hours of conversation, it was time for Joe and Martha to head home for dinner.

As the couple got up, Ziggy rose from his chair and said, "I owe you both my life. If it wasn't for you, I'd be sitting on death row right now."

Joe responded, "Once I'd convinced myself you didn't do it, I felt I didn't have a choice. I had to help. Besides, Marty here was dying to be Theda Bara." The comment provoked Martha to cringe and playfully slap her husband's arm.

"I've learned a lot from you. Some Irishmen can be as smart as us Jews, and goyem can be worthy of trust. I am in your debt."

The operation to help free Ziggy had consumed most of Joe's waking thoughts for over a week. Now his attention could shift back to his father's murder. There were several open questions that Ziggy could help answer. Joe asked, "How're you going to handle Moishe?"

"Tomorrow, I thought I'd pay him a visit and apologize. I'm sure he wanted to kill me when he saw those pictures. Hopefully, he's cooled down and realizes it was my only play to save my skin."

"When you meet him, see if you can get some more details about why they chose you to take the rap. I'm thinking there's got to be a connection to the actual killer."

"Joe, I'll do my best. Let's meet back in this joint on Friday at five."

‡

As soon as Ziggy walked into the butcher shop, Moishe took off his blood-stained apron and went over to him. The two hugged each other vigorously. Withdrawing from the embrace, Moishe kissed Ziggy's forehead.

"You know I made a mistake, and I want you to forgive me. The Sicilians asked for you personally. You need to be careful and think about who you've disrespected there."

"Moishe, I also want to ask for your forgiveness. I hated doing what I had to do to save my life. I knew you were involved because you're the only person who knew I was in Orange that day."

"When Steinberg came back and showed me the pictures, I was furious. Then I realized how smart you are and how you could be doing more in the business. I felt a sense of pride that maybe I taught you a few things."

Ziggy felt encouraged. Maybe Moishe had put the blackmailing behind him. While they were on the subject, he figured he'd try to get more information. "Your approval means a lot to me. Just one question—I thought you hated the wops. What're you doing talking to them?"

"It's true. I don't like dealing with them. If you can believe it, the Sicilians, the Irish, and the Jews are talking to each other about managing

Prohibition. We all believe there's more money to be made by cooperating than waging war for the business."

"That's hard to believe. Why'd they ask for me?"

"This arrogant guinea Romano got way ahead of himself. The syndicate that was formed gave Orange to him for distribution. He's got an inside guy on the force there. Romano asks him if there is anybody who he thinks might get in the way of future business. One name comes back. Romano winds up having the cop killed and stages this post office incident, so it doesn't look like the mob whacked him. Romano gets the Irish on his side with a plan, and he demands you as the sacrificial Jew to play the part of the anarchist Red. You know Armando Romano?"

"I don't know him, but I was shtuping Angela Romano a while back. I stopped when I found out she was only sixteen."

Moishe chuckled. "Nice to hear someone else is getting into trouble with a shiksa. Stay away from their women. They're looking for any excuse. I'm sure you can find a nice Jewish girl around here who likes to fuck."

"I've learned my lesson." Ziggy decided to stop there with his questions. This would be good information to share with Joe.

Moishe said, "Wait a couple of minutes—I'll be right back with a present." He stepped into the back room, where the butchering was done, then returned with a small, wrapped piece of meat in his hand. "Enjoy the brisket with your mother. Take a few days. When you're ready, come back and we'll talk about giving you some new responsibilities. Mazel tov."

‡

Two days later, Joe was set to meet with Ziggy to talk about the murder. While there was no guarantee that he would even show up, Joe's anticipation was building. That day at the jail dragged on forever. Finally, it was time to leave for the day.

Joe didn't mind the walk from the county jail to Harrison in pleasant weather. It usually took him a little over a half hour to get home if he didn't stop into any of the stores on Central Avenue. Today, heavy spring showers and strong winds from the east forced him to run in fits and starts, seeking cover under various canopies. Since Joe passed Lock Street, a rather heavy-set man in a gray jacket and a black cap on the other side of the street had been trying to keep pace with him. Joe wanted to know whether this was intentional, so he stopped and lit a cigarette, casually looking up and down the street. The black-capped man also came to a halt and was peering into a shop window. Throwing down the half-smoked cigarette, Joe ran two blocks as quickly as he could. Glancing backward, he could see the man speeding along on the other side of the street. He was being followed.

Rather than lead this fellow to where he lived, Joe decided a confrontation was necessary. He crossed Central Avenue and headed back in the opposite direction, toward the man, who had stopped a half a block away. Seeing Joe walking toward him, he took a few steps forward and then turned into a tobacco shop. Joe walked past it and ducked into an army-navy store a few doors down. There was quite a bit of glass, which would allow him to survey the sidewalk without being seen first.

Less than five minutes later, Joe saw the black-capped man walking past the doorway. He stepped forward and said loudly, "Sir, you've dropped something."

Startled, the man looked around, then bent over to search the rain-soaked sidewalk. Joe stepped forward and crouched down next to the hunched figure. "Let me help you."

Joe sprang upward and propelled his body into the man's torso, knocking him backward into the heavy plate glass store window. Putting his left arm under the hefty man's throat, he sensed he would not be able to restrain him for long, so he swung his right arm up between the legs of the man's baggy trousers and grabbed his testicles, squeezing hard.

With a thick eastern European accent, the man said, "What are you doing? Let go of me." His expression was one of intense pain.

Joe took a mental picture of the man's face and distinguishing characteristics: a gold front tooth, bushy black eyebrows, and a large scar on his thick neck under his right ear. Before speaking, he released his grip slightly. "I've got a message for the guy who sent you. Next time, I'm not gonna be so nice. I'll be sending his stooge back to him with his balls stuffed in his mouth."

In one swift move, Joe pulled on the gray jacket, released his hold on the stunned man, and pushed him toward the street. Joe knew there would be no way for the guy to follow him immediately. The rain had stopped, so he could get to the Bridge Street Bridge quickly. Proceeding with extra caution, he finally made it back home.

‡

Friday had finally come. Joe had arrived at Ralph's a few minutes early and took the table in the corner, nervously waiting for Ziggy. At ten minutes after five, the man walked through the door, got a beer, and joined Joe. He spoke first. "It all makes sense now. I've got answers to a lot of your questions."

"Well, that's good. You go first. I've also got a problem I need to tell you about."

Over the course of the next hour, Ziggy took Joe through every detail of his conversation with Moishe. The fact that Armando Romano had ordered for his father to be killed hit Joe like a freight train. His memory flashed back to when another Romano was trying to put the squeeze on Harry. On that November day, four and a half years ago, he'd shot two men without hesitation. Had he been a fool to think he'd gotten away without paying for it?

"Moishe didn't mention the name of the cop who gave up your father."

"I'm pretty sure I know who it is. I've got somebody who will confirm it for me. Now's my time to tell you about what happened on Wednesday night when I was coming home from work."

Joe recounted his encounter with the man and gave a detailed description of him. Ziggy said, "That's Ezra. He's one of the guys Moishe uses for muscle."

Once Ziggy had confirmed his suspicion, Joe asked a question he already knew the answer to. "Okay, why was he trailing me? Why didn't he just jump me somewhere?"

"Joe, I feel terrible. This could only mean one thing. He's after Marty, too."

"Yeah, it's eating me up inside just thinking about it. What are we going to do?"

"You're not going to do anything, Joe," Ziggy said. "It's my time to step up to the plate. I got the impression when I saw Moishe that he wanted to put the blackmail business behind him. Now it's obvious he wants revenge. There's a good chance I'm on his list, too."

"What are you gonna do about it?"

"I gotta figure this out. The less that you know, the better. If you don't see me in a week, threaten Moishe with the blackmail pictures."

Joe's heart was pounding. He'd never thought about the consequences of his scheme to free Ziggy. Now, both he and Marty were in danger. It would cost another man's life for this danger to go away.

‡

From the moment he left Joe at the tavern, Ziggy put every ounce of his mental energy into figuring out a way to take out Moishe without getting caught. First, it was critical to keep the element of surprise. This had to be done quickly. Ziggy knew the man was a creature of habit. He observed the Sabbath and did not work on Saturdays. However, he went to the butcher shop around 5 a.m. the next day to prepare cuts of meat to be used for Sunday dinner.

After two sleepless nights, the day to act finally came. The night before, Ziggy had stuffed a large envelope with papers and sealed it. He brought that, along with his mother's best carving knife and a sack of spare clothes, to the butcher shop. Upon arriving, he heard chopping in the butcher's room, just like he'd expected. He opened the door and greeted Moishe, who was busy carving up some steaks on the other side of the narrow wooden table.

"Zig, what are you doing here so early?"

"I couldn't sleep, because I can't stop thinking about what I did to you. I figured the only way I could get your full trust was to give you the remaining set of pictures and negatives."

With a look of surprise, Moishe took the envelope from Ziggy's outstretched hand and, after wiping his hands on his butcher's apron, laid it on the table. He began to open it.

Ziggy knew he had one chance to strike a fatal blow. He leaned over the table and, wielding the carving knife like a pirate cutlass, sliced his former mentor's jugular vein. Moishe immediately clutched his neck but could not stop the blood from spattering everywhere. His body continued to convulse as it lay on the floor. Moments later, all movement stopped, and red rivulets flowed toward the floor drain.

Covered in blood and unable to control his shaking, Ziggy went into the office to compose himself. He could barely light a cigarette. He had a little less than two hours to chop up the body and stuff it into the canvas bags used for disposing of waste.

Overcoming his initial hesitation and reflex to throw up, Ziggy commenced the task and finished with time to spare, dragging the bags into the meat locker. After changing, he went to the office and looked where he suspected that Moishe had stashed money. Carefully lifting a floorboard in the corner, which wasn't nailed down, he saw cash piled in neat one-inch-thick rows. He grabbed five twenty-dollar bills and stuffed them in his pants. Until Moishe's body was disposed of, he wouldn't risk taking any more.

When he was finished, he locked up the butcher shop and put the "Closed" sign on the door. Moishe's associates would assume that he was spending time with one of his girlfriends if they saw it. Ziggy's biggest worry was Miriam expressing concern to the police. However, he was reasonably certain that any kind of investigation would happen well after the body had been taken from the butcher shop. He planned to dispose of the parts early Monday morning, when Moishe usually went to the slaughterhouse for meat, so the Tabachnick business truck riding on the streets would not draw attention. He retreated to his mother's apartment for the rest of the day.

‡

Despite all the care Ziggy had taken to drain the blood at the butcher shop, a considerable amount leaked from the canvas bag and dripped onto the metal railing of Jackson Street Bridge, He intended to drop half of Moishe's remains along with rocks into the river there, and the other half a mile north at the Bridge Street Bridge. By daybreak, the job was done. He returned the truck and cleaned out the remainder of the cash stashed in the office.

Ziggy decided to wait a few days before he went to see Joe at the jail. He would send the blackmail pictures to Miriam anonymously, suggesting that her husband might have run off with another woman. Now that the deed was done, he began plotting how he might replace Moishe as leader of the local crime enterprise.

‡

When he received word that someone was in the prison foyer with a message for him, Joe raced through the cell blocks, past the warden's office area and final security, to the entrance.

As soon as he appeared, Ziggy rose from his chair and walked up to Joe. He began speaking in a hushed tone. "I wanted you to know Moishe has mysteriously disappeared. He won't be a problem for you and Marty."

The tension that had built up in Joe's body since his Friday meeting with Ziggy dissipated. Over the weekend, he struggled with the moral dilemma of whether it was right for him to turn a blind eye to the killing of the man who'd threatened the lives of both him and his wife. After considerable thought, Joe finally rationalized it as a casualty of war, one which he did not start. His focus turned back to the Orange police force.

"I appreciate you coming to tell me. I couldn't tell Marty, but she knew something was up because of the way I was acting."

"You take care of that beautiful wife of yours."

"I will."

"You know I got to leave now, and what I'm gonna try to do puts us on opposite sides of the fence. Just because we can't be friends doesn't mean we aren't brothers. You and Marty are my family, and I will do anything in my power to help you until the day I die."

"Thanks, Ziggy. You're a smart guy, and I think you'd be successful in whatever you put your mind to. You don't have to do this line of work."

"I could say the same thing about you. Why is a fucking smart guy like you wasting his talent in that jail? Come work with me. We'll be rich."

Joe answered with a laugh. "Last couple of days taught me I'm not cut out for that kind of life. Besides, Marty would leave me in an instant."

"I figured as much. Good luck getting to the bottom of who killed your dad. When you find out for certain, I can help you with that problem, too. Oh, and by the way, I'm dropping the Ziggy and going back to using my real name, Abe. Ziggy is a kid's name."

‡

The first chance Joe got, he made the trip to Orange to see his mother. He did not have to work this Saturday and decided he would get over to the family apartment in the morning before breakfast. His mother was in a talkative mood and told him of the movement's plans to put pressure on their local congressman to vote for the woman's suffrage amendment.

Biding his time until she stopped talking to have a sip of tea, Joe asked, "Did Pat Maloney come and see you?"

"Yes, he did. We talked for a good long time. He told me so many wonderful things about your father."

"Did you ask him about Tom Sullivan?"

"I did. Pat said that Tom is a disgrace to the uniform. Says he's being controlled by the local Italian mob. There's nothing he won't say or do to help them get what they want."

While he was certain that Tom Sullivan was the man who'd given up his father, Joe wanted this confirmation. In his mind, a jury had just convicted Sullivan, and he was ready to pass sentence. He then shared the information Ziggy had been able to extract about his father's death and the post office incident.

"Mom, we both know he did it, but there's no way to convict him in a court of law. He's got to pay for killing Dad."

"I don't know how you did it, but you did a good thing getting that young man set free. Your father is up in heaven smiling because of it. He also knows Tom will get his someday."

"I can't do nothing."

"As much as I want justice, I know it won't bring him back."

"Mom, I am struggling with the fact I know who did it and—"

Margaret quickly interrupted her son. "And you must swear to me you'll not lift a hand or plan to avenge your father by physically harming Tom Sullivan. He may not get his punishment in this life, but he's sure to get it in the next."

"It's hard for me to make that promise, but I swear I won't harm him."

"Focus on being a good husband and starting a family. Let God take care of justice for this man."

CHAPTER 22

THE REUNION

It was 1923. Prohibition was in its third year. Joe, at last, received an opportunity for advancement and began working full time as a policeman in the Newark First Precinct in the Central Ward. This was the rookie beat, where the opportunities to line your pockets with organized crime bribes were far fewer than with other assignments in the city. There were a diverse group of legitimate businesses along Central Avenue, and no illegal drinking establishments known as "speakeasies," which paid off the police to stay in business. The area had a growing population of negroes, who had migrated from the South during the war to help fuel industrial production in Newark.

Balancing the demands of the job with his family life left little time for Joe to engage in gambling the way he had in the past. His success at cards over the years had cultivated in him a strong desire for that type of action. He was in frequent contact with bookmakers on his beat and started making small wagers on a weekly basis on boxing, baseball, and horse racing. As calculating as he was with cards, he was the opposite when betting on sports. He was always taking the long odds and looking for the big payoff.

When he won, Joe enjoyed splurging on Martha and the kids. He learned how to brush off the losses, which forced him to juggle his cash flow and delay paying his debts. Tom had gotten him out of a few jams, but Joe always paid him back quickly, keeping the debtors under control and his wife in the dark.

Martha, meanwhile, had taken to motherhood naturally. Her first experience was taking care of Minnie's little boy, Russell, in 1919. The following year, she was changing her own little girl, Gladys's, diapers. Less than a year later, she gave birth to a son—Joseph Sebastian Junior. Refusing to call him Junior, she gave him the pet name Joel.

Joe and Martha put their plans for getting their own place on hold because of her lost wages and the unpredictable nature of the money Joe brought home every week. The house in Harrison was always abuzz with activity until they put the children to bed. Wilhelmina loved having her three grandchildren there and taught them German so they could communicate with each other better. The only irritable one in the house was Fred, the Wolffs' youngest and only male child. Now a strapping twenty-one-year-old, he still harbored resentment against Martha from the time their father had beaten him for striking his sister.

‡

Joe was used to being greeted by his wife and kids almost as soon as he opened the door when coming home. This was not the case today. He climbed up the two flights of stairs to find her sitting with the kids in their bedroom.

"Marty, what's wrong? You've been crying."

"Joe, we're going to have to move. I'd rather not get into the details. Trust me, we need to get out of here as soon as we can."

"I thought things were going well at the house. Sure, it's crazy with three kids running around, but everyone gets along pretty well, don't they?"

Looking her husband straight in the eyes, Martha responded, "I'll tell you why, but you have to swear to me you won't do anything about it."

For a moment, Joe was confused. Then he pieced things together and asked, "What'd Fred do?"

"Promise me. Please, Joe. I don't want you to hurt him."

"I promise. I'd love to teach him a lesson, but I won't, out of respect for your mother."

"I caught him beating Joel with a belt. I'd put him in the parlor in his crib. I ran up to Fred and told him to stop. It was one o'clock in the afternoon, and he said he'd been taking a nap to get ready for work. He said Joel wouldn't listen, and he needed to teach him a lesson."

Over the past four years, Joe had had to restrain himself from confronting Fred many times. Since his father's death, Fred had started acting like a privileged, spoiled brat. He was inconsiderate and annoying, but in the end, his behavior had been harmless. Now he'd crossed the line.

"That makes me so mad. The kid isn't even three yet. Why couldn't he just find you to quiet him down?"

"I've never trusted Fred. I think he wants to pick a fight with you. Fred and I've never gotten along, and I think he resents you and how close you've become with my mother."

"Maybe this is a blessing in disguise. I've always wanted us to have our own place. Things'll be a little tight money wise, but we can do it." Joe was hoping to reassure his wife, but he was quite concerned about their ability to afford an apartment. His thoughts immediately went to how things would be better if he won on a big bet.

Fred usually came home from his second shift at the General Electric Lamp Works factory between 11 p.m. and midnight. Joe was sitting on the porch on that chilly September evening, smoking a cigarette, when his brother-in-law opened the gate and started walking up the stairs.

"Fred, you have your wish. We'll move out as soon as we can. In the meantime, if you lay a hand on one of my kids, you'll be saying goodbye to some of your teeth."

"Oh, is that right, you cocky mick bastard? This is my house. I'll do anything I damn well please."

Thoroughly provoked, Joe got up from the chair and took a step toward Fred. Remembering Marty's words, he turned around and walked slowly into the house.

Burning with anger, Fred called after him, "Don't give me the air. I'm not done talking to you."

Still tempted to finish the conversation with his fists, Joe forced himself to join his family upstairs instead.

‡

After that evening, Joe's impatience to leave the Wolff house drove him to increase the size of his wagers. His hunch about the Washington Senators beating the New York Giants in the 1924 World Series presented him with a nice payout. That enabled him to pay off all his current gambling debts and provided enough money on top of that to move.

While discussing their plans for the new place, he took a twenty-dollar bill and gave it to Martha. "Tuck this away for now. Save it in case the kids need something."

"You're worried about expenses, aren't you? We should have plenty of money to pay the rent and buy food on your salary. I think you've found a wonderful place. It's small, but really cozy." Joe had found a furnished one-bedroom apartment on the second floor of a red brick row house on Summit Street in Newark and had paid the rent through the end of the year.

"Marty, you're right about the money. I just worry about the unexpected."

Joe had made a vow to himself that he would stop gambling now that he had completely caught up and could pay the bills and put food on the table. The apartment would be fine for the time being, but there really wasn't enough room to live as comfortably as they had done in Harrison.

‡

No, it can't be, Joe thought as he gazed at the stocky colored man buying a newspaper in front of Schulman Tire on Central Avenue. "Ulysses?" he called out.

The man turned his head and looked at him. "Joe, I knew the good Lord would help me find you. Look at you." He gestured at Joe's clothing. "You done traded one uniform for another."

"My goal is to get rid of the uniform and eventually become a detective," Joe said. "Well, I'm not all that surprised to see you. Back in New Mexico, you told me that maybe you'd come up my way."

Ulysses Thompson had left the army just as he had pledged and moved back home to South Carolina. Tired of being treated as a second-class citizen after his tour in the army, he convinced his brother Lincoln and his family to join him in the move. Using the money he'd saved from the army, he'd gotten them all to Newark and rented an apartment in the Central Ward. Lincoln had already found employment in the tire store. Ulysses was still looking for a job.

"Let me guess—you're all hitched up with that girl you always talked about."

"Hitched up with two kids, a girl and a boy." Joe smiled proudly and continued, "My brother Tom runs a funeral home not too far from here. He's always looking for help because no one wants to work around the bodies. What d'you think?"

"Well, those dead white folks can't complain about me! If your brother is half as good a man as you, I reckon he'll be a good boss."

"He's a good man. Why don't you stop by the house for dinner tonight? We eat about 6:30. I'll get in touch with Tom to see if he can stop by and meet you."

‡

"Now, what is this child's name? I hear you calling him 'Junior' and 'Joel.'" Soon to be three, the toddler was laughing and bouncing up and down on Ulysses Thompson's knee.

"Both," said Martha. "I'm the only one that calls him Joel, because I hate calling him Junior." She smiled. "He sure does like you. He's fascinated by your deep voice and laugh, I can tell. Look, now his sister is getting jealous."

Four-year-old Gladys beckoned for Ulysses to pick her up, clearly wanting to get in on the fun. "Let me put Joel down, and I'll pick you up, darlin'. Y'all are making me feel bad that I never settled down and had me a coupla kids to take care of. I love how both of them are so friendly."

"It's not too late for you, Ulysses. Any woman would be lucky to have you as a husband," Joe said, right as a knock came at the door.

After a round of introductions, Tom O'Mara, fresh from work and dressed in his undertaker's black suit, crammed in at the small table. There was an opening at the funeral home because the previous caretaker had died.

Tom said, "Ulysses, Joe has told me about you and what a fine soldier you were. I've had a hard time finding dependable workers of late. There's a small two-room apartment in the home's basement with an icebox and stove. It's right next to where we do all the undertaker work. I'd like to offer you thirty-five dollars a week and the apartment. Your responsibilities would include care and cleaning of all parts of the funeral home, odd jobs, and driving. You just need to be able to handle being around blood and dead bodies. It might take a bit to get used to."

"Mr. Tom, you have yourself a worker. It sounds like I'll have some very quiet neighbors." Ulysses then took on a more serious tone. "I've seen quite a few dead bodies as a soldier and think I can handle it. Your offer is very generous. My brother Lincoln is getting twenty dollars a week, and he knows the white guy who does the same thing is getting thirty."

"I offered you the same money that I paid the last man."

"You won't be sorry. I can start whenever you want me to."

CHAPTER 23

ANOTHER FALL GUY

"Officer, come quick. There's a nigger going wild in the tire store. They're trying to hold him back. You need to come in here and settle him down before he hurts Mr. Schulman."

A clerk from the office of Schulman Tire Store had run out onto Central Avenue and caught Joe's attention while he was on duty. Joe rushed inside the store to see two of the white workers restraining a furious colored man. Lincoln Thompson was considerably taller than his brother and looked like he could have handled himself well in the boxing ring.

Joe introduced himself. "I'm Ulysses's friend, Joe. I'll sort this out. Will you calm down?" He could see the fury in the man's eyes abate.

"Yes."

"Gentlemen, please release Mr. Thompson. I'm responsible now."

"Are you sure, Officer? He's one crazy nigger. You better have your night stick ready."

After the Camp Logan Mutiny in Houston, Joe cringed when he heard the word nigger or other derogatory terms used to describe colored people. So many white people just used it as part of their speech for no reason. The white men in front of him were both hateful and stupid. Didn't they have enough common sense not to use the term in front of an already angry man?

Joe answered, "I'm sure. Perhaps if you treated him with a bit more respect, he wouldn't be so crazy. What's the problem here? I'll start with Mr. Thompson."

"Officer, every day I've been coming to work, doing my job while taking shit from these white folks. They boss me around like I was their child. Now, being from South Carolina, I'm used to that, and it don't mean nothin' as long as I get my money. But when the supervisor came to pay me, he only gave me fifteen dollars and told me I hadn't earned the full amount this week. I got hoppin' mad and told them I was going to see Mr. Schulman. We made a deal at twenty."

Joe now turned to the men who had been restraining Lincoln. "Is this true?"

"It's true about the money. We had a slow week, and the boss cut all of our pay. When I told old Lincoln here, he was about ready to explode, and we grabbed him when he said that he was going to go see Mr. Schulman, 'cause we thought he was headed to hurt him."

"I'm going to go with Mr. Thompson and see Mr. Schulman."

Joe and Lincoln walked upstairs to the second floor and followed a long, dimly lit corridor to a large open area at the back of the building. In that space stood a wooden table and six chairs, intended for meetings. Past the table, there was an office. Joe encouraged Lincoln to have a seat while he went to check if Schulman was inside.

Joe knocked, and a balding man in his late forties of medium build came to the door. "Officer, glad that you got here quickly—my secretary alerted me to the problem downstairs."

Before speaking to the store owner, Joe noticed there was someone sitting on the chair in the corner of the office. He looked over at the man, whose gaze had locked onto him. It was Tom Sullivan.

"I see you are taking after your father, Joe," Tom said. "I hope things are going well for you here in Newark."

As the years passed after his father's murder, Joe found it easier to accept that justice had not been done. He could focus more on the memories of his father than on the hatred he had for Tom Sullivan. Seeing the man's face unexpectedly brought his revulsion to the surface once again. Rather than display his true feelings, he put on his poker face.

"Things are good. Just trying to be half the cop my dad was. So, what brings you to this neighborhood?"

"Oh, the chief has me out shopping tires for the paddy wagons and such."

"Ah, I see. Sorry to interrupt your visit, but I need to speak with Mr. Schulman."

Joe closed the door and went to sit at the table, where Schulman had already taken a seat across from Lincoln. Schulman started the discussion. "Lincoln, I heard you were quite upset."

"Yes, sir, I surely was. We had a deal at twenty dollars a week. You didn't say nothin' about cutting pay."

"Well, this has been my practice for quite a long time with all of my employees. If I don't have the income coming in, I can't afford to pay you the same."

"Mr. Schulman, when you have a busy week and make more than expected and the men have to work harder, do they get paid more?"

Schulman looked at Joe incredulously, as if he spoke a foreign language. "I'll not press charges against Lincoln, but I'm going to have to fire him. I can't have a man with that size temper working for me."

Lincoln stood up and banged his fist on the table. "Don't want this job anyway. I can't work for somebody I can't trust."

Joe empathized with Lincoln. If he had been in his shoes, he might have been just as mad. He needed to send a message to Schulman that he wasn't doing Lincoln any favors. He said, "For the record, Mr. Schulman, there are no charges to press. A man getting upset with his employer for screwing him isn't against the law. Your men downstairs assumed the worst, but there were no threats made to you."

Joe and Lincoln left the building and walked outside.

"Thanks Joe. I have a temper, but I'm not stupid. I wasn't gonna hurt anybody."

‡

One week later, authorities discovered Irving Schulman's lifeless body, stabbed to death, on the corner of Henry and Frankfort in Orange.

"Sir, why can't they question him here in our precinct? Why do they have to bring him to Orange?" Joe pleaded with his superior, Lieutenant Bradley.

"Joe, they have every right to bring the suspect to Orange, as they found the body in Orange. It'll be easier for them to question this fellow there and maybe have some witness provide an identification."

Joe had a good relationship with the lieutenant but knew that he had jumped the chain of command past his sergeant and was testing Bradley's patience. The lieutenant needed information regarding Sullivan's character to make a good decision. Unfortunately, Pat Maloney had retired over a year ago, and his father was dead.

Joe continued. "There's something that just doesn't smell right about this. I saw Sergeant Sullivan meeting with Mr. Schulman in plainclothes at the tire store. I'm sure he heard the disagreement between Mr. Schulman and Lincoln Thompson. One week later, Schulman is dead, stabbed four times, and Mr. Thompson is a suspect. Sounds like too much of a coincidence to me."

"Joe, don't you think the police should bring Mr. Thompson in for questioning?"

"Yes, for questioning. He might very well have an alibi for the time when the murder was committed."

"Then that'll come out during the questioning. If the shoe were on the other foot, I wouldn't want to be taking orders for a murder which I was responsible for solving in my jurisdiction."

"Sir, I have reason to be quite suspicious about Sergeant Sullivan and his motives. I believe he has strong connections to the Italian mob in that area."

"That's quite a serious accusation. Do you have any proof?"

"Unfortunately not. If my father were alive today, I'd encourage you to speak with him. I think you should ask the police chief in Orange about Sullivan before you send Mr. Thompson there."

"Joe, you are a smart young man and a good cop. Your father was a credit to the uniform, a real straight shooter. It's not a coincidence that things have calmed down in the Central Ward since you started. I hear what you're saying, but I won't get in a pissing contest with the Orange police chief over this colored man. Bring Mr. Thompson to the station this afternoon."

Joe knew the decision was final and that he had to keep his cool. He left the building. Perhaps he was overreacting, but his gut told him otherwise. He would have a discussion with Lincoln on the way back to the station, so he would be as prepared as possible for the interview.

‡

That night, Joe slept very little, thinking about all the bad things that could happen. Lincoln Thompson would be an easy person to pin a murder charge on and get a conviction. There was motive and witnesses who could testify to his anger at Schulman. Joe imagined the trial and the all-white jury looking at Lincoln in the defendant's chair. They would think he was guilty before the trial even began. Then there was Tom Sullivan. Lincoln was clearly a suspect because of what he'd overheard at the tire store.

Joe decided that as soon as he got to the precinct, he would ask his sergeant to call over to Orange to find out how things had gone with the questioning the previous afternoon. Once he received word from Sergeant Cross, he raced to Hannifin's Funeral Home.

"Joe, what happened? I can't believe my brother is dead." Tears were streaming down Ulysses's face as Joe broke the news to him.

"I was worried about this police sergeant in Orange. I tried my best to convince my lieutenant they should question Lincoln in Newark. He didn't agree and allowed Lincoln to be taken to Orange. The police there say the suspect tried to escape right as the questioning began by trying to strangle an officer. Because he was so big and strong, they said they had to shoot Lincoln in self-defense."

"Lincoln had a hot temper and was strong as an ox, but he wasn't stupid. Colored folk down South get plenty of training on how to behave with the police if they want to stay alive," Ulysses said.

"I know their story is bullshit. I gotta figure some things out. Is there anything I can do for you?"

"Git the guy who done this to my brother."

Joe closed his eyes and nodded like a schoolboy being scolded for playing hooky. He felt like an absolute failure. Thinking back to his conversation with Lieutenant Bradley, he wondered if there was anything else he could have possibly said or done to prevent this tragedy from occurring.

After leaving Ulysses, he went to see his brother in the funeral director's office. Immediately, Tom gave Ulysses time off to grieve and spend with Lincoln's widow and family. Upon Joe's urging, he picked up Lincoln's body at the morgue and reviewed the coroner's report. Later that day, Tom called Joe at the station to let him know his findings.

"Joe, I don't think I can fix Lincoln up enough to have an open coffin wake. I promised Ulysses we could have a small ceremony here before we brought him to the colored church and burial. His face was beat up quite bad. I'm no doctor, but I suspect that this man may have died from wounds sustained before the listed cause of death, which reads from the coroner's report as two fatal gunshot wounds to the abdomen."

The next step was obvious to Joe. He needed to find out more about Schulman and would use his contact on the opposite side of the law.

‡

After the murder of Moishe Tabatchnick, Abe Livosky made a bold play to take control of the Newark-based Jewish mob. Abe appealed to Moishe's boss, Stan Gertz, who was based in New York and part of the Arnold Rothstein crime empire, to employ him for a three-month trial, guaranteeing 10 percent higher revenues than his predecessor. Recognizing the presence of disgruntled associates in Moishe's organization, Abe secured their loyalty by promising a higher percentage of the take, reducing his own share. Because the associates of the crime enterprise were highly motivated, Abe's plan worked from the start. Then Prohibition exploded the size of the opportunity, securing his position leading the local mob while making him rich. Ironically, he continued to use the butcher shop as an office.

"So, what brings you to my office today, Officer O'Mara?" asked Abe Livosky, who was dressed in a dark blue tailored suit, a white silk shirt, and a red tie.

While he hadn't seen Abe for some time, Joe was confident that if he knew something, he would be forthright and share the information. Making note of the man's fancy attire, he said, "Even though I'm in uniform, I'm not here on official police business. You made a promise to me some years ago, and I'm looking for your help."

"Of course. That offer holds for life. I think about you and your wife often."

"What d'you know about a merchant on Central Avenue named Schulman? Was he clean?"

"Oh, you mean the stupid putz who got himself killed because he was being too greedy?"

"Tell me more."

"Cops look the other way with booze unless the Feds come in, and then they try to make a show of it—breaking bottles and taking axes to barrels of beer for the camera."

"Yeah, I knew that."

Abe explained bootlegging, covering the entire process from the moment imported whiskey and spirits were acquired in international waters off the coast of New Jersey near Sandy Hook, to the speakeasies in Essex County where citizens would indulge in drinking them. The Irish mob picked up the booze once it got to shore and brought it to distribution warehouses. The Italian and Jewish mob were responsible for sales to the illegal drinking establishments.

"Irv Schulman had a warehouse, mostly filled with Canadian whiskey. The Irish report cases they deliver. Guys in the warehouse make sure everything is jake. The Irish get paid, and so does the warehouse. Businesses like Irv's get dollars for each case. Schulman supplied the Italians for distribution in the Oranges and North Newark. They come into his shop for tires and come out with cases of whiskey."

Joe thought back to Schulman's business practices. He had all this money coming in for warehousing booze, and he still screwed the employees in the tire store out of their week's wages. He asked, "You said he was greedy. What do you mean by that?"

"He's making a good buck with little risk. Everyone knows there're going to be some losses. Glass breaks. I've heard the Schulman warehouse has three times the amount of loss that the other warehouses do. The Sicilians catch wind Schulman has a couple of juice joints in Elizabeth he's selling cases to. It's peanuts when it comes right down to it, but Irv didn't have to pay for the booze, and he was always trying to make an extra shekel or two."

Here was the connection that Joe was looking for. Schulman was dirty and had wronged the Italian mob. Sullivan had ties to the Italian mob.

Joe asked, "Now it just so happens that the cop who's visiting Schulman is the same cop who gave up my father to Armando Romano— you know, the guy who asked for you to take the rap. Does it make sense to you that the Sicilians would send a cop rather than one of their own to talk to Schulman?"

"If Schulman was fucking with me like this, I'd go see him and tell him to stop being stupid. I'd tell him he's getting two bucks less a case until I think we're even. Now, maybe the wops look at this differently. They say the sheeny disrespected them, and if they ignore it, there's a loss of honor. For the relatively small amount of money at stake here, I'm not sure they'd kill the guy . . . but maybe. Why was the cop there meeting with Schulman instead of one of them? Not sure about that."

‡

After leaving Abe's office, Joe began a slow walk home. He looked in the various storefronts on Prince Street and Springfield Avenue, trying to distract his thoughts from what he knew to be the truth. By the time he'd gotten to the residential section on High Street, his anger took over. He stopped walking and stood in the middle of the sidewalk, unable to move. Joe felt fully responsible for Lincoln's death.

He thought of the recurring dream that had haunted him for years. He was in the audience watching the executioner place a bag over Tom Sullivan's head. When the switch was lowered and electrical current pulsed through the man's body, causing it to convulse for minutes, Joe started to clap because justice had been done. In the real world, he'd listened to his mother and let this monster of a man walk the streets.

He thought of his friend Ulysses and his request for justice.

‡

The following morning, Lieutenant Bradley came down to the locker room to see Joe as he was preparing to begin his shift.

"Joe, I'd like to see you in my office."

"Yes, sir. Let me finish changing, and I'll come up." The visit had caught Joe completely off guard. He was anxious about speaking with the lieutenant and did not have any idea what it could be about. He made his way upstairs, went into the office, and shut the door.

"Joe," the man said once they'd settled, "the whole matter of the negro's death in Orange has been quite disturbing for me. I didn't follow your advice, and I'm sorry. Police bureaucracy rose above the advice of a valued member of the force. I made some inquiries of my own concerning this Tom Sullivan. He's been under investigation for some time now because of his alleged association with organized crime. The supposition that Sullivan could actually have taken the life of this colored man to cover up for his own dealings did not surprise the Orange police chief. Because this matter would be almost impossible to prove in a court of law, we felt the best course forward would be to fire him from the force. Effective today, Tom Sullivan has been relieved of his duties. I thought it was important to give you this news in person."

Mixed emotions flooded Joe. It was good they'd fired Sullivan, but they should have taken his badge away a long time ago. Joe himself knew of two murders Sullivan was responsible for. Despite corruption and a suspected murder, there would be no investigation. Sullivan was getting off easy. Trying hard to hide his disappointment, he said, "Thank you, sir. I appreciate you telling me this." He turned and started to walk out the door.

"Not so fast—I'm not finished yet. I know you have ambitions to become a detective. You're doing a solid job as a policeman here, but I feel your talents are a bit wasted. We've created a special position of junior detective to get you involved in investigating and learning from some of the older detectives who'll be retiring soon. There is also a substantial increase in pay. Do you accept the assignment?"

"Lieutenant Bradley, I don't know what to say."

Joe needed a minute to collect his thoughts. All those years paying his dues in the prison had fully prepared him for spending years proving himself as a police officer before they would consider him for detective. Then he thought about his father and how proud he would be for his son.

"Yes, this has been my dream. Thank you for your confidence in me. I won't let you down."

"When they see your youthful face over at the Fourth Precinct, they may ask a lot of questions about why you got this job. Frankly, I don't care what you tell them, but I'd ask that you keep this matter regarding the Orange police force to yourself. I'd be very disappointed if I heard otherwise."

With Bradley's last comment, Joe got a clearer picture of why he was getting this break. In a roundabout way, the lieutenant had admitted he had made a mistake and used his influence to get Joe a promotion to buy his silence. Perhaps the lieutenant felt responsible for Lincoln's death, and this act was one to clear his conscience.

"Sir, I understand," Joe told him.

‡

One month later, while having a cup of coffee before breakfast, Joe was reading the *Newark Star-Eagle*. A headline caught his eye: *Retired Orange Police Sergeant Found Murdered*. He read through the brief article on page three that described the discovery of Thomas Sullivan dead in his bed at home. The body was in a decomposed state. He had taken one gunshot to the head. The police suspected organized crime because of the execution-style killing.

After finishing the article, Joe immediately thought about his mother. He knew she read the paper religiously. What would she think after reading this?

PART FOUR

CHAPTER 24

ADDICTION

It was Joe's first day as a junior detective, and he was having his initial meeting with his assigned mentor. It appeared to Joe that Carmine Dotti was playing a game as he gave his opening soliloquy of sorts. He talked about how the mayor really didn't give a shit about the detective force and the stupidity of the *mouilinyans* for getting themselves hooked on dope. As he spoke, a cigarette burned between his fingers, producing a pillar of ash that would get long, then curl and eventually wind up on the floor or his trousers when he gestured with his hands.

"Kid, I'm gonna level with you. You're gonna see some awful shit you won't believe human beings could do to each other. You'll go home some days wondering, 'Why the fuck did I ever take this job?' Just remember one thing: if you do this right, you're doing God's work, just as much as the priests who put their parishioners to sleep with their sermons on Sunday morning."

Joe chuckled. "I've caught a few winks on Sunday morning myself."

"It's a living. The pay ain't bad, not as dangerous as being out on the street. Know when to leave, though, because you can spend twenty-four hours a day here. Told them I've had enough. Got enough money together to move with the Mrs. down to the shore to be out fishing and breathing sea air instead of all these foul odors from the factories in town."

The ash from his cigarette fell right on cue. "Connor's told me I'm supposed to take you under my wing and show you the ropes so you can take my place when I leave. There're some pretty pissed-off patrolmen downstairs who think you jumped the line and took their spot. Don't expect any love from them for a while, but it'll eventually blow over—unless you're a real asshole."

Despite Carmine's long-windedness, Joe valued his perspective and found pleasure in conversing with the experienced detective. Carmine was quick to give him praise but did not hesitate to provide constructive criticism when he thought Joe was drawing conclusions without enough evidence. Joe missed the times when his dad would give him a bit of fatherly advice and, while Carmine was nothing like James, his feedback definitely brought back nice memories.

Within a few weeks, Joe felt like a contributor rather than just a tagalong.

‡

With his higher salary, Joe could afford to move. Tom and Ella had been living in the family apartment in Orange with Margaret and decided they were going to buy a large house on Ward Place in South Orange, right near Seton Hall College. Given the crowded conditions in their place, Joe jumped at the chance to take the place in Orange. He had some convincing to do with Marty, because she would not be able to walk to Harrison to visit her mom and sister. Joe's mother closed the deal by talking about how much she would love to babysit for them.

Joe felt the extra room and having his mom closer were well worth the additional time it would take to get to work. After all, he had gotten used to the much longer walk to the Fourth Precinct from their small apartment on Summit Street. He realized soon after starting this commute from Orange that it was more challenging than he'd expected, given some of the late nights he ended up working. Tom would give him rides occasionally, and as his brother was dropping him off one morning, Joe realized that if he had a car, life would be so much easier. That he was now making seventy dollars a week was helping, but he didn't have enough money saved up yet.

Despite his self-made pledge not to go into the hole ever again through gambling, Joe placed some long-shot bets on the hope he could acquire enough cash. He wouldn't gamble over five dollars a week, and he'd see what happened.

‡

The weather in February 1925 was cold and wet, and Joe's patience with the commute soon wore thin. He raised his bets to $20. After three weeks of increased wagering, he hit on a number's bet for $275, which netted him about $200 after paying off the accumulating short-term debts.

Joe remembered how his old boss, Harry, used to buy cars that people couldn't afford to fix and resell them. He took a walk to the shop early Saturday morning before going to work to see if there was anything available.

"Aye, Joe. Things are well. Business is booming. I bought this Oldsmobile that somebody forgot to change the oil on a few months ago and haven't had time to fix it. It's going to need an engine overhaul, but it'll be a fine car once that's done. It's an eight-cylinder, and it should do over sixty."

The boxy black 1916 Oldsmobile 44 sedan was not what Joe had imagined for his first car, but it would be very functional for the family.

It might take him some time and money to fix it, but depending on what Harry wanted for it, it might just be the perfect solution.

"How much for the car as it is now?"

The old man looked at Joe and laughed. "Joe, I know what you're probably thinking. This old Scot's going to try to get every penny he can. Maybe I'm getting senile, but I want you to have it. I paid $150, as I figured it needed about ten hours of my time and not too many parts. I thought if it ran well, I'd get at least $400 for it—probably more. You can have it for what I paid for it. Work on it here and use my tools after we close on Saturday afternoon and on Sunday."

"Harry, what a surprise. I'll take it." Joe opened his wallet and handed the cash to him. "I'll be back this afternoon to get started."

During his time in the army, he had learned a trick to free motors that had severely overheated and had motor oil sludge caked up on the pistons. Provided the pistons and cylinders were not too damaged, that might be all he needed to do to get the Oldsmobile on the road. He filled the crankcase with some of the kerosene in the shop, which was still used for the wall lamps. In the warm garage, he waited an hour for the sludge to thin. The engine could barely crank once. Joe drained the sludge kerosene mix and was happy to see some semi-moist black chunks make it out into the drain pan.

After the third time of repeating this procedure, the motor continued to run past the first stroke, with Joe turning it off after about twenty seconds. He drained the kerosene sludge mix and pulled the head cover to inspect the cylinders and pistons. Things were cleaned up. They looked a bit worn, but he had seen much worse in the heat of the southwest prairie. It should run. How well? He was going to find out.

After filling the crankcase with oil and topping off the gas tank, Joe left a five-dollar bill and a quick note for Harry explaining that he'd fixed the car. He was going to drive this a bit to test the compression. If he could get up over fifty miles per hour, he would be satisfied he didn't have to do any more work on it. Knowing he couldn't drive like that in Orange, he tried to think of some place where it was less crowded, somewhere with fewer intersections. He recalled a wide street in Glen Ridge with stately homes that wasn't too far to drive to in case the car broke down.

The Oldsmobile shuttered and shifted roughly for the first mile, but the engine smoothed out, and Joe's confidence was building by the time that he hit Ridgewood Avenue. There were no cars on the road, and Joe decided he could put the throttle down. It had been some time since he'd driven, and he felt an exhilaration going faster than he ever had before.

Suddenly, Joe noticed a tiny red traffic light and a line of cars crossing Ridgewood Avenue, less than a hundred yards ahead of him. He tried to slow down by pressing and then literally standing on the brake pedal, but he could not appreciably reduce his speed. The car veered to the left as Joe began engaging the emergency brake. He could barely keep it from skidding into the intersection with Bloomfield Avenue. When it finally stopped, he breathed an enormous sigh of relief, making a right turn toward Bloomfield Center and then back to Orange.

Joe parked the car in a lot near his home. It was just after 5 p.m. After bounding up the steps, he opened the door and walked in, finding his wife standing in the kitchen with a strange expression on her face.

"You smell like kerosene. What's going on?"

"It's too late now, but I have a surprise to show you. First thing tomorrow."

"Joseph Sebastian, after all these years of marriage, I thought you knew me better by now," Martha exclaimed, pretending to be offended.

Margaret was visiting and helping Martha put the finishing touches on dinner. With a big smile on her face, she said, "Joe, I must agree with your wife. That's no way to behave. I'll watch the children. Take Martha out to see this surprise of yours."

Martha grabbed her coat, and Joe raced down the wooden steps and waited for her at the bottom. He took her hand and escorted her to the lot. Four feet in front of the black Oldsmobile, Joe proudly pointed at it like a little boy would to his first bicycle. "This is our car. Been putting a few dollars away with my extra pay, and I got a great deal from Harry, my old boss. I had to do some work on it today to get it running. It'll be fine for us. I got it up over fifty when I took it for a drive."

"Well, Mr. O'Mara, you *are* full of surprises. I won't ask if you robbed a bank to get the money, because I know you didn't. It's wonderful, and the whole family can fit in it. Where are we off to tomorrow?" Martha asked in her usual playful manner.

"After church, I was thinking maybe Harrison, because you haven't seen your mother lately. I'm planning on using this to get to work, and it wouldn't be hard to drop you and the kids off whenever you want. I know Gladys and Junior miss Russell."

"I don't want you to take this the wrong way. I love the fact that you got a car. It's a pleasant surprise, but I think I'd rather be involved in what you're thinking than be kept in the dark."

Joe apologized, feeling guilty about how he got the money. "I'm sorry, Marty. You know I'd never want to hurt your feelings."

‡

Lieutenant Francis Connor was a strictly by-the-book cop who had worked his way up to lieutenant from patrolman by aligning himself with the right people and faithfully following their orders. A slight man with somewhat feminine features, Connor dressed in fashionable suits and never had a hair out of place. Carmine Dotti had developed significant resentment toward the far less experienced Connor when they promoted him ahead of Carmine five years ago. Carmine maintained that the only thing Connor was good at was taking credit for other people's work. Behind his back, he called him "the weasel."

Heroin had been a problem in the Newark area for years. Until 1914, the sale of it was unregulated. Ten years later, it became completely illegal. Similar to Prohibition, organized crime now saw heroin as an opportunity. Unlike illegal alcohol, the mob targeted heroin sales toward the poor, with a disproportionate number of the negro population becoming addicted. Theft and burglaries increased exponentially because of the growing population of addicts who stole to pay for their habits. Influential local merchants had had enough and promised the mayor that his bid for reelection would fail unless he did something to stem the tide of these thefts.

Lieutenant Connor called both Carmine and Joe into his office. With an unnerving stare alternating between both men, he began, "I have a special project for you. The mayor's been putting enormous amounts of pressure on the police chief, and now this pressure comes to us." He cleared his throat several times. "Over the last six months, thefts and burglaries have become an increasing problem in our city. Repeat break-ins have been occurring in businesses, and valuable items have been stolen. Uniformed police have caught some of these thieves. Almost all of them were colored."

Connor's manner almost made Joe squirm in his chair. His pace of speech had slowed to a crawl. After making a point, he would turn to gaze at each man, seeking some gesture of acknowledgement. Joe nodded his head when this happened but tried not to show any emotion.

"We all know there's been quite a rise in the negro population here in Newark since the war. Why the sharp increase in theft over the past six months? Heroin. The mob can't resist making money from forbidden fruit. Since the drug became illegal last year, they've been preying on the colored community and building a customer base of hopheads. Once hooked, they break into businesses, take whatever they can, and go to pawn shops to sell the goods for cash."

Joe knew that heroin was a problem in the area. Because he'd grown up in an apartment above a pharmacy, he was aware of the many break-ins to steal drugs. He hadn't realized the mob was involved now. He knew Abe was making a fortune from Prohibition and wondered if he was involved in the drug racket as well. He asked, "Lieutenant, I think the money they're making from the heroin is tiny compared to what's being made on booze."

"Detective O'Mara, that's absolutely correct. However, given how challenging it is to enforce Prohibition, there may come a day when they decide to repeal the law. These gangsters want their hands in everything and may be planning for the future."

Joe felt his curiosity peak. Why was Connor only talking to the two of them if this was so important? Why wouldn't he put a dozen detectives on this?

Connor continued, "We need to stop this at the source, as we cannot hire more cops or focus our efforts exclusively on catching the coloreds. In Newark, the drug's being distributed by the mob led by a gangster named Abe Livosky. We *must* make an example of this man and put him in jail. This is your job—get Abe Livosky charged and convicted. This'll go a long way toward showing the police are actually doing something about the problem and will take pressure off the mayor."

Carmine had been unusually silent throughout the lieutenant's explanation. Now he said, "We could go out right now and catch one of Livosky's men doing something illegal and lock him up for it, but it's going to be damn near impossible to get Livosky. I'm sure he's miles away from the action."

"Exactly. That's why I need you both to figure out a way to get something on him."

"To be clear, Lieutenant, everything's on the table to nail this guy?" Carmine asked as he lit a cigarette.

"Everything that'll hold up in a court of law is on the table. Report progress in a week to me, verbally. I don't want to know any details, just whether you're making progress."

A half hour later, Carmine asked Joe to meet him in the interrogation room. When Joe walked in, he saw his mentor leaning back in a chair, puffing on a cigarette. He would never have described Carmine's disposition as sunny, but there was a scowl on his face, which was uncharacteristic even for him.

"Joe, you know what the weasel wants us to do and not tell him?"

"He wants us to come up with a plan to do a search and find something illegal on Livosky."

"Yeah. The newspapers get involved, then put his mug on the front page. Maybe he gets convicted, maybe not. The important thing is it becomes news. Connor gets a pat on the back, and we run the risk of getting the boot. I can't believe this piece of shit made lieutenant, and they passed me by."

"Carmine, let me sleep on this. I might have an idea, but I need some time to mull it over."

"Make sure we don't get killed or go to jail in this plan. Okay, Joe?"

‡

Joe made a detour over to Prince Street on his drive home and went to see Abe in his office in the Tabatchnick Butcher shop. Two well-dressed gangster types were seated outside the office, looking as friendly as two junkyard dogs.

"We don't know you, Mr. Why'd you want to see Abe?"

"Tell him his old friend Joe wants to see him."

One of the men opened the door to the office to check with Abe, while the other held a staring contest with Joe.

"Boss says to come in."

The finely tailored clothes that Abe wore reminded Joe of his economic status. However, he found it quite amusing that someone who looked like they were dripping money was still heading operations from a dingy office in the back of a butcher shop.

"To what do I owe the pleasure today, Joe?" Abe asked.

"Abe, let's talk. The short story is, you've pissed off the police and they're fixing to arrest you one way or another."

"Well, I appreciate you warning me. Not sure how they're going to do that. I stay clear from anything that's not kosher."

Joe explained the big problem heroin was causing in the city and the pressure being put on the mayor to make something happen. Because he wanted to get Abe's reaction to the problem first, he stopped short of talking about what Connor wanted them to do.

"Fucking Rothstein! I pleaded with him not to do this because it'd endanger our other businesses. Moishe liked to use the word *finesse*. Rothstein uses the term *strategic*. He said the drugs were important to get established to hedge our bets on Prohibition. Well, I can put the brakes on this and dry up the supply, at least in Newark. Rothstein will listen to me, at least for a while. It'll take some time, but robberies should come down as the coloreds move to Orange where the wops are selling it."

Joe reflected for a moment on how this might impact his family, pulling out a pack of cigarettes and offering one to Abe as he mused. "But that won't be enough. The public wants an arrest, someone to blame. That someone's you."

"I know you just made detective. How d'you know about this?"

"My partner and I have been instructed to come up with a plan to get you arrested. This'll go a long way toward showing the public the police aren't just sitting on their asses."

Abe became silent and nervously started fiddling with the papers on his desk. He then took out the last cigarette from a pack, which he immediately crumpled into a small ball. He stood up and threw it as hard as he could against the back wall. "So, I gotta be the scapegoat."

"Well, if my partner and I don't get this done, it's gonna be a lot worse. Somebody else will stage a raid and plant some heroin in your office. You'll do major time for that."

"So what's your idea?"

"How about catching you with some booze at one of your warehouses? You can even stage it so that not much of it gets confiscated. They arrest you and you're out on bail that day. If convicted, maybe you do a little time. A few months at most. Not years."

"Joe, you continue to be my guardian angel."

The comment caught Joe the wrong way. The main reason he'd come to see Abe was to avoid doing anything illegal. In addition, he was angry. Obviously, Abe was rolling in dough. Did he really need to get involved in selling heroin?

"Guardian angel? I'm protecting my ass because I want nothing to do with planting evidence on anybody. I've always thought that deep down, you were a good guy. Now you're hep to all the awful shit with the heroin business. You gotta get it off the street *today*."

"You're right. Haven't thought about what the dope's doing to anybody. I'll be straight with Rothstein about it and maybe he can talk some sense into his Italian friends. Remember, without supply, there're going to be some crazy people running around. It'll get worse before it gets better."

"Are you in?"

"Give me some time to talk to Steinberg and have everything ready at the warehouse. I'll contact you about when the raid should be."

‡

After he'd met with Abe, Joe decided he had to confide in Carmine and tell him the story of why he had a connection to one of the biggest mob bosses in the area. He did not want his mentor to think he was in his pocket. Joe got to work early the next morning and asked Carmine to join him in the interrogation room.

"Okay, tell me about this plan of yours, Joe."

"I met Livosky when I worked in the jail. He was on the fast track to getting fried for killing a cop. That cop was my father. Found out he was framed, and I helped him beat the rap."

Carmine almost jumped out of his chair. His expression was one of complete disbelief. "Whoa, wait a second. You went to see this gangster?"

Joe understood. Carmine was going to retire soon and wanted to leave with his head held high. He didn't want the stench of any controversy surrounding him. In a reassuring manner, he said "I knew he'd listen. He agreed that he'd stop selling dope in Newark and take the fall in a warehouse with some booze. He wasn't thrilled at first, but now he's jake with the plan. Best part is, we're not involved in planting evidence or doing anything illegal."

"Well, Joe, I hate to break this to you, but what you did was not too kosher. Just seems a little too easy. You swear to me what you told me is true? I can't have this backfire on me, not this close to retirement."

Joe knew Carmine was anxious because they had only been working together a short time, unable to build the trust which partners develop over years. "Carmine, you're a good cop. Trust your instincts. I'm not on the take from Livosky. I helped him because I knew my father wouldn't want to see an innocent man go to the chair for his murder. Abe's a criminal, not a monster. I promise this won't backfire on either of us."

Carmine took a handkerchief from his pocket and wiped his brow. He scanned the room and ceiling as if he was searching for a fly to swat. He finally stopped, lit a cigarette, and looked Joe directly in the eyes. "I needed to hear that. I believe you, kid. Let's do it your way."

‡

Upon hearing from Abe a week later, Joe notified the police sergeant of the Fourth Precinct that he had received a tip from an informant, and they needed to raid a small warehouse on Broome Street to enforce the Volstead Act. Four police cars appeared at the scene and arrested Abe Livosky and two of his associates. The police seized and destroyed about fifty cases of Canadian whiskey. Livosky's attorney posted bail the same evening, and all three men spent the night at home.

Lieutenant Connor called Joe and Carmine into his office a day after the arrest. He patted them both on the back as they took a seat. "Good work, men. I'd have loved to catch this son of a bitch with drugs, but this isn't bad. It happened quickly, which is just as important. All the papers are posting his picture and writing about his alleged association with other rackets. The mayor is thrilled."

"I used an old informant of mine who had a personal grudge against Livosky," Joe explained. "He let me know he'd be there, as it was part of his weekly routine."

"I had my doubts when Bradley spoke to me about taking you on, since your sum of police experience was not that great. Detective O'Mara, I have to tell you, I'm quite impressed."

‡

They convicted Abe Livosky and his two associates at a trial held two months after the arrest. A sympathetic judge sentenced the men to just one month's incarceration at the Essex County Jail.

Word got around that the local mob businesses were jeopardizing their largest moneymaker by selling heroin, and they placed a moratorium of sorts on such sales. Eventually, the crime rate fell to more standard historic levels.

CHAPTER 25

FRANK, JEFFREY, AND JASMINE

As soon as Carmine retired, Lieutenant Connor began assigning Joe to a variety of cases, which were typically more complex than the standard investigations of thefts, burglaries, and assaults that crossed the precinct desk. Joe worked over ten hours a day, and on most Saturdays, he would come into the office until about two in the afternoon to keep up with the paperwork required for the cases in his file. He still felt significant resentment aimed at him in the department, particularly from the uniformed police. When he asked for information or a favor like the other detectives would, there was always an excuse, never a helping hand. Detectives in his area started calling him "Golden," resenting what they perceived as his golden-boy status with the lieutenant.

After a busy morning investigating a break-in at a doctor's office on Mount Prospect Avenue, Joe figured he could take a brief break before he started in on the paperwork that was piling up on his desk. Because of his distance from the lieutenant's office, he didn't notice the door opening.

Standing in the doorway, Connor called out, "Detective O'Mara, I would like to see you right now."

Joe stubbed out the cigarette he had been smoking, closed his file, and made his way over to a chorus of smooching noises. As he entered the office, shutting the door behind him, Joe thought about the day when one of these jokers would need something from him.

"Thank you, Detective. I have an immediate matter which'll require your full attention."

"Sir, I've got six active cases at the moment. Should I just stop working on them?"

"Yes, you'll bring your case files to me. I'm going to reassign them. The matter which I'm going to discuss with you has to be kept under wraps. I'm not blind to the fact that the other detectives haven't accepted you as one of the boys yet. That's the reason I've chosen you for this investigation."

Joe was wary of Connor, to say the least. At that moment, he decided that if Connor suggested he engage in some activity which could be considered illegal, Joe would challenge his superior to tell him how he could deliver on the request *legally*.

"The mayor of Jersey City, Frank Hammond is a powerful man well beyond the confines of his city. As I'm an old high school friend of his from our days at St. Peter's, he's requested a personal meeting. I'll warn you, Frank is very straitlaced, so watch the swearing—and absolutely no smoking in his office. I'll drive today, as city hall is close to where I used to go to school."

‡

After they'd waited a short time in the reception area, a door opened, and a tall, thin gentleman appeared with his pocket watch in hand. He was rather stern faced, balding, and dressed in an old-fashioned black suit.

"Francis, it's so good to see you. It's been way too long."

"Mayor, yes, it has been. Let me introduce the man who'll run the investigation. This is Joe O'Mara. He was the lead detective on the big Livosky arrest some months back."

"Oh, I see. Pleased to meet you. Come inside, where we can speak privately."

The trio walked back into what Joe thought looked more like a room in a palace than a mayor's office. The walls were painted a deep shade of red and decorated with rather large paintings with ornate gold framing. Mayor Hammond led them to a beautiful mahogany table and seated himself at the head. Perhaps it was just his imagination, but Joe felt that the mayor's chair placed him well above his two guests. The two policemen waited for him to begin.

"As much as this pains me to talk about, it's important that we get started. First, I need you to promise me you will only discuss this matter with me. As you will learn today, everything is of a highly sensitive nature, and if it got out into the papers, it could do serious damage to my reputation. Do I have your word, Detective O'Mara?"

"Yes, Mayor Hammond. You have my word."

"Good. Thank you."

Rather than getting into the details of the matter, the mayor gazed at Joe, and in a harsh tone said, "Rest assured that if this gets out and I can trace it back to you, your career will be ruined, and you'll have trouble finding work of any kind."

Joe felt he had already given his word and didn't need to acknowledge the comment. Realizing that the mayor was a bully by nature, he sat and waited without expression until Hammond was ready to begin.

Clearing his throat several times, Hammond opened a large envelope that had been sitting on the table and passed over a set of photographs and a coroner's report to the two men. A Newark Office of the Coroner stamp was on each of them. "I have the good fortune of knowing many people in the area. Thank goodness the head coroner of the city of Newark and I go way back. I got a call from him to come down to his office urgently. The person you see in those pictures is my youngest son, Jeffrey, whom the coroner recognized."

The mayor paused, taking a handkerchief to wipe his sweating brow. "I want you to investigate the murder of my son and find out who was responsible. It's important I alone know who did this. Your discretion in this matter is required because of the nature of these pictures and the murder. This cannot get out in the news."

Joe and Lieutenant Connor began looking at the photos. At first, Joe thought he was looking at a very pretty young woman, wearing a great deal of makeup and the short, bobbed hair of a flapper, until he saw the pictures where the wig and makeup had been removed. It was remarkable to Joe how easily the mayor's son could pass himself off as a woman.

He skimmed through the coroner's report to find out what the cause of death was. "Mayor Hammond," he began, "you said he had been killed. It says in the report it's from a lethal injection of heroin. What gives you suspicion it was murder?"

"My son was not a drug addict. If you look further in the report, you'll see there was no evidence of any other needle marks on his body. You can speak to the coroner yourself, but that is highly unusual for someone who dies of an overdose."

Connor jumped in. "So, this is the primary reason you suspect foul play?"

Barely acknowledging his former high school chum's question, the mayor cleared his throat again. "Let me get into a few more details about Jeffrey. He was a very talented young man. He picked up the French language on his own and developed a fascination for art, specifically art history. His dream in life was to go to France to study. Because of the war, he couldn't realize that wish and instead attended Yale. He transferred to the Sorbonne in 1920 to finish out his final two years. Jeffrey was always a quiet young man, very serious and soft-spoken. Those two years in Paris changed him. He became much more social and far more independent. He continued to live at home but would spend considerable time away. I had many arguments with him about getting serious about his life and starting a career. My wife intervened and said Jeffrey needed some time to find his way, just like so many other young men his age. I reluctantly agreed."

Pouring a drink of water from the pitcher on the table, the mayor continued in a distressed tone. "After I identified him, I made arrangements for the body to be picked up and brought to Jersey City. There'll be a wake and a funeral during the coming days. The cause of death in the obituary will be leukemia . . . and that is the way it will stay."

‡

Lieutenant Connor suggested Joe work as a private investigator rather than show his badge when questioning people in public. He provided him with a hundred dollars to use for getting information and assured him that more could be obtained if necessary.

The obvious place to start was at the coroner's office. Joe needed to confirm what the mayor had alleged regarding the overdose and get information on exactly where they'd found the body. He followed the mayor's instructions and only spoke with the head coroner, who told him an anonymous phone call to the hospital had led to the discovery of the body in an apartment on Chapel Court. When police arrived at the scene and discovered the body, they notified the coroner's office.

The next step was not as apparent to Joe, because he really knew nothing about female impersonators or homosexuals. While he was growing up, all of this had been quite taboo and never talked about. Now he knew for a fact there were a few speakeasy clubs sprinkled throughout the city that featured female impersonators as entertainers.

After visiting two establishments, Joe found that the going rate to buy his way in was ten dollars. Once inside, he noticed a rather well-dressed clientele of couples there to drink, dance, and enjoy themselves. He tried speaking to the female impersonators and anyone who worked at the place by showing a cropped version of the coroner's photo of Jeffrey Hammond as a woman. Given Jeffrey's social standing, he thought it would be smart to start with these high-class establishments first. However, this approach did not yield any leads, as no one recognized the victim.

Next, he tried The Bohemian on Halsey Street, attempting something different at the front door this time. Instead of waving money as a first step, Joe introduced himself and showed the picture of Jeffrey.

"Oh my goodness. That's Jasmine. We were wondering where the girl had disappeared to. This is terrible news." The tall, colored, heavy-set female impersonator grabbed Joe by the hand and took him inside the club. "Let me get somebody to cover at the door, and then I'll come back and talk to you. I'm Ruby. I was one of Jasmine's closest friends."

"If you knew Susie, like I know Susie . . . Oh, oh, what a girl," sang a very tall colored female figure dressed in a white gown. She was standing in front of a ten-piece band dressed in black tuxedos. Each member wore red cloth devil's horns on their head, complementing their formal attire. Instead of the upbeat tempo that Joe was used to for this song, they played it adagio so that it sounded more like a torch song, taking advantage of the singer's rich, soulful voice.

Sitting at the table waiting for Ruby to return, Joe looked at the dance floor in amazement. He noticed men dressed like women. Unlike Jeffrey, some had facial hair that gave them away. In contrast, there were women who wore fake facial hair and dressed like men. Couples were switching partners, and some just danced to the music by themselves. Joe had been to parties and some clubs over the years, but had never seen anything close to this before.

"Sorry, baby. I got back here as quick as I could. Were you one of her boyfriends? I knew her type, and boy, you are it." Ruby drank from her champagne glass and placed a cigarette in a holder. Joe lit it and then his own.

"No, Ruby. My name's Joe. I'm a dick working for someone who wants to understand what happened."

"I'm guessing it's her parents. Jasmine was drunk one night and told me her father was a very important man, but she couldn't tell me who."

Joe paused for a moment, thinking it wise to neither confirm nor deny this and just proceed with his questions. "The cause of death was an overdose of heroin. Were you aware of her doing drugs?"

"Jasmine was a smart girl. We did our share of drinking together, but she'd never put a needle in her arm. We smoked some hashish, and she liked to get a little crazy with cocaine, but she'd never do heroin." Ruby paused for a moment, grabbing Joe's hand. "Where are my manners? Let me get you a drink. What do you like?"

"Jameson or Bushmills neat, if you got it?"

"We've got both. I'll be right back." When Ruby returned, she pulled her chair closer to Joe's and put her hand on his leg. Considering she was going to be a wealth of information for him, Joe decided he would play along.

"You mentioned Jasmine had boyfriends. Tell me more."

"Jasmine was a party girl. Once she got to know you and liked you, she wanted to have sex with you. She'd sleep with both men and women. She preferred men, though . . . just like I do. There's this mulatto boxer she used to see fight who was her main boyfriend."

Joe immediately thought of a very light-skinned heavyweight named Eddy Price. "Was this boxer jealous and possibly—"

"Stop right there. Eddy's a brute in the ring, but he's the gentlest soul on earth. He knew all about Jasmine's appetite for love. I can tell you that firsthand, as we've had a ménage à trois on more than one occasion."

"Do you know anyone who wanted to hurt her?"

Ruby got visibly emotional for a moment. "I can't. She was so much fun. Made the people around her feel good. I can't imagine what monster did this to her. You find them and make them pay."

"Thanks, Ruby. You've been really helpful. Next, I'm going to see Eddy Price. If you see him, please clue him in that I'm just looking for information. I'd appreciate it."

"Joe, you're a nice man. Thanks for playing along and treating me like a lady. You've probably got a wife and kids."

Joe winked at Ruby as he got up and walked out of the club.

On his drive back to Orange, Joe thought about the evening and how he could possibly even begin to tell the story to Marty. In his time as a policeman and detective, Joe had experienced different kinds of human behavior at its worst. Tonight, he'd observed a different kind of human behavior, but there was no crime. All the people at the club were having a great time and doing whatever pleased them. Unlike the upscale speakeasies, where the only colored people worked as servers or performers, white and colored people were completely mixed at The Bohemian, and not thinking twice about it.

When Joe got home, no one was up, so he crawled into bed, trying not to wake his wife. It did not take long for him to fall asleep.

‡

Joe attended Eddy Price's next fight, a three-round knockout of a vastly undermatched opponent. He waited patiently at the back door of Laurel Garden Arena, where the fighters would leave after cleaning up in the locker room, until Eddy arrived. Seeing the boxer come out, he walked up to him and said, "That was one helluva fight, Eddy."

"Thanks, appreciate it."

"Have a few minutes? I need to speak to you. My name is Joe. I'm a private dick."

"I've been expecting you. Let's head back inside and find a place to talk."

The pair took a seat in the emptied arena about twenty rows back, looking ahead at the ring. This was as private a place as any to ask questions. "Thanks for taking the time to speak with me. I understand you were close friends with Jasmine."

"Hey, listen. You don't need to beat around the bush with me. I'm not ashamed of what I am. I don't want you to spread it around town, as it'd hurt my career, but I won't apologize for it."

"Okay, got it. How long did you know Jasmine?"

Eddy spoke eloquently as he told the story of how he had met Jeffrey while attending Yale. Eddy was the son of a former ambassador to Jamaica who'd fallen in love with a negro woman and married her. He'd been able to attend Yale despite his race because his father was an alumnus and had connections to President Taft. Jeffrey, a shy, lonely boy, had gravitated toward the mulatto boxer with no friends, and eventually they became lovers. When Jeffrey went to Paris, it broke Eddy's heart. Upon his return from France, he'd been a completely changed person.

All the information Eddy provided was consistent with the story the mayor had told. Joe could tell Jeffrey's boyfriend was quite upset when speaking about him, but decided to just ask questions directly rather than trying to be delicate. "I understand you knew Jasmine had more than a few lovers."

"Yes, I did. It was a bit of a sore point with me, as I wanted him to want me exclusively. However, the person who returned from Paris was so joyful and always the center of attention and attracted so many interesting people. I just went with it and enjoyed myself."

"I understand Jasmine would come to your boxing matches. Did people know she was your girlfriend?"

"Absolutely everyone knew he was my *girlfriend*. Of course, there were people who disapproved of us being together, but that was only because of my color. She explained so persuasively that people in Paris were colorblind and saw people for who they were inside. As far as I know, everyone who met her thought she was a woman."

This was not a surprise to Joe, thinking back to the set of pictures. "So no one knew she was really Jeffrey Hammond, the son of the mayor of Jersey City?"

"Jasmine came to visit me as Jeffrey a few times. He attended a match with his father and sat in the front row, right in back of my corner. He was making a spectacle of himself by cheering me on, his voice rising above everyone else's. My manager noticed him and put two and two together. He made a comment later that night that I needed to keep my dirty little secret under wraps or it'd destroy my career."

"Do you think your manager could be involved in hurting her?"

"Joe, I've thought about it, but I'd have to say no. I know your next question. Would he have told anybody else? Maybe."

"Right, keep going."

"Only thought I have is he might have mentioned it to Tony. I have an excellent sponsor who's been very generous to me. Galvano Construction is the company, and Tony Galvano is the head of the firm. They're involved in quite a few state projects for roadworks. Tony's a former boxer. He treats me really well, and I'm grateful for that. I don't ask questions, as I don't need to know any more."

This was the lead Joe had been looking for. He knew firsthand that organized crime, specifically the Italian mob, controlled some construction companies bidding for roadworks and other big projects.

"Thanks for being honest and sharing all you did. I'm sorry things ended this way for Jasmine. Please know I won't be telling anybody anything about you—other than that I think you're a great fighter."

"Thanks, Joe. I've had a rough time dealing with his death. Good luck finding out who did this."

‡

Joe had not been reporting in at the precinct. He knew Connor was usually the first one to get to work in the morning and decided to catch him before the rest of the detectives started filling their desks. His door was open, and Joe walked in without knocking.

"Lieutenant, I have a few questions to ask you about Mayor Hammond."

"Detective, I hope you're not going down the proverbial rabbit hole. Are we making progress so I can report back to the mayor?"

"Yes. I've talked to several of Jeffrey Hammond's close friends and have developed a few theories."

"Well, tell me what you have."

Joe had expected there would be some resistance from the lieutenant regarding some of the facts that needed to be presented. He was cautious about how he communicated what he'd found, but he debriefed Connor on the information he'd gotten from the interviews.

"So, what you are saying is Jeffrey Hammond was a fairy masquerading as a woman, sleeping with anyone he met. You didn't mention animals—any animals in there, Detective? I expected more from you than this. How can I share this with Mayor Hammond?"

Joe had foreseen the man might react this way and listened to the tirade calmly before responding. "Lieutenant, you didn't instruct me to come up with bullshit. The mayor wanted the straight story. Finding out about Jeffrey Hammond's other life is the only way to get that."

"Detective, forgive my outburst. I'm just expecting the conversation we'll have with Mayor Hammond. He's just so conservative. I'm positive he'll have a hard time accepting the facts about his son."

Joe thought back to Carmine's special name for Connor. "Weasel" sure fit him well. The lieutenant was quick to criticize but offered no suggestions as to how to get a result that was more acceptable. This was typical of what Joe has observed from him.

"I'll leave you to figure out how we break the news to Mayor Hammond," he said. "I think I'm close to something here but need information to confirm. I think you mentioned the mayor's a powerful man in this entire area. You think he has enemies?"

"Detective, any man of power is going to have enemies. Frank Hammond has plenty. However, most of his enemies are too scared to lift a finger against him."

"If the coroner hadn't been a good friend of the mayor's, someone would've likely identified the body. The newspapers would be involved, and a lot of mud would've been slung at Mayor Hammond," said Joe.

"Yes, I see where you're going with this. I agree someone could want to kill Jeffrey to discredit his father."

"The people I've talked to made me believe he was very well-liked in his Jasmine life. He didn't hide the fact he was with many lovers, so I've ruled out jealousy as a motive for the time being. I've got one other lead I need to explore. Can you get me access to construction bids for roadworks in this area for the past two years?"

"Detective, that'd be like knowingly going into a pit of rattlesnakes. You could get out without getting bit, but no one in his right mind should go in there in the first place."

"I'll take that as a no."

Joe knew he was on his own with this investigation. He thanked the lieutenant for speaking with him, then went to his desk to plan his next steps.

‡

Joe's initial impulse to get more information on Galvano Construction and any potential ties to the mob was to go see Abe Livosky and pick his brain. However, he wasn't sure Abe would be knowledgeable about this, and he really wanted to keep his distance from him if at all possible. Joe had heard that Abe had recently moved out of the city into a fancy gated house in West Orange.

Instead, his brother might be a good place to start. Tom's had become one of the top funeral homes in the area, and it seemed like he knew everyone.

Joe made an early night of it because he was spending so much time on this case. He returned right after the kids got home from school and took them over to Tom's house. He knew his mother would be overjoyed to see her grandchildren, and Marty would appreciate having a break.

"Hi, Mom. I thought I'd bring the kids over to see you. I wanted to chat with Tom."

Joe Junior and Gladys ran into the open arms of their grandmother. "It's always a good time to bring these children over. Your little boy is the spitting image of Tom at that age. I can't quite figure who little Gladys looks like yet, but she sure is my cute cuddle kitten."

"Do I hear correctly that my brother is paying me a visit?" said Tom, walking to the front vestibule. In a cheeky tone, he proclaimed, "I think today is the day he'll tell me he's finished with this detective work and can now come to work with me!"

"Brother, I've been working some long days. Marty is none too happy with me, but I'm not at that point yet. I actually wanted to get your thoughts on a few things."

"Of course. Let's move into the parlor."

The two men left their mother and went into the next room. Joe made note of all the fine furnishings here, a contrast to the eclectic group of shabby furniture in his apartment. Yes, Tom was doing really well.

"Joe, what'd you want to talk about?"

"I'm working on a rather odd case. I'd love to give you more details, but I can't. Do you know anything about Mayor Frank Hammond of Jersey City?"

"I've never met the man. I know that his son recently passed from leukemia. Sad story, someone so young."

"Heard he's a pretty powerful guy and has his hands in everything."

Joe watched his brother's mood darken as he talked about the shady practices that Jersey City had instituted regarding funeral homes, despite the fact that there were no formal regulations. Tom said that the funeral directors were furious at Hammond because inspections conducted by his cronies always found fault, which warranted a fine. If there was resistance to paying, they shut down the homes.

Taking all of his brother's comments in, Joe asked, "Would you expect he is doing similar things in building projects?"

"Joe, you know we're all Republicans because our father loved Teddy Roosevelt and our mother hated Wilson for getting us into the war. It's not because Hammond is a Democrat, but from what I've heard, he's the most crooked politician in New Jersey, and that's saying a lot. I'd be shocked if he wasn't involved in big building contracts and benefiting from it."

"Thanks, that's really helpful. Do you know Tony Galvano?"

"Sure do. Helluva nice guy. I know him through our brother. John told me Tony helps keep his parish afloat and is very active in supporting the orphanage."

"So he's clean? No mob connections?"

"I didn't say that. I don't know. I'd assume he probably has to go through the same shit most businesses do around here, paying protection money to somebody."

‡

Joe firmly believed Frank Hammond had screwed someone out of a substantial amount of money. This person must've been so infuriated when they learned about his son's dual life that they murdered him and had his secret identity exposed to the mayor. After all, it was only a bit of luck that had actually prevented the affair from becoming public.

Now how was he going to establish who was responsible among so many people who could have that motive? First things first, it was important to determine who'd been with Jeffrey on the night he died. Joe decided he should go back to The Bohemian.

When he arrived, he was happy to see find Ruby checking patrons in. She looked up and saw Joe, a smile flashing across her face. "Darlin', so nice to see you again. Making any progress on the case?"

"Yes and no, Ruby. Got to ask you a few more questions."

"Of course. Come inside with me and you can ask me anything. Bushmills, neat, wasn't it?" Joe nodded and followed Ruby inside. It was 9 p.m., right before the place got packed. The band had just started warming up.

"Sorry for the wait, Joe," Ruby said when she returned a couple of minutes later. "What do you need to know?"

"Was Jasmine here the night she died?"

"Yes, that's easy to answer. She was here every night unless she was with Eddy."

"Was she with anyone that night?"

"I don't remember exactly if it was that night. She had a fling with one of the regulars just before she died. Good chance she might've been with Lillian that night. Lillian is a woman. She's slept with all the girls that work here. Told me she doesn't like actual women . . . Can't get enough of that you-know-what."

"Is she here?"

"Yes, she's the blond sitting in the corner smoking a cigarette and drinking champagne."

"I'm going to go over and ask her a few questions."

"Joe, if you go over there and say that, she won't tell you a damn thing. Tell her you want to fuck the best-looking girl in The Bohemian, and she'll open right up."

"Thanks, Ruby."

Joe approached the woman, who was doing her best to look as if she hadn't noticed him. He asked innocently, "Mind if I join you?"

She'd been far more attractive from a distance. Up close, he saw that she had applied an excessive amount of makeup, and it hadn't been carefully done. She had long white gloves, and it looked like she had slept a night or two in her red flapper-style dress. Following Ruby's advice, he repeated the recommended opening line to Lillian.

"You must be desperate, Mr. I look terrible. Do you really want to fuck me?"

"I noticed you from across the room. I'd like to get to know you. You seem on edge and upset."

"I am. I want to be around people . . . music. Lotsa noise." Lillian pulled out another cigarette, which Joe lit for her. She gave the impression of being sedated. It appeared the makeup had been used to cover up her red eyes, which had been doing a lot of crying.

"Why are you so down?"

"One of my best friends died and . . . it was my fault."

"Oh, that's terrible. Let me get some champagne for you." Joe wanted to ask more questions immediately, but he realized that if he didn't progress slowly, she would clam up.

The champagne came with two glasses. Joe poured them each one and waited a few minutes before proceeding. "It helps to talk about things sometimes. Maybe it'll help if you tell me about it."

"You're sweet and very good-looking. Under normal circumstances, we'd be in bed right now and I'd be riding you like a cowgirl."

Joe acknowledged the comment with a smile. He waited, thinking it best to let Lillian continue at her own pace. She finished the glass of champagne and poured herself another.

"The friend I mentioned was my favorite lover. I had never met someone as wild at heart as I am. We would spend hours together and never say a word. We smoked opium and snorted cocaine together, and it made our sex . . . indescribable. I brought the heroin to our bed, suggested we only try it once, just to experience it. We did, and now my beautiful lover is gone."

"Your friend was Jasmine?"

"Yes, did she know you?"

Joe felt it was best to lie and nodded his head.

"It happened so quickly. My head was in the clouds, and I panicked. I ran from the apartment and called the hospital, but I knew she was dead when I left."

‡

After leaving The Bohemian, Joe needed some time to think things through before he went home. He went to his car and sat there, staring through the windshield at a brick wall. Things came quickly. He immediately decided telling the complete truth wasn't an option. Neither Connor nor Hammond would want to hear about Jasmine and the way she had lived. If he fingered Lillian and said that she was the person who'd introduced Jasmine to heroin, Hammond would consider it murder even though it had clearly been an accident. If he concocted a story in line with what both of them wanted to hear, perhaps he could make this all go away. Of course, Joe had no evidence.

‡

Joe woke up the following morning planning to see Connor early despite being thoroughly exhausted. The weasel's response would be predictable. However, he felt apprehension about meeting with Hammond, since odds were even whether he would ask Joe to drop the investigation or ask for proof and ultimately a scapegoat.

Joe knocked on Connor's office door and took a seat after being told to come in.

"What is it, Detective?"

"Lieutenant Connor, I'd like to conclude the investigation. I'm afraid more digging and interviews will open up the possibility of this whole affair becoming public."

"Well, we don't want that. What have you learned?"

"The facts point to a mob-backed contractor who was angry over the loss of a construction contract and blamed Mayor Hammond. To retaliate, they cooked up a scheme where they kidnapped Jeffrey, forced him to dress like a woman, and then gave him a lethal dose of heroin. Only the mob could do something so horrible to discredit the mayor."

"Excellent work, Detective. Would you mind paying a visit to Mayor Hammond this afternoon? I won't be able to join you."

Fully having expected Connor to worm his way out of making the trip with him, Joe replied, "Not at all, Lieutenant."

‡

Joe knew that he would have to put on an even better act to convince the mayor. Connor let Joe bring the news to Hammond because he had nothing to lose, regardless of the outcome. If Hammond became irate after the meeting, Connor could blame Joe and his poor detective work.

Joe nervously sat in the chair outside the mayor's office and waited to be called in. Once settled at the big mahogany table, Hammond began,

"Detective O'Mara, thank you for coming. Please brief me on what you've found."

"Mayor Hammond, please accept my condolences for your loss. I have two children of my own. I understand the pain you and your wife must be going through."

Joe felt the mayor relax a bit as Hammond shrugged his shoulders and mouthed *thank you.*

"Mayor, the first thing that I did in my investigation was to validate your assumption of foul play. I confirmed your son was not a drug addict. Therefore, we assume it wasn't an accident, and he didn't take his own life."

The mayor's mood shifted back to one of impatience. "Yes, Detective, that's hardly new ground."

"With some investigation, I was able to find places your son used to frequent and some people who knew him well. I showed them the picture of him dressed as a woman, and it surprised them. The people I spoke with all liked Jeffrey and mentioned he had quite a few romances with women. He also went by the last name of Hall to protect his true identity."

"I see. It's comforting to know he wasn't one of those fairies. So no one knew he was my son?"

"Not the people I talked with."

"Good. Proceed."

"I ruled out Jeffrey being killed by a jealous boyfriend, for example. There would be no reason for him to be found dead dressed like a woman. The only thing that makes sense is for someone to have killed Jeffrey knowing his true identity and looking to discredit or seek some kind of revenge on you."

"I see."

"Who would have such a motive and be capable of committing such a terrible crime? My first thought went to city works projects, since there's a lot of money at stake and, as the mayor, they might hold you accountable for decisions. Organized crime is connected with quite a few of these companies, and they can be quite brutal in their methods. I asked Lieutenant Connor if I could access to some recent project bids in the Newark and Jersey City area to identify a short list of potential suspects. He told me this wouldn't be possible."

A long period of silence ensued, broken only by Mayor Hammond tapping a pencil against his desk. Joe attempted to stay as calm as possible, trying not to look anxious.

"Detective, you did exactly what I asked you to do. You conducted this investigation hush-hush at my direction, which placed limitations on you. As much as I'd dearly love to find out who did this to my son, I know it won't bring him back to life, and we run a risk of having mud thrown on his legacy and my office. I think your instincts are probably correct about where to look first, but I sincerely believe it'll do more harm than good to my family to proceed any further. Please consider this investigation closed unless you hear otherwise from me."

"Thank you, Mayor Hammond. I'll let Lieutenant Connor know."

Joe left the office feeling better than if he had just won a big wager. He could drop this case and not create a trail to person who had been involved in an accidental death. His strategy for handling the mayor had depended on the fact that Hammond was dirty. Joe wondered if he even cared about his son or if all he wanted was revenge.

CHAPTER 26

ROCK BOTTOM

The daily stench of the factories, which bellowed smoke into the skies of Newark and its surrounding area, was replaced with despair. Despair emanated from every face in the soup kitchen lines and from legions of laid-off workers lining the streets, holding signs begging for work of any kind. Many men wore their army uniforms from the Great War, perhaps as a reminder that if they'd survived that horror, they could persevere through this one. It was 1931, and the Great Depression was in its second year. There was no end in sight.

‡

In the years leading up to the Great Crash in 1929, Joe had been doing well in his career and even had two younger detectives reporting to him. This helped lighten his workload so he could spend more time with the family and take frequent trips to Asbury Park to enjoy the amusements, ocean, and beach. Joe suppressed his desire to gamble, taking part of the money from his paycheck every month and depositing it at Essex & Hudson County Savings and Loan, which was a few doors down from the precinct. Remembering Martha's comments about being kept in the dark about money, he made sure she knew where he kept the passbook. They built a nice little nest egg they could use to buy their own home in the next few years. Joe was proud of the fact that he was doing things his way without seeking help from anyone.

Things happened so quickly in October 1929. The stock market crashed. People became afraid for their money and tried to take it out of the banks, causing a run on funds that lead to the closure of many institutions. The Savings and Loan where Joe banked went under in early 1930. He visited it frequently, hoping to find the doors open so he too could withdraw his money. Finally, one day there was a note on the door explaining that the institution was permanently closed and that all deposited funds were now lost. With a heavy heart, Joe went home to break the news to his wife. Their plans for buying a house had just gone up in smoke.

"Marty, our money's gone. The bank shut its doors permanently. They put a note on the door apologizing, but it's all gone."

"What are we going to do?"

"Marty, as bad as this is, I'm going to keep my job. I guess the city'll have to do some cutting back, but I'm pretty sure they won't touch the police."

‡

Almost as quickly as the financial institutions melted down, Joe dug himself a hole by starting to gamble again. The compulsion took hold of him, and he made one poor bet after another in April and May 1930, until the vig, the interest he had to pay to the bookies, cut his salary by over a half.

At first, Joe went to his brother help, but soon realized Tom's business was hurting as well. As he put it, "People are still dying, they just can't pay for it anymore."

After that, Joe started juggling their bills, soon owing money to just about everyone in town. He started making partial payments and then no rent payments. When the landlords' patience ran out, the O'Mara family began bouncing from place to place, trying to stay in the area so the children could attend the same school. Martha tried to keep things positive for their sake, but when she had to move into this dingy apartment on Dodd Street in Orange, she lost her temper.

Tears streamed down her face as she yelled at her husband in a fit of rage, "This is the absolute last place I'm going to move to with you. I feel like we're a bunch of gypsies floating around town because we can't pay the rent. The kids aren't in one place long enough to make any friends. Your brother's offered to help, but you're too damn proud to take any more money from him. My next move will be back to Harrison with the kids."

Martha rarely got angry. She had endless patience with and was always encouraging the children, and she never complained about having to make do with lesser things. Joe knew he deserved every second of her rage. However, her ultimatum was a tremendous jolt to his psyche. He realized he had no choice but to tell her everything.

Grimacing as if he was going to choke on his words, he whispered, "Marty, I screwed up. I don't want you to leave. That'd break me."

Joe wanted a reaction from his wife. She was standing there looking away from him and appeared to be in deep thought. When she finally turned toward him, it was obvious her fury had subsided. She said, "You know, if I left, I'd still love you. I don't want to leave. I want to stay and be your wife. How do we fix this?"

"I don't know. I dug myself a deep hole by trying to win back the money we lost at the bank. I made one bonehead bet after another. Right now, I got everyone in town paid off except for the bloodsucking bookies. I owe them just under eight thousand dollars, which is more than fifty a week in interest."

"I knew you had to be gambling. It was the only thing that made sense to me. I wanted you to come to me and tell me. You're a stubborn, prideful ass sometimes." Marty walked over and kissed him on the cheek.

Joe's heavy mental burden got lighter as he talked things through with his wife. Usually reluctant to share his innermost feelings, today he wanted to keep going and lay bare his soul. He wanted Marty to know everything. "When I'm wrong or screw up, I don't like to admit it, not even to you . . . I can't just gamble a little like most people. Either I stop completely, or this other part of me just takes over. All I can think about is how the next bet is going to solve the problem."

Joe knew there was plenty of work they needed to do to figure things out together, so with the kids off at school, he went down to the drugstore to call out sick. When he returned, Marty was at the kitchen table, scribbling down figures on paper with a cigarette burning in the ashtray.

"Jeez, you look like an accountant," Joe told her.

He started off by explaining that in order to get the debt forgiven by the mob-backed bookies, he would need to do certain favors for them. The favors would get bigger with time. He adamantly stated that he'd did not want to be a dirty cop and be in anyone's pocket. Additionally, he wanted to maintain his distance from Abe Livosky, since the newly formed Internal Affairs had been investigating corruption on the police force.

The couple figured out how much money they could bring in if Marty went back to work and Joe took a second job fixing cars. When adding up the figure, they quickly realized their new earnings would hardly make a dent in their debts.

Martha collected all the papers they had been using to make calculations and put them in a neat pile. After lighting a cigarette and taking a drag, she looked squarely at her husband. "Who do you want me to ask, Tom or Abe? You and I both know that's the only way out of this."

Surprised by his wife's sharp tone, Joe struggled to answer. He eventually responded, "Neither."

"Then there is no other way out of this mess than move back to Harrison and hand over your paycheck to the mob every week. Whether you like it or not, I'm going to ask Abe. You came up with the plan to save his skin. I was an equal partner in getting him out."

Joe knew Marty was right. Maybe it would be better if she went in case his place in West Orange was under surveillance. "Okay," he finally said. "I don't think Abe will ask this, but if he does, I'm not doing him any favors."

Marty shot back quickly, "Joe, he's not gonna ask. What should I tell him when he asks why I'm here and not you?"

"Tell him I'm embarrassed about being a putz, as he would say, and ashamed that I put my family through hell. Tell him what I did, so he understands."

‡

Martha asked Margaret to be there when the kids got home from school, then went to the corner drugstore to look for Livosky in the phonebook. After finding the number, she called and, to her good fortune, was able to speak with Abe and request a meeting. From there, she got a cab to take her to the address on Mountain Avenue in West Orange.

"Marty, you're making my day," Abe said when she arrived. "It's such a pleasure to see you."

"Please forgive me if I slip and call you Ziggy. Joe's told me you only go by Abe now."

"Yes, but Abe remembers when he was Ziggy and how two people saved that young man's life. Abe wouldn't be here in this house if it wasn't for you and your husband. I'm a little curious why Joe's not with you today. I hope he's not mad at me."

"Abe, Joe's a little embarrassed because he said he's been such a putz."

Abe let out a loud laugh. "I knew I had some influence on him. What did he do?"

"We'd been saving money to buy a house. We lost everything when our bank failed. Joe had a hard time accepting that and started gambling to win it back. He dug himself quite a big hole we can't climb out of. He owes eight thousand dollars."

"Marty, can I let you in on a little secret?"

"What?"

"I knew this already. Not the exact amount, but I'm quite aware Joe is in too deep. Most of the people he owes money to work for me. Their bosses came and asked me what we should do about this deadbeat detective. I told them if anyone lays a glove on him, they'll have to answer to me personally."

Upon hearing this, Martha began to cry. She admitted to Abe that she'd finally figured out he must have been gambling, but never realized that he might actually get hurt.

"Marty, I'd never let anything happen to Joe. I figured out at some point he'd run out of options and have to come to me. I'm guessing that's the reason for your visit."

"Eight thousand dollars is so much. I feel terrible asking you."

"Marty, my driver is going to take you home with the full amount today. By the time Joe pays off all his gambling debts, I'd guess about half the money'll find its way back to my pocket. It's not a big deal. However, there's one condition."

"Abe, I know Joe doesn't want to be supplying—"

Abe interrupted her. "I want the both of you to be guests at my wedding."

"Congratulations," Martha told him. "I'm so happy for you. Who's the girl?"

Grinning from ear to ear, Abe went to get a picture and passed it to Martha.

"She's beautiful."

He took out a pack of cigarettes and offered her one, which she accepted. "It's a bit of a long story, so let me tell you about it."

"Please, go on. I'm going to accept your invitation."

"Marty, I don't know how much you know about what's going on in Germany these days."

"I read the German papers occasionally, and I know how bad things were there even before the Depression started. There seems to be a fight brewing between the Reds, this new group called the Nazis, and the existing government. My mother said she doesn't trust Hitler because he's Austrian. She thinks only Germans from Prussia are real Germans."

Abe became emotional as he started explaining the circumstances of his impending marriage. Coincidently, his family was from the same area of north central Europe that Martha's parents came from. His mother had stayed in touch with family and friends who had remained in the area, now part of Poland. She'd learned about a tragic event that befell a young Jewish family visiting the free city of Danzig on a shopping trip. Nazi brownshirts attacked the four of them, beating the husband so badly he eventually died from his wounds. When Abe's mother found out about their misfortune, she asked him if there was anything he could do to help. Moved by the sad story, Abe offered to bring the widow to the States and marry her and adopt her children. She immediately accepted.

Martha asked, "So you haven't met her?"

"It's just like the old days—an arranged marriage. Do you think I'm good-looking enough for her?" With a whimsical expression on his face, Abe stood up and twirled around, displaying his expensive gray suit.

"Abe, don't be silly. I'm sure that you'll get along wonderfully. The poor thing has been through so much. Give her some time and be patient."

"There's one other thing I want to tell you. Years ago, I offered Joe a job. He told me he couldn't take it because he was afraid of losing you . . .

because of the business I'm in. Joe is a putz with gambling, but he loves you with all his heart."

"I know that. I love him too."

"Now that I am going to be a husband and will have two children and hopefully some more of my own, I've been doing some thinking about this life I lead. Now's the time to invest in some legitimate businesses. I have a plan to quit and become a respectable business owner. What d'you think?"

"I'd love to see it happen."

"Maybe then, your husband would feel differently about being my partner. It'd do my heart proud to see your family in a home like this."

"Abe, you're making me cry again. Thank you so much for getting us out of this jam. Can I tell Joe about how you've been keeping him safe?"

"Marty, let that be our little secret. Do tell him about my plan to get out of the racket."

‡

Joe was sitting at the kitchen table, waiting for his wife to come home. He recalled the many times Abe had reminded him that he would help them whenever they needed it. Despite believing him, he was still anxious, but soon Marty walked through the door with a big smile on her face. She placed an envelope filled with money on the table and went to hug him. Joe asked how the meeting had gone, and she filled him in on everything except her little secret with Abe.

"I'm not going to dillydally with paying off the bookies," Joe told her when she was done. "It shouldn't take long, and then let's go see if we can get our old apartment back. I saw a sign on Miller's pharmacy the other day, and I think it's still vacant. I know how much you hate it here."

"Joe, do you really think Ron would let us move back? We left suddenly, and he was none too happy with us, as I remember."

"My dad rented that apartment from Ron's father well before I was born. The O'Maras have been good tenants and always paid on time until yours truly took over. I'm going to be straight with him and let him know it won't happen again. Having you with me will certainly help our chances."

"Thank you for trying. It'd be swell if we could move back. You know, we're in this together. Always remember that, and it's okay to admit you're wrong."

"Marty, you and the kids mean the world to me. When you told me you'd leave me, I got the jolt that I needed to get some sense through this dense Irish skull of mine."

After some initial reluctance, their previous landlord agreed to rent to Joe and Martha again. The three months' security and the fact that he hadn't been able to find new tenants since the O'Mara family left made his decision much easier.

CHAPTER 27

DE REGNO CAESARIS
VEL DEI?

The impact of the Great Depression was still in full force in 1932. Herbert Hoover was the Republican incumbent president, and his popularity was at an all-time low. Little shanty towns of unemployed workers called Hoovervilles were popping up all over the country. More and more people were starting to consider extreme suggestions from both the far left and far right as viable approaches to fixing the ills of the nation. Franklin D. Roosevelt, a charismatic speaker and the Democratic Party nominee, was promising a new deal for Americans if he was elected. Other populist voices were making their opinions known on the radio airwaves that came into so many American homes.

"I don't know what's gotten into my mother these days," said Joe to Martha as he helped corral the kids and get them into the back seat of the Oldsmobile. They were going over to Tom's house for Sunday dinner. Waiting for his old car's engine to smooth out, he continued, "You know her. The woman has opinions. These days, it seems like she wants to pick a fight with you if you don't agree with her completely."

As the family walked up the steps to Tom's front door, they could hear the RCA radio blaring and a rather defiant, resonant voice echoing through the parlor window.

"*And we have no one to blame but ourselves if we let the communists force us to look away from our God and the international banking community prevents us from feeding our families.*"

Martha, with the kids at her side, knocked on the door. Margaret, who was holding her finger up to her lips, slowly opened it. "Shhhhhh . . . It's almost over. Come in, but please be quiet for five minutes."

Joe gestured for Marty and the kids to follow him into the kitchen. His brother was standing there waiting with his hands on his hips. The look on his face suggested he found this all very amusing. In a soft voice, he said, "What? I thought you'd want to sit with Mom and listen to the good father. What are you doing in here?"

Joe knew his brother was trying to be funny. He asked, "What's gotten into Mom these days?"

Tom shrugged. "Our mother needed a cause to get behind. Since women can vote and most of Ireland is now independent, she's been searching for something. One of her lady friends told her about Coughlin's program on Sundays, and she started listening about a month ago."

This made complete sense to Joe. His mother was passionate about those causes. "What's this guy about?"

The broadcast now over, Margaret walked into the kitchen and overheard Joe's question. "Your mother will answer. Your brother Tom is not too fond of Father Coughlin because he won't take the time to listen."

Tom responded, "Mom, I won't say anything. You tell Joe all about him."

Joe noticed Martha had taken the kids into the parlor and was visiting with Ella. He would have preferred to join them rather than listen to his mother at this moment, but decided to be the good son. "Okay, Mom. What's he about?" he dutifully asked.

She moved closer to Joe. "Although Coughlin is originally from Canada, in my book, he is still a patriot," she began, in a tone reminiscent of the one from her catechism teaching days. "He reminds me of brave men like Charles Parnell, who fought to bring home rule to Ireland. I've had it up to here with these Republicans. All they care about is big business. Father Coughlin's out for the common man. He says they've stacked the deck against ordinary folks, and he's going to fight to get it unstacked."

Joe wondered why Coughlin seemed to bother Tom so much. Given all the crimes Joe had seen committed by ordinary folks who had become desperate because of the Depression, this actually sounded very positive. "Well, it sure seems like Dad would have supported him," he told his mother.

Margaret came over and patted him on the back. "Well, the first thing your dad would've said is, 'What's more important than our family sitting down to have a Sunday dinner together?' We can continue this conversation in the dining room after we say grace and have our meal. Ella and Martha, will you help this old lady put the food on the table?"

After a meal of pot roast, potatoes, string beans, and fresh bread—and banter back and forth about every subject except politics—Margaret surprised everyone by requesting they resume their earlier conversation. Standing up, she proclaimed, "Ladies, before your loudmouth husbands take the floor, I'd like to get your thoughts on Father Coughlin and the upcoming presidential election. Your opinion matters now that you're citizens who can vote. My lovely daughter-in-law Martha, please start us off."

Joe watched as his wife assuredly stood up and said, "I like what Roosevelt has to say. Hoover's had his chance and did nothing to help. I've never listened to Father Coughlin, but I've been doing plenty of reading.

He's made a lot of comments against communists and Jews. A man of God shouldn't be attacking members of another religion."

Joe was impressed, and too embarrassed by his own lack of knowledge to voice an opinion.

Margaret offered a rebuttal to her daughter-in-law. "Coughlin's vehemently against communism because they're godless. Because so many communists were Jews—like Marx, Lenin, and Trotsky—I believe when he talks poorly about the Jews, he's only referring to the ones who are communists. When Jesus was on earth, He was Jewish, and I'm sure Father Coughlin respects their faith as a good Catholic."

The discussions continued in a spirited but good-hearted way. Everyone agreed that the country needed a change and said they would vote for Roosevelt. Tom voiced his concern over Coughlin, arguing that "a priest should be a priest and not a politician." Margaret did not rebut this time, saying everyone was entitled to their opinion.

While the other members of the family gave their views, Joe considered what he wanted to say. When it was his turn, he turned to his mother. "I can see how important this is to you, Mom. Right now, I don't have an opinion, because I don't know enough about Coughlin. Give me some time and I'll come back and tell you what I think."

"Thank you, son, for taking this seriously. I look forward to chatting with you about it."

‡

Joe hadn't really given that much thought to politicians and the difference between the parties until recently. He had great respect for Tom's opinion and wondered why his views were so at odds with their mother's. Marty's comment about Coughlin was also concerning. He decided he would take a long lunch one day this week and go visit John at his parish on Mulberry Street. Although Joe had never been close with his oldest brother, he had a tremendous level of admiration for him and the work he was doing in the neighborhood.

On Tuesday, Joe walked over to the soup kitchen next to John's parish, almost certain he would find his brother there, and when he arrived, it turned out he'd been right. Father John O'Mara, the eldest and most studious of the five children, was entering his mid-forties, his dark brown hair graying around the temples. His demeanor radiated complete piety, and he spoke in a soothing voice. When he saw Joe waving at the back of the soup kitchen dining room, he took off his apron and welcomed his brother with a radiant smile.

"Joe, what a pleasant surprise. Is everything okay?"

"Yes, things are great. I was hoping to get your thoughts on something if you have the time."

"Of course. Please come with me to the office in the back of the church."

When settled in the small room, which was used for counseling, they started the conversation by exchanging a variety of family updates. In his experience as an investigator, Joe had learned how important it was to ask the right question if he wanted a truthful answer. Without preface, he asked, "What are your thoughts about Father Coughlin?"

John nodded. "Interesting that you bring him up. I was just discussing this with a fellow priest, who had a very different opinion than mine."

Joe had always found John very difficult to read, and today was no exception. He couldn't tell whether his opinion was positive or negative.

"Joe, don't look so concerned. I'll answer your question. I would have to say my views align more with our brother's than with our mother's."

Joe laughed. "So, you've been talking to them. What don't you like about the guy?"

John explained that, for him, the role of a priest was simple because there was such a logical model for behavior: Jesus. During his time on earth, Jesus spent his time teaching love and acceptance and tried to lift the poor and downtrodden by giving them hope.

"When his enemies were trying to trip Jesus up and get him to comment on politics, He simply answered, 'Render to Caesar the things that are Caesar's, and to God the things are God's.' That's clear direction for me."

"So, you think Coughlin shouldn't give his opinions?" Joe asked.

"I believe he intentionally keeps the religious aspect tightly woven into his political views, and that is wrong. He's using the pulpit to influence Catholics in this country. Believe me, this country needs hope, and his message provides comfort to folks that need it. However, he plays fast and loose with the facts, like a shady politician would."

After their discussion, Joe understood why his mother was so captivated by Coughlin when she could be so critical of most politicians. It was most certainly because of the collar. She wasn't putting Coughlin through the same scrutiny because she equated him with the good priests who had touched her life—possibly even John.

‡

Joe knew that Tom and Ella usually went out on Friday nights, so tonight he could catch his mother alone and have that chat. He didn't want to let too much time go by before he got back to her. When she answered the door, he noted that she seemed to be moving slower than usual.

"Mom, is this a good night to have that talk? You look a little tired." She was now in her sixties, but she usually gave the impression of having lots of energy.

"I haven't been sleeping well these days. You know me—I'm no drinker, but I've been having a whiskey or two, which helps. Will you join me?"

After getting the drinks and sitting down on the sofa in the parlor, Margaret told her son, "To be honest, I really don't care whether you agree with me. I appreciate the fact that you didn't make up an answer or tell me what you thought I wanted to hear. If we did anything, your father and I raised our kids to think for themselves."

"For sure, Mom." Joe fully recognized that she was going to listen and was not interested in a debate. Rather than speak about Coughlin, he chose to just communicate an observation.

"As long as I can remember, you have always been talking about politicians. You have been so critical of their words and actions. Since Father Coughlin is talking about politics and world affairs, just make sure you listen to his words like you would with Taft or Wilson."

Margaret came over and kissed her son on the cheek. "Son, that is good advice. I'm so happy I've got a new member of the family to discuss these matters with. Thank you."

CHAPTER 28

WANDA'S MISTAKE

On January 30, 1933, in a shrewd political maneuver, Adolf Hitler became chancellor of Germany. Shortly afterward, Nazi sympathizers organized rallies in US cities with large German American populations. The organization supported by the regime called itself "Friends of the New Germany."

In March 1933, the people of Newark elected a Jew to be the mayor—Mathias Edelstein, who had previously been an attorney, a Golden Gloves boxer, and a collegiate wrestler. Since the Depression started, over six hundred factories there had closed their doors, and payrolls had shrunk to less than half of their pre-Depression levels. Unemployment was rampant, and there was significant tension between all the ethnic groups who lived in and around the city.

‡

Over his years working for Lieutenant Connor, Joe had learned the cardinal rule for dealing with the man: "Make sure a problem is already solved before you make Connor aware of it." Joe felt his own instincts as a detective were far better than his boss's, so he preferred to handle things by himself with his two direct reports. He watched the weasel frequently lose his patience and scream at his fellow detectives, who obviously hadn't figured out how to best handle him. Because Joe's dealings with Connor seemed low-key compared to his colleagues', his Golden moniker remained, and his relationships in the department were strained at best.

As soon as Joe sat down in the lieutenant's office after being summoned, Connor addressed him, not looking up from his desk. "Detective O'Mara, the mayor's secretary has been trying to reach you to arrange a meeting. The only reason I even know about it is because she gave up and instead talked to my secretary, Helen."

"Sorry sir, I have been out doing case work the last few days. I can assure you I have no idea what this is about."

"We have a chain of command for a reason. This is highly unusual. I can appreciate the mayor is new, but he should know better."

"I'll brief you when I get back."

Connor handed Joe the slip of paper with the phone number and mumbled, "That'll be all, Detective. I need to get back to this report."

Back at his desk, Joe thought it best to figure things out before he called to arrange the meeting. It was clear Connor was upset because he was being excluded. And he was right—at the very least, the mayor should have requested a meeting with Joe through Connor. After trying to come up with a single reason Mayor Edelstein might want to see him, Joe gave up and called to make the appointment. He'd be finding out what this was all about at 2 p.m.

It was a nice spring day in early May, and Joe decided to walk rather than spending time coaxing his old car to run. The fresh air would do him good. He got to the office a few minutes early, and the mayor welcomed him in promptly at two.

"Detective O'Mara, please come in. It's a distinct pleasure to meet you." Mathias Edelstein was dressed in a gray double-breasted pin-striped suit that did not hide his athletic build. He gave the impression of being much younger than his forty-five years, with not so much as one gray hair visible.

Edelstein's friendly manner immediately put Joe at ease. He thought back to the prickly manner of the mayor of Jersey City, whom he'd met earlier in his career. While Edelstein's office was nicely furnished, it did not have the air of the palace chamber where that mayor used to conduct his business.

"Thanks, Mayor Edelstein," Joe said once he was seated. "I was looking forward to meeting you and finding out what you had on your mind."

"I'm sure you're wondering why I've asked to speak with you alone. The short answer is I have a rather challenging assignment, which requires someone who I can absolutely trust. From what I know about you, I think you're that man."

Joe didn't know how to respond. He actually felt he knew less now than when he'd walked over to the building. "Sir?"

"Sure, I've looked at your personal file. You have an exemplary record as a detective. However, the reason I think you're the right guy is our mutual friend, who speaks of you highly. He describes you as a man of great integrity."

Joe let the comment settle, but still felt completely in the dark.

"Joe, I can see from your face that you're quite puzzled. It's Abe Livosky. We are both members of Temple B'Nai Abraham. I attended his wedding in 1931, just like you. I know what you must be thinking. Let me explain."

Joe listened attentively while the mayor went into great detail rationalizing his association with a known criminal. While Edelstein did not condone Livosky's illegal business dealings, he highlighted the incredible generosity and good work that he was doing for the underprivileged Jewish community in the Newark area and his support for the emigration of Jewish families from Nazi Germany. Edelstein felt it unwise to have police work to incarcerate Livosky just to have him replaced by some heartless thug like Dutch Schultz or Lucky Luciano. Finally, Livosky had pledged to him to be out of illegal operations by the end of the year.

While Joe was surprised the mayor would admit to having an association with a criminal, it made sense. Abe was going legitimate, and there was a strong possibility that Prohibition would end this year as well. Still, Joe needed to make one thing clear. "Mayor, I understand what you're saying. Why Abe and I are friends is a long, complicated story. I want you to know that I had no connection to his illegal business dealings in any way."

"Abe told me that. He told me how you and your wife supported him in his time of need when there was no compelling reason for you to get involved, other than to protect an innocent man. That's why you're my first choice for this assignment."

Joe liked Mayor Edelstein. Very few of his superiors over the years had treated him with this level of respect. He was putting the pieces together. Edelstein's secretary had reached out to Joe directly because the mayor couldn't trust Connor. "It's about my boss, isn't it?"

Edelstein smiled. "You're a quick study. Yes, it is. But frankly, I fear it's a lot bigger than that."

"Just curious, sir—why wouldn't you give this to Internal Affairs?"

"It's a matter of trust. I need to know how big of a problem we have today. I don't have time to build trust in their investigators."

The mayor believed he was sitting on a powder keg of ethnic hostility in the greater Newark area. Since Hitler had come to power, the number of anti-Semitic crimes had risen in the city. Edelstein knew for a fact that agents of the Nazi government were trying to recruit members of the German American community to the cause. Enraged by the horror stories of what was happening in Europe, the members of the Jewish community, including its criminal elements, were bonding together to fight back. Edelstein felt confident that they could suppress the aggression that was occurring on the streets. His biggest worry was Nazi sympathizers infiltrating the police and the emerging antisemitism in the Catholic community, especially given the high percentage of Catholics on the force. If he lost control of the police, he would lose control of the city.

The rise in anti-Semitic crime was not news to Joe—he'd noticed it in his job. He wasn't sure about the mayor's concern about Catholics, however. He and Marty had listened to Coughlin on the radio a few times recently. While the man mentioned his disdain for the Jewish community and their attitudes, it seemed his main beef was with communism and international bankers, who he believed had caused the Depression. Marty explained that, based on what she knew from the articles she'd read, Coughlin was also attacking Jews when he mentioned those groups, because of his perceptions and biases.

"Mayor, what do you want me to do on this assignment? I'll be honest with you. I'm not crazy with the idea of being a rat."

"Joe, please trust me on this. The stakes are high. I've reached out to the Feds already, and they told me they don't have the resources to help. Hoover was very dismissive and said that because I was new in the role, perhaps I was being paranoid. I need an investigator who will be totally objective and interested in finding the truth, whatever it might be."

Joe remembered how his father's advancement had been curtailed because he called his own shots and did things his way. Joe worked in a similar fashion but was being tapped on the shoulder for a special assignment by the mayor of the largest city in New Jersey.

He looked Edelstein directly in the eyes and reached out his hand. "You've got your man."

First, the mayor briefed Joe first on his suspicions regarding Lieutenant Connor. He believed the Nazis had recruited Connor, who was acting as an agent on their behalf. The mayor felt it was important not to reveal how he got the information, as he was looking for independent validation. He mentioned that Connor's connection to the regime was through his wife, who was originally a German citizen. They'd met in Boston when Corrina, the daughter of a wealthy family from Bavaria, attended Wellesley and Connor was at Boston College.

Regarding Catholics on the police force, the mayor wanted Joe's opinion on whether a threat was imminent. As a Jew, he admitted that there was a possibility he was being overly sensitive because of what was going on in Europe. Edelstein felt that Joe, as an Irish Catholic, would have an easier time getting answers than an outsider.

"This isn't about making arrests. As a citizen of this country, Connor has every right to be a Nazi. However, given his position, he is privy to sensitive information and controls day-to-day operations for quite a few detectives. I need to know if he's using his position for their benefit."

"Sir, I promise I'll inform you regularly. I'm glad it's getting late so I can just head home. I need to cook up a good story for Connor."

"Oh, about that matter with my secretary. My apologies for making things more difficult for you. This is Wanda's last day. I gave her explicit instructions to only give you the message, and while I suspect no bad intentions, she was lazy. I need someone I can trust in that job."

An idea flashed through Joe's head. "I have someone in mind who I know you can trust. She might not be the best typist, but she's smart and will work hard for you."

"She sounds wonderful. Who is it?"

"Of course it's her decision, but I think my wife Marty would be perfect. She might say no only because her work clothes are dated, and she might feel embarrassed. The other thing you should know is that her family is from Germany, but her mom despises Hitler and thinks he's ruining the country."

"Joe, if I assume that all German American citizens have Nazi sympathies, I'm sinking to their level. Tell Marty she's hired if she wants the job. See if she can stop by at 11 a.m. tomorrow to meet with me. I will provide an advance in her pay so that she can go out and buy clothes. Of course, there is the added benefit of us having a direct line of communication with each other through her."

Head abuzz from the conversation, Joe walked to his car and headed home. He was thrilled that he'd come up with the idea for Marty and hoped she would be as excited as he was.

‡

That evening, while both kids were in their rooms doing homework, Joe and Martha sat in the kitchen and discussed Joe's meeting with Mayor Edelstein. Martha jumped at the opportunity to work for the mayor and came up with a plan for their children. They could stay with their grandmother at Tom's house after school—the walk was only fifteen minutes longer. There were also plenty of public transportation options for her to go to and from work when Joe couldn't drive her.

"Joe, thank you for mentioning to him about the clothes. It's such a great opportunity. I probably would've still said yes, but would've been really self-conscious."

"You're gonna like working for him. He's really easy to talk to. Plus, we get to work together on this case. Let's have dinner and talk the rest through after the kids go to bed."

After tucking in their kids at eight thirty, the pair sat back down at the kitchen table. Martha had put out a tablet of paper and started taking notes when Joe began recapping the discussion from earlier in the day.

In a frustrated tone, he said, "The more I think about this, the harder it seems. The guys at the precinct would sooner confide in a rabbi at Temple B'Nai Abraham than in me."

"They think you're buddies with Connor. They can't stand him, so naturally they're not gonna like you. Start doing what they're doing to get yelled at in front of them. I'd be surprised if that didn't do the trick."

"That's a great idea. I'll get him good and pissed off at me. The weasel can't help himself with the yelling and screaming."

Marty got up from the table and went to the cabinet where they kept a bottle of Jamison's Irish Whiskey. Because good whiskey was in short supply and expensive, they reserved it only for special occasions. She poured two glasses and took a cigarette from the pack on the table. Lighting it, she blew smoke up at the ceiling. Looking down at her notes, she asked, "What are you gonna tell Connor about your meeting?"

"Now, I was thinking if you're this Nazi agent, you already know why I'm going over there. So whatever I tell him he knows is bullshit. I'm betting he will barely talk to me. Now if he's not an agent, the Connor I know will want me to spill every word that came out of the mayor's mouth. What d'you think?"

Martha took some time to mull the question over. "Yes, I think you're right. It won't prove anything, but we'll figure out where to go after that."

‡

Joe awakened suddenly at four in the morning. He looked at his wife cuddled up next to him and listened to her snoring ever so slightly, which reminded him of the purring of a cat. He felt that the turmoil they'd navigated through together had strengthened their marriage. His new assignment was disrupting the mental tranquility he had been enjoying since he'd paid up his debts and stopped gambling. However, Marty seemed so excited about the chance to get involved, so maybe it was all worth it.

Moving quietly out of the bed and into the kitchen, he decided to put on a pot of coffee.

"Hon, is everything okay? It's really early." Martha, wearing her nightshirt, slowly came in sat down next to her husband, clearly still half asleep.

"I couldn't sleep," Joe said. "I guess I'm nervous about coming up short on this assignment. I was thinking that I've never been one of the guys. Not when I was a kid, or when I was in the army, or now. I gotta do an acting job like Gary Cooper to pull this off."

"You know you can do this, but you're going to have to do things differently. You need to work slow, plant the seeds and let the information come to you."

"Marty, that's great advice. I won't be able to get this done in a week, and probably not in a month."

Joe dressed and headed to work early, trying to get there before Connor. Over the years, he'd been able to predict his boss's reactions in most situations. If, after seeing Joe at his desk, the lieutenant declined to summon him into his office first thing, something was definitely up.

The office was empty when Joe arrived. He pulled out his active case files to look busy and started listening for Connor's arrival. A few minutes before eight, he heard footsteps hurrying upstairs and put his head down to give the impression he was hard at work.

"Good morning, Detective O'Mara."

Joe did not raise his head. "Mornin', sir."

Connor briskly continued up to his office, turned the light on, and shut the door. Joe looked at his watch. He would wait one hour to see if he was called into a meeting. When the time was up, he would knock on Connor's door and offer him an update on his conversation with the mayor.

Just after nine, he went up and knocked on Connor's door. "It's Joe, can I come in?"

"Yes."

After taking a seat, Joe said, "I wanted to fill you in on the meeting yesterday. It was only—"

Connor cut Joe off mid-sentence. "I'm sorry, Detective, but I'm knee-deep in work. We can have this discussion another time."

"Okay, sir, I just wanted to mention that—"

Raising his voice, Connor told him, "Another time, Detective. Another time."

"Yes, sir."

Back at his desk, Joe knew that step one of his plan was complete. The mayor had a right to suspect Connor. Getting proof was going to be much more difficult.

CHAPTER 29

SPORTS COSTUMES

Joe decided that for the rest of May, he would take a staged approach to test Lieutenant Connor's patience by increasing the amount he interacted with him. All the cases he deemed urgent, he delegated to his two junior detectives.

One afternoon, when Connor seemed to be in a particularly foul mood, Joe asked for direction on a recent arson case. All evidence pointed to the owner setting the building ablaze to collect insurance payments. The same fellow had even tried this before, three years back. The fact that Joe seemed to be perplexed by this simple investigation provoked Connor to no end. After a flurry of expletives, he told Joe not to waste his time. As this had happened out in the squad room, several detectives witnessed the incident. Over the next weeks, Joe repeated his act, appearing to remain oblivious to whatever Connor said and asking numerous questions. Eventually, the lieutenant lost all patience and began to seethe. Later in May, he reached his boiling point.

Connor's office was usually a private place to talk. Conversations at speaking volume were not audible to detectives sitting at their desks, but that day, they all heard Connor yell at Joe.

"Do you think you can continue to play these fucking games with me without consequence? You think the mayor will save you? Well, I've got connections too, and I'm starting the process to have you fired."

Joe walked back to his desk. The room was completely silent except for the sound of his footsteps. As soon as he sat down, Detective Brannigan appeared at his desk. "Golden, what'd you do to piss him off so much?"

"Stop calling me Golden. I'm in the doghouse, just like you when you screw up."

"What's was Connor saying about the mayor and you?"

Joe realized that this was his first chance at finding something out from the force. He would put out the bait and see how far he could go. "It's a long story. We actually have a mutual friend, some Jew I served with in the army in Mexico. The mayor seemed okay, but he's a Jew. You know their kind. They can't be trusted."

"For sure. All these greedy Jew bankers fucked up the stock market, and now we've got to suffer. My brother with three kids is holding on to his place by a thread. Since they laid him off at the hat factory, he works any-where he can. He's lucky when he can get two days a week."

Joe nodded, trying his hardest to project empathy. "Do you think Roosevelt's gonna do anything to help? Lots of people are hurting."

Brannigan shook his head. "Too early to tell. I voted for him because there was no other choice. Father Coughlin supports him, and that's good enough for me."

"Right. Coughlin's a patriot. He supports the little guy, not big busi-ness." Joe felt pangs of conscience as he parroted his mother's words.

After that day, he began reaching out to his colleagues regularly. Their conversations were about sports, family, or just the weather. He refrained from asking for their opinions. Soon, he received an invitation to go to a speakeasy with some of them on a Friday night. He was at a table with four detectives and two policemen, and after a few drinks, he regaled the group with a collection of stories from his time in the army, mixing in imitations of Patton and his old mate Donnie Walsh. The six men howled with laughter. He then told a story about Carmine Dotti and Lieutenant Connor, imitating both of them while doing it.

"Joe, that's gotta be the last story. I'm laughin' so hard I'm pissin' in my pants."

"Yeah, Joe. Save some for the next time. My stomach hurts."

He left with every man slapping him on the back, telling him he needed to be a regular on Fridays from now on. When Joe got back home, he couldn't wait to tell his wife her plan had worked. They talked things through, and they both thought it was the right time to move to the next phase of the operation.

‡

Word spread quickly through the precinct about Joe being a regular guy after all. Whenever he interacted with the detectives and the uniformed police, he would throw out racial innuendo, focusing mostly on disparaging remarks about Jews. When he posed the question "What do you think will happen if the things Roosevelt is doing now don't work?", it surprised him how many of his Irish Catholic brethren said they looked to the leadership of Coughlin.

As June was coming to a close, Joe felt he had talked enough to both the detectives and patrolmen. He thought his precinct was typical of ones in the rest of the city, so the mayor could draw some conclusions.

After putting the kids to bed, Joe and Marty once again sat at the kitchen table. Marty had out her notepad and was ready. Joe began. "Quite a few of the police blame the Depression on rich Jews. I'd say most of the guys who said that also listen to Father Coughlin. He gets them pretty riled up." Joe waited for Marty to catch up with her notes.

"For now, most of the guys are giving Roosevelt a chance. They like what he did with the banks right after being elected and the fact he's taking action. He's got some time, maybe a year, to get people feeling better about the country. Just a few of them said they think Roosevelt is too soft and going too slow and they'd prefer somebody like Mussolini or Hitler."

Marty finished writing and looked up at her husband. She crinkled her brow and deepened her voice, attempting to sound masculine. "What's your conclusion, Detective?"

"Tell the mayor nothin's goin on with the cops right now. If things take a turn for the worse, that could change."

The next day, Martha relayed that information to Mayor Edelstein. He was pleased. His message to Joe was to focus on Connor and try to get proof of his connection to the Nazis.

‡

Throughout the summer of 1933, tensions between the Friends of New Germany and a variety of Jewish American and communist organizations intensified in Newark. Almost every day, the Newark daily newspapers were publishing stories of the ostracization of Jews from all aspects of German society. During this time, the chapter of the Friends organization in Newark grew to one of the largest in the nation.

On his way to see Abe Livosky at his home in West Orange after work, Joe took some detours and drove through the areas with high populations of German Americans. His attention was drawn to the prominent swastika signs advertising a rally for the Friends of New Germany celebrating the eighty-fifth birthday of the German president, the powerless figurehead Paul von Hindenburg, commander of German forces in the Great War. It was to take place right outside of Newark, in a German American club in Irvington called the Schwabenhalle. Ironically, the areas where they placed the signs were next to one of Newark's major arteries, where many Jewish merchants had their shops.

Joe arrived at Abe's residence. The groundskeeper opened the gate for him, and he parked his Oldsmobile near the front door. Ewa Livosky and her two daughters greeted him when he stepped out. In a very deliberate, halting manner, she said in her heavy Polish accent, "It is so nice to see you again, Joe."

He spoke intentionally slowly. "Good to see you, Ewa. You're making good progress with your English."

Abe's wife closed her eyes and shook her head, then uttered, "Very hard."

Dressed casually today, sporting slacks and a sweater, Abe came down the stairs and greeted Joe. "I hired an English tutor for Ewa and the girls. She speaks much better with just me. She gets nervous about making mistakes and freezes up. Luckily, we can speak Yiddish to each other. Let's go into the living room to chat. I need to make you aware of something."

After they'd sat down, Abe continued. "Edelstein gave me the lowdown on your assignment. You're going hard trying to get something on Connor and will attend some of these Nazi rallies. I know you can take care of yourself, but there's something you need to know."

"Abe, I'm all ears."

Leaning back in his comfortable chair, Abe explained how he had been on the sidelines for some time and his protégé, Longie Zwillman, had been running the business and dealing with the organization in New York. He then warned Joe. "Zwillman's organized a group of the fucking scariest Jews in Newark. These tough guys are from the third ward and used to be my muscle. Two ex-fighters and a bunch of other mugs are planning to disrupt that Friends' meeting. You've heard about the communist organizations showing up at Nazi rallies to protest and hand out papers . . . a scuffle here and there. That's going to change. Nate Arno and his crew are coming with clubs to beat the shit out of any Nazi they can find."

"Thanks for the tip, but I still gotta go. I'll be at the Schwabenhalle meeting in Irvington on the thirtieth."

"Joe, stay out of their way. Trust me, you don't want to go near them."

‡

Joe watched as about three hundred members of Friends of the New Germany filed into the hall in Irvington. To his amazement, many of them were dressed in uniforms with brown shirts adorned with armbands displaying a swastika. As he approached the building, he noticed that there were at least twenty-five men congregating in a nearby alley—probably the people Abe had warned him about. He counted only four Irvington policemen in front of the building, there to ensure the event remained peaceful.

Joe made his way into the hall and found a place to stand on the left side, where he had a reasonable view and could remain relatively inconspicuous. While the hall displayed the American flag, they'd decorated the auditorium with an overwhelming number of swastikas. A large red Nazi flag prominently hung on the wall directly behind the speaker's podium.

At the front of the hall groups of people were still filing in. A very tall, fashionably dressed woman walked slowly toward Joe with a man in a fedora, whose face he couldn't see, trailing closely behind her. Joe recognized the woman's face but couldn't recall from where. She brushed past him, followed by her male companion. When they were ten rows ahead, Joe finally recalled seeing that face in a picture that Connor had on his wall. It was his wife! His next thoughts were whether the man in the fedora was Connor and if he'd noticed him. Joe moved closer, since he was too far away to make a positive identification.

The leader of the Newark chapter of Friends, Albert Schley, came out to thundering applause, accompanied by four men in full Nazi uniforms. They flanked Schley, two on each side. To Joe's shock, his brother-in-law Fred was standing closest to Schley, stiff as a board, ready to salute anyone who mentioned Hitler's name.

Joe had lost track of Marty's brother, as he had not been part of their lives for some time. His focus needed to be on Connor, so he put Fred out of his mind for the time being. He had to do whatever it took to reach a place where he could spot Connor's face and then exit the hall as fast as he could.

Schley began the proceedings innocently enough by commemorating the fallen soldiers from the Great War from all nations. It was followed by a long moment of silence.

The next speeches drew parallels between Roosevelt and Hitler, and the hard jobs each man had to do to rebuild their nations. Eventually, the speaker's rhetoric became more accusatory, and he provided justification for why strong measures needed to be taken against the Jews and communists who were infesting Germany and causing hardship for all.

On that cue, stink bombs were rolled into the hall. As they began to explode and fill the auditorium with the strong odor of rotten eggs, chaos broke out. A horde of people ran in front of Joe as he watched his targets flee to the opposite side of the building. Quickly realizing it would be impossible to get a better look at the man he thought might be Connor, he headed for an exit and tried to muscle his way out.

However, about a dozen angry men, each armed with a foot-and-a-half long piece of iron pipe wrapped in newspaper, burst through the door that he'd planned on using. Joe stopped and immediately ran toward the center of the hall. More men armed with pipes swarmed in from all available doors except the front, where the police had been located. Joe pushed and shoved as needed to make his way past the speaker's podium, from where the Friends' leadership had departed at the first sign of trouble. He thought he recognized Nate Arno, who was leading a group toward the large Nazi flag, which was guarded by ten unarmed men in uniforms. The four policemen who had entered the building were also trying to make their way toward that same area, where most of the fighting was taking place.

Joe beat the Jewish vigilantes to the back. Out of the corner of his eye, he noticed Fred had reentered the area and was beating a man senseless with his fists. Nate Arno, now a few steps behind Joe, was racing toward Fred.

Joe finally made it to his brother-in-law and horse-collared him to the floor. "You're under arrest." He pulled out his detective badge and flashed it at Nate Arno, who was seconds away from taking Fred's head off with a pipe. The former fighter backed off and ran toward his cohort, who were fighting with other uniformed men.

Joe looked down at Marty's brother. Fred's haughty facial expression, combined with Joe's recollection of the man's cruelty toward his young son, pushed him to the brink. At the last moment, instead of landing a punch to erase the air of arrogance from his face, Joe said, "Better you spend the night in jail than in the morgue, Fred."

"What are you talking about? Why am I going to jail?"

"Because you're fucking stupid. Always have been. You should thank me. Didn't you see the mug—who was twice your size—coming to take your head off with that pipe? If I hadn't come over and arrested you, he might've killed you."

Since there were so few police there, they could catch none of the Jewish vigilantes and only arrested a handful of Nazi sympathizers that evening. Ambulances collected quite a few people who had been roughed up and brought them to a nearby hospital.

Joe led his brother-in-law out to the paddy wagon that had arrived at the scene. Despite realizing that Corrina Connor and whoever she was with were probably long gone, he still searched for them in the crowd. After most people had left the scene, Joe walked to his car, which was a few blocks away, feeling tired and discouraged.

‡

Martha was up waiting for him when he got home. "Are you okay? You look like they've run you through the mill."

"Tonight was crazy." Despite feeling exhausted, Joe began to recap the evening's adventure in animated fashion. He shared his frustration at not being able to identify Connor and his amazement at seeing her brother. He told her how he'd saved Fred in the bedlam but had been pretty close to taking out of few of his teeth.

Martha looked shocked. "I'm sure my family doesn't know about Fred being a Nazi," she exclaimed. "He's just moved back home because his wife kicked him out of the house."

Joe went to the small cabinet in the kitchen and pulled out the bottle of whiskey. "Would you like one?"

"Not tonight. You had a rough night—why don't you have mine as well."

Joe sipped his whiskey and exhaled loudly. "Ya know, I'm disappointed that I didn't make the weasel tonight, because that would've put an end to this investigation. Tell the mayor tomorrow exactly what I told you and see where he wants to do next. You also need to tell him about your brother. Maybe Minnie can keep an eye on him for us?"

"Let me talk to Mayor Edelstein about it. Either way, I have to tell Minnie, for Russell's sake."

‡

The following morning, Joe got up with a terrible headache. Marty said she would take a bus to work rather than make him drive. Prior to facing Connor, Joe believed it would be wise to get guidance from the mayor, leading him to take a sick day. Connor's secretary picked up when he called and said she would relay the message when the lieutenant came in. Joe found it strange that the weasel was not at his desk yet, since it was almost nine o'clock.

Curious to see how the paper covered what had happened last night, he bought a copy of the *Newark Star Eagle* downstairs. Back in the kitchen, Joe unfolded the paper and perused the article about the incident, which was featured on the front page. When asked why so many members of the Friends chapter were wearing uniforms adorned with swastikas, Albert Schley had replied they were sports costumes. After reading that line, Joe howled with laughter. Then, pretending to be a reporter asking a follow-up question, he said out loud, "Herr Schley, may I ask you—what fucking sport were they playing?"

‡

Joe could not remember a day during a workweek when he had done so little. He read the newspaper cover to cover and spent some time listening to a variety of radio programs. By early afternoon, he started feeling better and walked to Our Lady of the Valley grammar school to pick up his kids when school let out at three.

When they passed the grocery store, which now stood on the vacant lot where Joe and his dog Teddy had won the day against the bully, Joe Junior asked, "Is this the spot, Dad?" Junior, soon to be twelve years old, was running into the same difficulties Joe had encountered as a child, and he had recently told the story to help build his son's confidence. Shortly after, they went up the stairs to their apartment.

When they entered, Marty stood to greet them. Joe immediately noticed how sophisticated his wife looked in her new business dress and seamed stockings. After planting a big kiss on her husband, she said, "I've got so much good news, I don't know where to start."

"Well, start with the best first."

"You're not gonna believe it. Connor handed in his resignation letter today. He must've concluded you definitely saw him last night, because he noticed you. The investigation is over for now."

Joe's eyes lit up, and he clapped his hands. "Wow, that's great. I suspected something might be up since he wasn't there when I called. No more weasel to deal with. Now, you've got more good news?"

"As a thank you to both of us and in recognition of a job well done, the mayor and his wife want to invite us for a night out on the town in New York for dinner and a Broadway play."

Joe felt happy and knew Marty deserved as much recognition as he did. He was overjoyed that the mayor had been thoughtful enough to choose a reward that would acknowledge her contribution as well.

While listening to Marty talk excitedly about seeing a show, Joe thought back to the young woman he had fallen in love with. Over the years, Joe had put her to the test in so many ways. It dawned on him that she was the head of their household. She was the one who'd been able to hold everything together through adversity of every kind.

"Joe, are you listening to me? What show do you want to see?"

"Hon, I want this to be your night. I'll be happy to go to whichever one you pick."

CHAPTER 30

THE PRODIGAL SON

One of the great pleasures Margaret O'Mara indulged in was taking a hot, soapy bath in her large high-backed claw-foot tub right before she retired for the evening at around nine o'clock. This was when she allowed herself to indulge her senses and relax rather than scurrying about Tom and Ella's house dusting, cleaning, and cooking.

While soaking in the tub on a cold January evening in the new decade, she felt a tiny lump in her left breast. Since she hated going to the doctor, she told herself it was probably nothing. She'd experienced so many changes in her body lately. Over the next three years, she noticed the lump getting bigger, but justified not going to the doctor because she felt just fine.

By the fall of 1933, Margaret had started turning in for the night earlier and getting up later. She'd always been proud of the fact that she'd maintained roughly the same weight since she was married, but recently, she'd noticed her garments felt a little baggy on her. She asked Ella for a recommendation and made an appointment to see Dr. Apfelbaum on the other side of Seton Hall, just a short walk away.

"Mrs. O'Mara," he told her, "I don't like what I'm feeling on your left breast. This concerns me greatly. It could be nothing, but you must have it checked. I recommend you schedule a biopsy at Mountainside Hospital in Montclair. I went to medical school with Dr. Byrne, and he is up to date on all the most modern techniques for performing biopsies to detect breast cancer. My assistant will call today and make an appointment for you."

"Do you think that I have breast cancer?"

"I think it's a strong possibility."

The doctor's assistant was able to schedule an urgent appointment with Dr. Byrne for the following day. Tom had a large funeral to orchestrate and could not break free, so he asked Ulysses to pick up his mother and bring her to the hospital.

Margaret counted sixteen needles that were stuck into various areas around her left breast and underarm. Dr. Byrne committed to calling her with the results no later than Monday afternoon.

When he saw her exit the hospital, Ulysses said, "Mrs. O'Mara, are you all right? You look mighty pale. Take my arm as we walk to the car."

Margaret started to cry. Ulysses stopped walking and tried to comfort her. She put her head on his chest, and he wrapped his arms around her the way he would console a member of his own family. "I can't die, Ulysses. I've too many things that I still need to do."

"Ma'am, I know you're a woman of faith. The good Lord has a plan for you. You might not understand it, but He'll take care of you."

"I believe that. I'm just afraid."

‡

Dr. Byrne was punctual with his call on Monday morning. "Mrs. O'Mara, I don't have good news. You have breast cancer. The biopsies have shown it has spread outside the breast area and into the lymph nodes. We treat this cancer with a surgical procedure called a radical mastectomy, where we remove the entire breast. I don't want to mislead you in any way. We can't know for sure how far the cancer has spread, so surgery will still have a low probability of eradicating it."

"Doctor, if I do nothing, how much longer do I have to live?"

"Everyone is different, and not knowing the extent of cancer in your body makes it very difficult to predict. If you were very lucky, you could live another two years. I think that in cases I have seen comparable to yours, a more reasonable expectation would be six months. I recommend surgery because it gives you a chance. It's very tough on the body, though. If we cannot remove the cancer completely, it'll come back quickly because the body is in such a weakened state. I'm so sorry to have to tell you this."

"Thank you, Doctor, for your candor. At this moment, I'm leaning towards not having surgery. I'll let you know if I change my mind."

‡

Margaret requested all of her children and their spouses gather at Tom's house that Sunday. Gladys and Joe Junior entertained Ellen's two young boys in the backyard while Margaret shared the news with her family.

"I got some bad news from the doctor. Unfortunately, some of the burden's going to fall on you, and I want you to be prepared." She paused for a moment to catch her breath. Tears rolled down her cheeks. "They've diagnosed me with cancer. I've elected to not have surgery because it probably won't help. The doctor said that I likely have about six months to live— two years at most."

Joe looked at his wife and closed his eyes as if he was in physical pain. He had noticed some changes in his mother but refused to acknowledge that something might be wrong with her.

Margaret took the time to make eye contact with each member of her family before continuing. "I see all of you are getting a little teary. You'll make me angry if you feel sorry for me. I've lived a full life and raised five precious children and have three other children by marriage whom I love dearly. You have blessed me with four beautiful grandchildren. I had the most wonderful husband a woman could ever have wanted, and I'll be joining him soon."

Joe was crying despite his mother's warning. He looked around at the rest of the family. There was not a dry eye among the eight adults who'd listened.

After Margaret had taken a few minutes to catch her breath, she told them, "I'm going to go for as long as I can and do things I enjoy. I don't want to be babied. There'll come a time when I'll lose my strength and the end will be near. I'll need your help to see me through."

‡

Joe and Martha visited Margaret frequently with the children. In the first month, Joe felt encouraged, because his mother was doing well and seemed like her old self on most days. He then saw a decline and, for his mother's sake, tried his best to hide his emotions. It was hard for him to hold back his tears when he realized how hard she was trying to put on as brave a face as she possibly could.

The entire family gathered often around Christmas. It was especially hard for everyone, since they knew this would be the last one they would get to share with their mother. By March 1934, Margaret could only get out of the bed using a cane, and only got up to go to the bathroom. Because Ellen had two young children and no one to watch them, Ella and Martha took turns providing care around the clock. Joe Junior would sit next to his grandmother in the bed and read his favorite Robert Louis Stevenson novels out loud to her. His youthful voice comforted her as she dozed in and out of sleep.

As spring came, Margaret could not get out of bed. She knew the end was near and wanted to spend time with each of her children individually. She did that in descending order by age.

Joe had not seen his mother for a little over a week. When he entered the room, which was painted a stark alabaster white, he noticed the religious items that decorated it. A nine-inch statue of the Virgin Mary had been placed on the dresser with a picture of Jesus displaying his Sacred Heart right above it. A large wooden crucifix hung from the wall over the mahogany headboard his mother was resting several pillows and her frail body against. He noticed her looking far more gaunt than she had when he'd seen her last. Joe knew it was taking all of her strength to force a smile for him.

"Joe, come on over and hold my hand. I want to have a good conversation with you. I'm not doped up right now. I stopped taking those pills to be able to talk to you." He took her hand and sat as close as he could to the bed to hear her every word.

"Do you remember the Bible story of the prodigal son?"

"Mom, I do. He's the one who ran off, got into trouble, and eventually came home."

"Yes, that's the one. I have two children who are devoting their life to the church. Ellen left home and got married to a wonderful man. Tom is a successful businessman and married Ella. I was always worried about you and how you would turn out, and yet you turned out just fine, choosing the perfect wife and raising two special children. You're my prodigal son. I have to admit, just like in the Bible, I love all my children the same, but you're my favorite. You remind me so much of your father. It's helped me get through losing him."

"Are you sure you're not telling the others that they're your favorite also?" said Joe, trying to lighten the mood. Deep down in his heart, he already knew her feelings for him, but he felt pangs of conscience. Joe and his father had shielded her from so much over the years. Perhaps if she knew the stark truth about the things he had done, she wouldn't be telling him this.

Margaret laughed hard for a few seconds, which made her cough. She then grabbed her son's hand even harder.

"I'm having last rites tomorrow. I want the parish priest, Father Dolan, to hear my confession rather than John. Your brother'll give my eulogy at the funeral. There's a matter I must discuss with you, and you have to promise me you'll be totally honest. Before I confess to a priest and stand before God, I need to confess to you."

Joe had a good idea of what his mother might ask him. At first, there had seemed to be an unspoken pact between them never to mention it. Then, as the years went by, it just seemed to be something that was buried deep and not worth talking about. But the part about her confession was puzzling to him, and he couldn't figure what possibly his mother would say.

"Joe, we've never talked about this. I must know the truth about what happened to Tom Sullivan. Before you tell me, I have to admit my sin. When we had that discussion years ago, when I asked you not to seek revenge, I didn't really mean it. There was a part of me that wanted you to take his life and make him pay for what he did. The man took my best friend away from me. James told me very little of his police work because he didn't want me to worry about him, but I knew enough about it to know that he was very capable of taking someone's life. If Tom Sullivan had done harm to a loved one, I don't think he would have hesitated to act."

She took a long pause to summon up the strength to finish. "I was being selfish, as I did not think about the consequences of the act and what it would do to you and your immortal soul. I have to know the truth about whether you were involved in Sullivan's death, and I can assure you that, whatever you tell me, I'll not judge you or love you any less."

To buy some time to think about what he should say, Joe got up and poured his mother a glass of water from the pitcher on the nightstand. He poured one for himself and took a long sip. His mother fixed her gaze directly into Joe's eyes, giving him the eerie feeling that she could actually peer into his soul and already knew the truth.

"Mom, when Lieutenant Bradley told me they were firing Tom from the police force, I was happy he couldn't use the badge to hurt people anymore. But the more I thought about it, the more it tortured me. I know he killed my father and was responsible for killing Ulysses's brother. Losing his job—that wasn't justice."

Joe choked up but forced himself to continue. "For two weeks, I had dreams of Dad being shot, his body thrown out of a car at the post office. It then switched to the interrogation room in Orange where Tom brutally murdered Lincoln Thompson."

Margaret gripped her son's hand even tighter and closed her eyes. Joe's voice cracked even more as he fought to hold back the emotions that roiled inside him. "Knowing that there'd be no investigation, I—I was the one who went to his apartment and shot him. I shot him after I told him why I was doing it and why he needed to pay for what he did. He didn't beg for his life. Tom looked me in the eye and told me to just pull the trigger, 'do it and get it over with.' I believe he really thought he was getting what he deserved."

Joe leaned over and hugged his frail mother, trying his best not to hurt her. He could not hold back the tears any longer and wept just as he would have as a young boy.

"Joe, you're a good man. We both know your act was wrong, but it doesn't make you evil. God will forgive you, but you're going to have to ask him for it. I want you to swear to me, so I can go to my grave in peace, that you'll confess this sin to a priest."

While still holding his mom's hand, Joe said, "I swear I'll do it. This promise to you I intend to keep."

‡

Four days later, with Joe and Martha sitting at her bedside, Margaret Keane O'Mara passed on to the next life. Tom's friend Jerry Healey took possession of her body, and they held the viewing at his funeral home in Orange.

At the funeral mass at St. John's Church, John gave a tear-jerking eulogy about Margaret and the impact she'd had on everyone's life. Some policemen from the Orange and Newark police departments were present for the service, along with the mayors of both cities. Ulysses Thompson and his brother's widow sat at the front of the church, right behind the O'Mara family, where Margaret had requested they sit. Abe Livosky and his wife were also in attendance.

As was the Irish tradition, a gathering of family and friends went back to Tom and Ella's house in South Orange for a celebration. Because the family had been so devastated when James O'Mara was murdered, there had been no wake. Tom thought it was a good idea to celebrate the life of their father today as well and invited Pat Maloney, his dad's friend from the force.

The entire downstairs of the large house was alive with people talking amongst themselves and making frequent toasts to Margaret's memory. Pat Maloney brought four of his cronies, and they positioned themselves in the parlor, close to where Tom had set up bottles of liquor for the guests.

Mayor Edelstein and Abe Livosky, after offering their condolences to each of the surviving children, were standing with Martha and their wives in the kitchen, having a conversation and enjoying a cigarette.

"Mind if I join you?" said Joe as he lit one and stood next to Martha.

"I loved what your brother John said about your mother. She was quite a strong woman. I wish I could've met her," said Abe.

"It was a beautiful service. During the eulogy, I have to admit that both Muriel and I were making good use of our handkerchiefs." Mayor Edelstein put his arm around his wife.

John, who was making the rounds and saying goodbye to everyone, came into the kitchen to announce he had to leave and go back to his parish.

"John, let me drive you back. I've only had one drink," Joe offered.

"Are you sure? Traffic's brutal this time of day."

"I'm sure. It'll give us a chance to talk."

"Thanks, brother. I'd like that."

The two men walked to the front door. Before opening it, Joe looked back into the parlor, noticing Pat and some men he didn't recognize sitting near the bottles of whiskey and carrying on in an embarrassing way. Holding back his anger, he followed John out. As Joe looked toward the heavens and saw dark gray storm clouds covering the skies, the sensation of loss took hold and began to overwhelm him.

The End

AUTHOR'S NOTES

I'll assume if you've gotten to this point that you have finished Newark Confessions. I want to personally thank you for taking the time to read it and I hope you've enjoyed the story.

I want to remind you that this is a work of fiction. While most of the events throughout the book are based in fact, not all of them are. I used reference books to write the sections on the Punitive Expedition, Father Coughlin, the Nazi movement in Newark, and the Jewish response. I did not use any specific historical references for the chapters covering Prohibition. I provide those sources for those who are interested on a following page.

To support a new independent author, I urge you to leave a review wherever you purchased the book.

If you would like to reach out to me personally with comments about Newark Confessions, my e-mail is rjkinch12@yahoo.com. I'll do my best to get back to you in a timely fashion.

If you would like to learn more about the real-life characters who inspired me to write the novel, please go to ww.rjkinchauthor.com.

ACKNOWLEDGEMENTS

I have found the writing of a novel to be a solitary act. However, the finished book has been helped by the following people who deserve to be recognized.

My dad was a big source of material which I used in the story. He never seemed to be put off as I questioned him about what it was like when he was growing up.

Dylan Garity was the perfect editor for me to work with.

I have been blessed by having a generous group of beta readers who kindly took the time to read my work and support my endeavor:

Dot Hall, Paul Petersen, my son Chris and daughter Julie, my wife Erica, Nancy and Ben Richardson, Dan Scavone, Pete Arndt, Micky Blask, Emily Campbell.

CREDITS

As much as I used reference books to build an understanding of the history, I read American authors from that time period to get a better understanding of the attitudes of the day. I would like to mention the three authors who helped me the most: Dashiell Hammett, Ernest Hemmingway and Thomas Wolfe.

I would be remiss if I did not mention the following works which sparked my idea for this novel. *The Berlin Noir trilogy* (Bernie Gunther series) by Philip Kerr, *The Many Saints of Newark*, written by David Chase and Lawrence Konner, directed by Alan Taylor, and *Babylon Berlin,* based on the books written by Volker Kutscher, written, and directed by Tom Tykwer, Achim von Borries, and Hendrik Handloegeten.

REFERENCE

Books

Grover, Warren, *Nazis in Newark*, New Brunswick, NJ, Transaction Publishers, 2003

Guinn, Jeff, *War on the Border, Villa, Pershing, The Texas Rangers, and an American Invasion*, New York, NY, Simon and Schuster, 2021

Hart, Bradley W. *Hitler's American Friends, The Third Reich's Supporters in the US*, New York, St. Martin's Press, 2018

Prieto, Julie Irene and Miller, Roger G. *US Army Operations in Mexico 1916-1917*, Washington D.C. , US Army Center for Military History, 2016

Movies

The 24th, 2020 written by Kevin Willmott, Trai Byers, directed by Kevin Willmott

Miller's Crossing, 1990, written by Joel and Ethan Coen, directed by Joel Coen

AUTHOR BIOGRAPHY

R.J. Kinch is a native of Essex County, New Jersey. After graduating from Rutgers with an engineering degree, he enjoyed an interesting career in science and business. Leaving that world behind, he decided to pursue his true passion, a lifelong love of history and literature, and undertake writing his first novel. During the creative process while researching the time period, he became thoroughly intrigued by the history of the so-called Lost Generation and inspired by the great writers of that period. He has begun writing a sequel to Newark Confessions.

Today, R.J. lives with his wife Erica and their faithful dog, Sophie, in Chester County, Pennsylvania. In their spare time they enjoy travel and the great outdoors.